continued . . .

Bundle of Trouble

"Engaging . . . [A] charming debut thriller."

—*Publishers Weekly*

"A stellar debut . . . Deftly plotted with a winning protagonist and a glorious San Francisco setting, *Bundle of Trouble* is a page-turning read. We will be hearing much more from this talented newcomer. Highly recommended."

—Sheldon Siegel, *New York Times* bestselling author of *Perfect Alibi*

"Anyone who's been a mother or had one will welcome the arrival of this entertaining new sleuth."

—Gillian Roberts, author of the Amanda Pepper Mysteries

"You'll love keeping up with this amazing mother and sleuth in the fun, fast-paced *Bundle of Trouble*."

—Margaret Grace, author of the Miniature Mysteries

"A charming, gutsy, wry character who will make you laugh so hard you'll forget the labor pains. Cigars all around . . . *Bundle of Trouble* is a natural-born winner."

—Louise Ure, Shamus Award–winner of *Liars Anonymous*

Berkley Prime Crime titles by Diana Orgain

BUNDLE OF TROUBLE
MOTHERHOOD IS MURDER
FORMULA FOR MURDER

Formula for
MURDER

Diana
Orgain

BERKLEY PRIME CRIME, NEW YORK

THE BERKLEY PUBLISHING GROUP
Published by the Penguin Group
Penguin Group (USA) Inc.
375 Hudson Street, New York, New York 10014, USA
Penguin Group (Canada), 90 Eglinton Avenue East, Suite 700, Toronto, Ontario M4P 2Y3, Canada
(a division of Pearson Penguin Canada Inc.)
Penguin Books Ltd., 80 Strand, London WC2R 0RL, England
Penguin Group Ireland, 25 St. Stephen's Green, Dublin 2, Ireland (a division of Penguin Books Ltd.)
Penguin Group (Australia), 250 Camberwell Road, Camberwell, Victoria 3124, Australia
(a division of Pearson Australia Group Pty. Ltd.)
Penguin Books India Pvt. Ltd., 11 Community Centre, Panchsheel Park, New Delhi—110 017, India
Penguin Group (NZ), 67 Apollo Drive, Rosedale, North Shore 0632, New Zealand
(a division of Pearson New Zealand Ltd.)
Penguin Books (South Africa) (Pty.) Ltd., 24 Sturdee Avenue, Rosebank, Johannesburg 2196,
South Africa

Penguin Books Ltd., Registered Offices: 80 Strand, London WC2R 0RL, England

This is a work of fiction. Names, characters, places, and incidents either are the product of the author's imagination or are used fictitiously, and any resemblance to actual persons, living or dead, business establishments, events, or locales is entirely coincidental. The publisher does not have any control over and does not assume any responsibility for author or third-party websites or their content.

FORMULA FOR MURDER

A Berkley Prime Crime Book / published by arrangement with the author

PRINTING HISTORY
Berkley Prime Crime mass-market edition / March 2011

Copyright © 2011 by Diana Orgain.
Cover design by Annette Fiore DeFex.
Cover art by Fernando Juarez.
Interior text design by Kristin del Rosario.

ISBN: 978-0-425-23988-9

BERKLEY® PRIME CRIME
Berkley Prime Crime Books are published by The Berkley Publishing Group,
a division of Penguin Group (USA) Inc.,
375 Hudson Street, New York, New York 10014.
BERKLEY® PRIME CRIME and the PRIME CRIME logo are trademarks of Penguin Group (USA) Inc.

PRINTED IN THE UNITED STATES OF AMERICA

10 9 8 7 6 5 4 3 2 1

For Tom Orgain

ACKNOWLEDGMENTS

Thanks to my wonderful agent, Lucienne Diver, and my fantastic editor, Michelle Vega, for your expertise and support. Special thanks to my mother, Maria Carmen Noa, and my brother, Tony Abad, for your creativity and help with brainstorming.

And thank you to all the readers who have written to me; your kind words keep me motivated to write the next story.

· CHAPTER ONE ·

To Do:

1. ✓ ~~Make holiday photo appointment for Laurie.~~

2. ~~Send out Christmas cards~~ Get them printed first—
   then send out Christmas cards.

3. ~~Complete~~ Start Christmas shopping.

4. Find a "Baby's First Christmas" ornament.

5. Get Christmas tree.

6. Finish background checks Galigani gave me.

7. Get new PI client. How do I do this?

I checked Laurie in the rearview mirror; she was sound
asleep. As usual, the motion of the car had lulled her into
slumber.

She looked adorable, wearing a tiny red satin dress with matching red booties. We were on our way to get her first holiday photos taken. I couldn't believe three months had evaporated; it seemed like she was born just yesterday. My best friend Paula had warned me the time would fly by, but this was ridiculous. How had I put off taking Laurie's holiday photos? Now it was the first week in December and I was hustling to get them taken, printed, and sent out as Christmas cards.

It's all right. From now on efficiency will be my middle name.

I cruised down the hill to the stoplight and stepped on the brake. Out of habit, I glanced in the rearview again and saw a silver SUV barreling down the hill.

Was the car out of control? It continued to speed and there was no telltale sign of the nose dipping as it would if the driver were braking.

They were getting closer! Almost on top of us.

I quickly looked for a way to avoid impact. The cars in front of me were waiting on the traffic signal and a steady stream of cross traffic moved through the intersection.

No! The SUV was going to hit us!

My eyes were transfixed on the rearview mirror. I held my breath, bracing myself for the crash at the same time that my brain screamed for a miracle.

Please stop in time. Please don't hit me and my baby!

Adrenaline shot through me, and everything felt as though it was happening in slow motion. I watched in horror as the SUV swerved violently to the right, but there was no way it could avoid hitting us.

The impact jolted us forward and I banged my head on the steering wheel. My seat belt caught and tugged at me just as we slammed into the car in front of us, then my entire body jerked backward, the base of my head smacking into the headrest.

Laurie let out a shrill wail, piercing into my heart. My gaze shot right and I locked eyes with the assailing driver. He was young, maybe only sixteen or seventeen, with longish brown hair and peach fuzz on his chin. His eyes were wide in shock. The SUV revved and tore off through the red light.

The light changed to green, and traffic—which had been stopped all around us—began to move again.

The passenger door of the vehicle in front of us opened and a woman jumped out. She rushed to my driver's side. I unfastened my belt with only one thing on my mind.

Laurie!

My hands were shaking from the adrenaline pulsing through my system. I pushed open my door.

The woman asked, "Are you all right?"

"I don't know. My baby! My baby!"

The woman's eyes widened as she focused on Laurie in her car seat.

Why wasn't she crying? She had cried out on impact but now she was silent.

My heart was lodged in my throat. I struggled with the door handle, my hands fumbling it. The woman reached over me and easily opened the door. I dove inside the backseat to Laurie's side.

Traffic sped around us. One vehicle slowed, then stopped. The driver yelled, "Is everyone okay? Do you want me to call a tow truck? The police?"

I swallowed past the lump in my throat and shouted, "Call an ambulance!"

My voice sounded near hysterical even to me. I examined Laurie, who upon seeing me started to fidget and then began to cry.

Was she hurt? Was I supposed to move her? Panic about spinal cord injury flooded my mind.

"What do I do?" I asked the woman. "I don't want to take her out of the car seat. What if it hurts her little spine?"

"Can we get the entire car seat out of the car? Traffic's not waiting, honey, and I want to get you two out of danger."

I unclipped the car seat bucket and pulled the carrier out. The woman grabbed the carrier, and we crossed a lane of traffic to the side of the road.

She set Laurie's bucket down on a bed of ice plants. "My husband went after the guy," the woman said. "I can't believe he just took off like that!"

I nodded distractedly, my mind and attention on Laurie. "He was young, a kid."

The woman blew out her breath in a sharp huff. "Probably on drugs!"

I leaned in as close to Laurie as I could without removing her from the seat, trying to soothe her.

"Did you see the plates on the car?" the woman asked me.

I rubbed Laurie's check, she rooted toward my hand. She was either hungry or looking for soothing. "No," I answered. "Just him. Long brown hair, peach fuzz, wide-eyed doe look on his face."

"Foreign diplomat car. DL? What code is that? French?" she asked.

Sirens screamed from up the hill.

Help is on the way!

I pressed my check against Laurie's and whispered, "Shhh, little angel, pumpkiny pie, Mommy's here and help's coming fast."

The woman said something inaudible and looked up in time to see an ambulance accompanied by a police cruiser pull up to the curb. The paramedics jumped out of the ambulance.

An officer stepped out of the patrol car and began speaking with the woman.

One EMT leaned over Laurie and me. "How are you?"

"I'm okay. I think. My baby is only three months old. I didn't want to take her out of the seat. Because, you know, I didn't know if it was okay to move her. I'm scared of neck or spinal injury—"

"Right, right," the EMT said, flashing a light across Laurie's eyes.

I knelt in the ice plant and hovered over them, not caring about the dew that soaked through the knees of my jeans and chilled me.

The EMT looked at me. "Her eyes are responding okay, but I can't tell much without taking her out of the seat. You want to go to the hospital? It's down the street."

I nodded, trying to shove down the hysteria welling inside me.

The EMT picked up Laurie's bucket. Laurie was now seemingly beginning to panic, too, and her cry turned into a shriek, her tiny arms flapping about.

It broke my heart to see her in distress, not really able to calm her. Every fiber of my being screamed to grab the bucket from him, pull Laurie out, and cradle her.

Please just be hungry or fussy. Don't be hurt, don't be injured!

The other EMT helped me up off my knees. The woman

seemed to be recounting the accident to the police officer. As soon as I got to my feet I followed Laurie into the ambulance. The EMT who had assisted me moved to the officer and said something I couldn't pick up.

The officer nodded and came toward me. He was slightly taller than me and had a stocky build. Somehow his build reassured me as though it made him sturdy and dependable. "Ma'am, I'll need a statement from you. If you leave me your information I can get it from you later."

I absently looked around for my purse. For the first time since the accident I saw my car. It was completely totaled. My trunk was smashed in and the hood looked like an accordion.

How had I walked away from that?

What about Laurie . . . Could she really be all right?

Tears flooded my eyes. "I don't know where my purse is. I can give you my number . . . Can you call my husband?"

The officer jotted down my home number. "I'll tell him to pick you up at the hospital." He looked at me for approval.

I nodded. "Thank you."

"I'll be in touch, ma'am. I hope your baby is all right." Anger flashed across his face and his jaw tightened. "Don't worry: I'm gonna get the guy who hit you."

I thanked him, then jumped into the ambulance, anxious to be with Laurie. She was still crying. Not knowing how to best channel my distress, I broke down and began to sob also, my brain trying to process the fact that this was the second time in Laurie's short life that we'd shared an ambulance ride together. The fact that this time was not my fault did little to settle my nerves.

Why had the driver left the scene? Sure, he was proba-

bly scared, but didn't he know a hit-and-run was a criminal act?

The EMT attending to Laurie put a small blanket over her and glanced at me. "Are you in pain, ma'am?"

I searched my pockets in a useless effort to find a pacifier for Laurie and shrugged at the EMT. "I want to hold her."

"I know," he said, almost in a whisper. "It's hard to listen to them cry. Did you know just the sound of a baby's cry makes your blood pressure go up?"

I shook my head.

He continued, "Yeah, in all mammals except for rats."

We rounded a corner and arrived at the hospital. Laurie and I were unloaded and ushered to a small room. A nurse freed Laurie from the car seat, before I could protest, and laid her on a table to take her vitals.

Someone in green medical scrubs was asking me if I had any cuts or abrasions. I shook my head and felt a blood pressure cuff go around my arm. My eyes locked on Laurie, I didn't even bother to look at him.

The nurse hovering over her asked, "How old is the baby?"

"Three months," I answered.

"When's the last time she ate?" she asked, stripping Laurie of her beautiful little holiday dress.

"A few hours ago."

The nurse attached small metal pads to Laurie's chest. Laurie let out a sharp cry.

"I'm so sorry they're cold, sweetie," she said.

The man attending me dropped my arm. "Normal," he said.

I glanced at him in disbelief, then read the digital display: 120/80.

I closed my eyes. Did this mean I was a rat?

Surely if I were any kind of decent mother my blood pressure would be through the roof.

"Can you take it again?" I asked.

The man frowned. "You're fine."

I didn't feel fine. I felt like a failure.

How could my blood pressure be fine? I'm a total and complete failure as a mom.

"Do you want to see a doctor?" the man asked me.

Again, I shook my head. "No. Just a pediatrician for Laurie."

He nodded and left the room. The other nurse turned to me. "Are you breastfeeding?"

I nodded.

She handed Laurie to me. "Why don't you nurse her now and see if she calms down a bit. All her vital signs are very good. Do you still want a pediatrician to look at her?"

"Yes, of course!" I answered.

The nurse nodded in understanding and left the room, promising to send the pediatrician on call.

I squeezed Laurie and fresh tears ran down my cheeks.

"Littlest! Please be okay. Please don't be hurt," I sobbed.

Laurie's hand entangled itself in my hair and she yanked at it, letting out a howl.

I laughed and let her tug at my hair. "If you're mad at missing a meal, then you're probably okay, huh?"

I bundled her in a blanket, nursed her, and waited for the doctor while replaying the accident in my mind. Was there anything I could have done differently? Why did he take off? I know he was just a kid, probably only recently got his license. But how could he abandon us like that?

The door to the room opened and my husband, Jim, appeared. I leapt out of the chair, still holding Laurie, and fell into him. His strong arms engulfed us and made me feel safe for the first time since the accident.

In a rush of words I told him about the hit-and-run. He listened to me while he watched Laurie.

There was a soft rap at the door, followed by the creak of it opening. The pediatrician, a tall man with smooth olive skin and dark hair, stepped in. He had me place Laurie on the exam table, which caused me to go into full sob mode again.

He peppered Jim with questions regarding Laurie's health, as he examined her. After a bit, he subjected me to the same battery of questions.

He finally said, "I think she's fine. Of course, we'll have to monitor her for signs of distress for the next forty-eight hours or so. But newborns are mostly cartilage; it's probably you, Mom, who's going to be hurting."

He handed me a checklist of symptoms to watch for, including: vomiting, diarrhea, and lethargy, and then left the room.

I rebundled Laurie. "What did the police tell you?" I asked Jim.

"Not much. He said the guy in the car in front of you followed the assailant. He ended up losing him, but was pretty sure it was a vehicle from the French consulate's fleet."

A vehicle from the French consulate?

What did that mean? Why did he speed off? Why not stop?

"Was the car stolen?" I asked.

Jim shrugged. "I don't know, the cop barely gave me the time of day. Told me to file an insurance claim and gave me an incident number." Jim stared at me with a dumbfounded expression—one I'm sure matched my own.

After a moment, he said, "Of course, I didn't press him much. I only wanted to find out about you and Laurie and how you guys were doing."

I nodded.

"Why'd you ask if the car was stolen?" Jim asked.

"It was a teenager driving it."

Jim exhaled. "So it's some diplomat's kid."

"Maybe," I agreed.

He squinted at me. "Let's go there."

"What?"

"Let's track down the snot nose that hit you and Laurie."

"Shouldn't we let the police do that?"

Jim clenched a fist. "They already know it's a car from the consulate. You think they're itching to get involved with some diplomat's pinhead son? If they were, they'd already be over there, right?"

I pulled Laurie close to me and pressed my nose into her soft cheek. She was asleep but my squeeze caused her little hand to reach out. I placed my finger in her palm and felt her small hand wrap around it.

"You know the police aren't going to do a darn thing," Jim continued. "They want us to open an insurance claim. Let us take the hit."

Anger surged inside of me. "We already took the hit. Literally! Laurie and I."

Oh God, please let my baby be all right.

The doctor had said to watch for signs of distress.

Didn't I always?

I would be even more vigilant now.

"What about Laurie? I want to get her home. Make sure she's okay. I want her to be warm and fed and content . . ." My voice caught as a sob bubbled in my throat. "I want her to be okay."

Jim pulled Laurie and me into an embrace. "She's okay, honey. She's gonna be fine," he said, his voice full of emotion "You heard the doctor: She's all cartilage."

"She not all cartilage. She's a person! A tiny defenseless little person, with a heart and soul and . . ." Tears rolled down my face.

He tightened his grasp around me. Laurie squirmed between us.

"It happened so fast, Jim. One minute you're there, stopped at a light, and then the next . . . What if . . ."

"I love you guys so much. I can't stand the thought. All I can do is fight, Kate. I want to find the guy who ran into you. Accidents happen, I know. But you can't just leave a mother and child in the middle of the road after smashing their car to smithereens."

I nodded, swallowing back my fears. I picked up Laurie's discarded dress and handed it to Jim. "Let's go."

•CHAPTER TWO•

We agreed that we'd drive by the French consulate on Bush Street and see if anything seemed obvious. Short of a smashed vehicle parked in front I wasn't sure what we were looking for.

I sat in the back of Jim's car, hovering over Laurie. Thank goodness we'd had an extra car seat. My car had been towed after the incident and the pediatrician had told me to discard the car seat that had been in the accident, as it was likely the harnesses were damaged.

We drove down Bush Street and spotted the consulate adjacent to the French school and Church of Notre Dame des Victoires. It had begun to drizzle, but when Jim turned the wipers on, there was only enough rain to smear across the windshield.

"Looks like they have a parking garage," Jim said.

"It's probably for staff only, right?" I asked.

Jim pulled the car up to the entrance and read the sign. "Yeah. You need an electronic key card to get in. Perfect place to hide a vehicle after a hit-and-run, huh?"

"Okay. Let's go home."

I was exhausted not only physically—every emotion in me had been pushed to the brink this morning.

"Not so fast. I want to check things out. I'm going in by foot."

We parked across the street at a meter.

Jim hopped out of the car and emptied all the change from his pocket into the meter. He frowned and tapped at it. "Busted. This is BS. What a day."

I watched as he crossed into the parking garage and slipped under the electronic arm. I stroked Laurie's cheek. She was sound asleep and breathing deeply.

"Don't be hurt, squirrel. Be like the doc said. Be just fine, okay, little monkey?" I pressed my lips to her forehead and smelled the baby shampoo I'd applied this morning. Had it really only been a few hours ago?

Jim emerged from the parking garage and ran over to the car. He bent down to my window. "You're not going to believe this: There's a silver SUV with a smashed-in front end, and it's missing a bumper!" His cell phone was in his hand and he opened it now. "You got that cop's number?"

I climbed out of the car.

"Never mind, I've got it here," Jim said, as he scrolled through his recent calls. His lips turned down in distaste as he waited for someone to pick up. "Voice mail," he said, shaking his head back and forth.

"Leave a message," I said.

Jim closed his phone. "Why bother? I'm going in."

"What?"

"By the time the cop gets down here, assuming he'll

even come, the rat could leave." Jim turned to cross the street.

"No! Wait! Jim, you can't—"

Jim's brow furrowed and he said, "Stay here with Laurie."

"If you're going in, then me, too. I mean, I saw the guy."

Jim squinted at me. "Do you feel up to it?"

"Yeah. Why don't you stay here with Laurie?"

"No way!" He leaned into the car and unfastened Laurie's carrier from the car seat restraints. "Let's go together."

He lifted Laurie's car seat out of the car and looked down the street for oncoming traffic. We crossed the street in silence.

At the entrance of the consulate, he asked, "So you think you'll recognize the guy?"

"I'm sure of it."

"Okay. If you see him, point him out to me. I'll do the talking."

I laughed despite myself. "What? You think I'm going to say the wrong thing?"

Jim pulled open the glass door. He waited for me to step inside, and as I crossed in front of him he said, "I have no idea what you would say, honey. That's why I'm going to do the talking."

We stepped into what looked more or less like a fancy hotel lobby. An elegant French lady about the age of twenty-five stood behind a huge counter topped with red marble.

She tapped her fingernails—which were painted a matching red—on the marble and said in a singsong, "*Bonjour.*"

Jim handed me Laurie in her car seat and stepped ahead of me and up to the counter.

"You speak English, right?"

The woman smiled and with a beautiful French accent said, "Of course."

"My wife and infant were rear-ended by a consulate vehicle a few hours ago on Lombard Street. The driver never stopped." He pulled out his cell phone and clicked to the photos. He pushed his phone toward her. "The SUV is parked in your lot. Can you get the driver out here for me?"

Her eyes widened at the photo, her face showing first shock then dismay. "*Mon Dieu! Un moment. S'il vous plaît.*"

Clenching the phone in her hand she pushed away from the counter.

"No. Not with my phone," Jim said sharply. He stuck his hand out.

She looked caught off guard, but nodded politely and handed the phone back to Jim.

She disappeared down a corridor.

"You didn't have to yell at her."

"I didn't yell at her. I stopped her from walking away with the only evidence we have and *accidentally* deleting it."

"Well, we know—"

"Listen, honey, I love you but this is exactly why I'm the one that's going to do the talking. These people are *not* your friends. They're not your buddies. They're obviously the kind of people who have no regard for smashing into a woman and child and taking off. So we're agreed, right? I'm doing the talking."

I gathered air in my cheeks, blew it out in a huff, and nodded. Giving up control is difficult for me, but it seemed an easier route than arguing with Jim right now.

The woman returned with a man by her side. He looked

to be in his late thirties. He had a square jaw and strong, straight nose. His dark brown hair was smoothly combed back and held in place with lots of spray or mousse. He wore a blue shirt that was unbuttoned one or two buttons too many. Dark curly chest hair peeked out as he swaggered toward us.

Before they reached us, Jim turned to me and quietly asked, "Is that the guy?"

"No. The driver was much younger. Like seventeen or eighteen."

When he approached us the man immediately extended his hand to Jim. "*Monsieur*, I am Jean-Luc Gaudet, the Deputy Consul General. *Mademoiselle* tells me you were a victim of a hit-and-run."

Jim looked at Jean-Luc's hand but didn't shake it. "My wife and infant daughter were in the car. Is that bashed-up SUV yours? The one with the missing fender?"

Jean-Luc seamlessly turned his outstretched hand into a gesture, shifting his palm faceup and motioning us toward a corner of the lobby that held some leather chairs and a small table covered in magazines.

We moved toward the chairs as Jean-Luc said, "The vehicle is registered in my name." He pointed to the leather chairs, indicating for us to take a seat. "Please."

Jean-Luc and I sat; Jim remained standing. I cradled Laurie's car seat bucket in my lap. An older couple entered the building, and Jean-Luc watched them as they made their way to the reception counter. He and the woman from reception exchanged glances, then the woman broke loose from us and returned to the reception area.

I tried to move Jim with my eyes, looking from him back to the empty chair and raising a pleading eyebrow.

Jim shook his head and mouthed, "Not our buddy." He broke eye contact with me and stared at Jean-Luc.

Jean-Luc rose to match Jim's stance. "Please accept my apologies. You've obviously been through some terrible trauma today. Unfortunately, I didn't go anywhere today, so I wasn't driving the vehicle."

Jim's eyes narrowed. "Right. Nice. Okay, someone on your staff obviously was. Someone has keys, access, whatever. Or are you saying it was stolen and conveniently parked back in your garage?"

Jean-Luc blew air from his lips in an exaggerated puff. He fixed his face in an expression of confusion and raised his hands and eyes as though searching for an answer from the ceiling.

Watching him play dumb made me want to rip out every last chest hair and shove them up his nose.

Jim clenched first his jaw then his fist. "My wife and baby had to be assisted out of our vehicle by the other party that got hit. They had to wait for the ambulance on a bed of ice plant, abandoned! My daughter's only three months old!"

Jean-Luc's face was unreadable.

Jim continued, "I just picked up my wife and infant from the emergency room. They got emergency rooms in France, right?"

"Pfft. Emergency room?" Jean-Luc's eyebrows creased. "Why? Because of a little bump? They don't look hurt—"

Jim closed the distance between him and Jean-Luc. "You interested in a visit to the emergency room today?"

Jim's face was inches away from the man, his meaning clear.

Jean-Luc's head turned toward the reception desk. The

woman was staring at us wide-eyed. The couple she was helping mirrored her expression.

Jim said, in a whisper that only Jean-Luc and I could hear, "My wife can identify the driver."

It was the final blow.

Jean-Luc lowered his eyes and cleared his throat. "*Un moment. S'il vous plaît.*"

He stepped toward the woman at reception and said something to her in French. She nodded and retreated down the corridor. He shook hands with the couple she had been helping. The older gentleman put a hand on Jean-Luc's forearm and pulled him close. Laughter erupted from them.

"Jerk," Jim said.

I glanced at Laurie and gently rocked the car seat back and forth. Her hand fidgeted but other than the small movement she was sound asleep.

"What was with the emergency room stuff? Were you threatening the guy?" I asked Jim.

The receptionist returned and handed a card to Jean-Luc. He approached us and handed the card to me. "Madam, please take my card. Our insurance information is on the back. We'll gladly pay for the repairs to your car and any bills you have from the hospital. Please accept our apologies."

We left the consulate in silence and crossed the street to Jim's car. I loaded Laurie into the back and secured the car seat carrier to the base.

I decided to ride in the passenger seat next to Jim instead of in the back next to Laurie. He seemed to need me more than she did at the moment, since she was still asleep and he was fuming.

I fastened my seat belt and waited. Jim didn't start the car.

"I would have liked to squeeze his neck until his head popped off," Jim said.

I put my hand on his thigh to soothe him. "Honey—"

"Then kick his head over the roof."

A nervous giggle escaped me. "That's awful!"

But hadn't I wanted to rip his chest hairs out?

Jim shrugged. "Is it? I think a hit-and-run is awful, cowardly. And then that guy trying to cover it up—it's reprehensible."

The doors of the consulate opened and two ladies exited. Both tall and slender, one a brunette, the other blonde. They were chatting and when they reached the sidewalk they turned away from each other and parted ways. I watched the blonde walk toward us.

"Hey, that's Nancy Pickett from Channel Five," I said.

Jim nodded. "The other one was Kimberly Newman."

Nancy Pickett, a serious investigative reporter, was the one always sent out to do a story during the eye of the storm or to report on the city's latest drug bust. As recently as last night, she'd been covering a major pet food chain store scam and had received an honorable mention from a neighborhood merchant organization for saving the lives of countless dogs.

Kimberly Newman, on the other hand, was a high-society girl turned weather woman, turned part-time journalist. She was always pictured on the news or in the paper and on the web at the tony Pac Height parties on someone's arm. I think her most recent conquest was a San Francisco city supervisor.

What were Nancy Pickett and Kimberly Newman doing at the French consulate?

·CHAPTER THREE·

To Do:

1. Call Dr. Clement for appointment. What if Laurie's brain is scrambled? The ER doc didn't test for brain damage, did he? Is there a test for that?

2. Call insurance.

3. Reschedule holiday photos.

4. Christmas tree, cards, shopping, decorating. Shoot! Behind again! NOT efficient.

5. Find stupid kid that hit us so I can give him a piece of my mind!

6. Finish background checks Galigani gave me.

7. ~~Get new PI client. How do I do this?~~ Forget it, focus on catching up first!

Once home from the consulate, I dialed Mom and then my best friend, Paula. I got voice mails and left messages. Jim and I decided on soup for dinner although neither one of us had much of an appetite.

I hovered over Laurie even more than usual, then finally upon Jim's urging went to bed early. Jim stayed up watching the news with Laurie. At one point in the night I got out of bed to check on them and found Jim singing and rocking Laurie. She was mesmerized by him, smiling and happily banging his face with her hands. I retreated back to bed, relieved that she wasn't showing any signs of distress listed on the sheet the emergency room pediatrician had given me.

I woke up when Jim climbed into bed.

"Where's Laurie?" I asked.

"In her nest," Jim answered.

I rolled over and sat up to peek into the bassinet by my bedside. Since Laurie had been born I'd become accustomed to sleeping with my side table lamp on and now wondered how I'd ever slept in the dark.

The light glowed on Laurie, casting a gentle shadow across one side of her face. "Is she okay?" I asked.

"I think so, honey. I really do. She seems fine," Jim said.

"Any vomiting, listlessness, diarrhea, melancholy, rash—"

"Noooo, honey," Jim said, in his best calm-down-and-don't-get-hysterical-on-me tone.

I laid back and snuggled into his arms. "Okay."

After a moment, he said, "Well, she did spit up . . . but that's normal, right?"

I sat up again. "How do you know it was spit-up and not vomit?"

Jim shrugged. "I don't."

I peered over at Laurie in her bassinet. "Can she sleep in here with us?" I asked.

Jim rose and crossed around our bed to the bassinet. He picked her up and then climbed back into bed. We nestled her between us.

"I love my girls," Jim said. "I'd do anything for you two."

"Yeah," I snickered. "Even have a showdown with an unsuspecting Frenchman."

"I don't think he's as unsuspecting as he'd have you believe."

The night-light illuminated his face and I traced a finger across his lips. He kissed my finger.

"Good night, honey. Get some rest. You went through a lot today."

"You, too."

Despite my best efforts for sleep, I woke every fifteen minutes and checked on Laurie. She slept great, only waking at midnight then at 3 A.M. for her normal feedings, which were actually so much more convenient with her lying right next to me.

Why didn't she sleep in our bed every night?

Was she showing any signs of distress? I reviewed the list in my mind. Vomiting, well, we weren't sure. I'd have to watch that. Listlessness?

Wait.

Listlessness? She had been sleeping an awful lot. Did that count?

I lay awake next to her and watched her snooze, poking her softly every so often to make sure her reflexes were still intact.

At 6 A.M. she woke up for another feeding. She had a wet diaper that had soaked through to our sheet. No wonder I didn't make a regular practice of bringing her into our bed.

I rose to change her diaper, my neck stiff and sore. Another reason she didn't normally camp in our bed. I could barely move my neck from side to side.

I scooped her up and took her to the nursery down the hall. I changed her soiled pink-striped pajamas to a clean white set with a bunny in a Santa suit on it. I tickled her.

She seemed pleased to be in clean clothes and rewarded me with a toothless grin.

After nursing her, I set her down on her play mat and proceeded to the kitchen to put on coffee. Jim materialized next to me as soon as the coffeemaker beeped to completion.

"What's wrong?" he asked.

"With what?" I asked, surprised.

"With you, honey, you're moving funny."

"I am? Oh. My neck is stiff. I must have slept kiddiwampus with Laurie in our bed."

Jim squinted. "Are you sure you don't have whiplash?"

"Whiplash? No. I'm fine."

Actually, now that he mentioned it, more than my neck hurt. My mid and lower back, and even my hips were sore, too.

I swallowed some Motrin with my morning coffee and tried to ignore the fact that if I had been injured in the accident then the chances were greater that Laurie had been injured, too.

Shortly after 8 A.M. Mom called in a panic. Thankfully I was in the shower so Jim had to deal with her near hysterics. She was coming right over Jim informed me as I toweled off and stared into my closet.

"Okay, good. She can obsess over Laurie with me," I said.

Jim snorted. "Laurie's fine. You're the one that needs to get looked at. Please make an appointment."

The doorbell sounded, interrupting our conversation. "That was fast," I said.

Jim left me to select some clothes and went to answer the door.

Paula's voice drifted down the hallway.

I threw on a pair of jeans and a sweater and rushed to the living room. My best friend, Paula, now eight months pregnant, was cradling Laurie above her massive belly. She studied Laurie's face. "I got your message," she said. "Pupils look fine. She looks alert and happy. Has she vomited?"

"I don't know. She spits up a lot. How can you tell?"

Paula's two-year-old son, Danny, clung to her leg and pulled on her maternity top. "It's kinda hard. But you can usually tell by the volume. Is she keeping anything down?"

"Yes. It must be just spit-up." I knelt down and extended my arms. "Hi, Danny!"

He rushed to me and wrapped his arms around my neck, sort of hanging from it. "Ouch! Oh, honey, wait." I disentangled myself from him.

Concern showed on Jim's face.

Paula looked at me, her brow creasing. "Are you hurt?"

"No. No. I'm totally fine. He caught me off guard is all."

The doorbell sounded again.

I moved toward it and pulled it open. Mom flung her arms around me and crushed me against her. "I'm so glad you're alive!"

I silently winced. My neck did hurt but no reason to cause a fuss.

Mom released me and rushed to pluck Laurie out of Paula's arms. "My love!" she said to Laurie, who cooed up at her. Then Mom instructed Paula "to have a seat before she went into labor."

"I wish standing caused labor," Paula said.

I rubbed my neck. Paula squinted at me. "I'm scared about brain damage," I confessed to her.

"Why are you scared?" She smiled. "You've lived your whole life with it."

I poked her arm. "Come on, idiot, not me."

Paula made a face. "Laurie? No way. She was in a five-point harness, right?"

I nodded and chewed my lip. "But what if her little brain was scrambled?"

Paula laughed. "She's not an egg. Babies are very resilient. She's fine. No brain damage. I promise." Paula wrapped her fingers around my arm. "You're the one whose gonna be hurting."

"I don't care about me," I said.

Jim put a hand on my shoulder. "We do, though. Make an appointment."

Paula agreed, then sat on my couch and put her swollen feet on the coffee table. Danny tried to climb into the little room left on her lap.

Jim plucked Danny off her. "Come with me, buddy. Let's make you a chocolate milk shake."

"Oh! I'll take one of those," Paula called after Jim as they headed to the kitchen.

Mom was doing an elaborate baby-calming dance for Laurie, who was giggling up at her. "Where's your Christmas tree?" Mom asked.

"At the Christmas tree lot," I answered, taking a seat on the couch next to Paula.

I put my head on Paula's shoulder and whispered in a voice that threatened to crack, "I'm a terrible mother."

"I know, you don't have your Christmas cards out yet," Paula whispered back to me.

We watched Mom making faces at Laurie.

A tear slipped down my check without me even realizing it. It touched my lip and I tasted the salt. "If I was a good mom I would have never let myself get rear-ended with Laurie in the car."

After a little prodding from Paula, Jim decided to take Danny to the Christmas tree lot to pick out a Christmas tree for us. While they were gone Paula hacked into my computer and printed out labels for my Christmas cards. It took her about three minutes and saved me several hours of frustration.

Mom helped out by executing a string of calls to my insurance company, trying to get through to a live person. She finally gave up when the garage called to notify me that my Chevy had been deemed a total loss. The mechanic said I should be hearing from an adjuster shortly.

Jim and Danny returned with the best Charlie Brown Christmas tree they could find. We spent the rest of the afternoon stringing popcorn, decorating the tree, and listening to Mom sing carols off-key.

Several days passed and I still hadn't heard from our insurance company. I'd made an appointment with our regular pediatrician, Dr. Clement, who concurred with the emergency room pediatrician and Paula. Laurie seemed completely unharmed by the incident. I, on the other hand, seemed to get progressively stiffer. Which Dr. Clement suggested was absolutely normal.

I snuggled next to Jim on the couch and tried to put the accident out of my mind. The day had been busy. Besides the appointment I was doing background work for Galigani, which although a bit mindless was helping me learn the general ins and outs of the investigation business.

Since giving birth to Laurie, I'd managed to be involved in several murder investigations and basically had decided to launch a private investigation business. But since I didn't have a PI license, Albert Galigani, an ex-cop and now successful private investigator, had more or less agreed, depending on his mood, to mentor me. He'd given me what he called "homework" to improve my skills, but the homework felt more like "penance." My eyes were tired from staring at the computer screen but every time I closed them I still saw typed text floating and scrolling.

I must have dozed off because Jim shook me awake. "Look at this, Kate!"

I pried an eye open and immediately looked for Laurie.

Jim indicated the television. "It's Nancy Pickett. She was found dead."

"What?" I sat to attention and stared at the TV.

"We are saddened to report that our colleague, Nancy Pickett, was found dead yesterday afternoon. Nancy had been with our station five years, reporting the best stories in the Bay Area." The anchor's eyes filled with tears. "Again, Nancy Pickett, dead at the age of thirty-five."

CHAPTER FOUR

"Wow!" I said to Jim. "What happened?"

"They found her body in Golden Gate Park. They think she was a victim of a mugging on her morning run."

Golden Gate Park! We lived so close to the park and I'd never thought of it as crime-ridden. It had always been a source of pure enjoyment for me.

I squinted at the enlarged photo of her on the television set.

"Mugged on her morning run?"

Jim nodded.

Well, that's a good reason to put off working out. Safety!

"Why would someone get mugged on a run? Most people don't go on a jog with tons of cash on them. Was she raped?"

Jim shook his head. "I don't know. They didn't say." He flipped through several local channels. All were reporting her death, either through the anchor or with a scrolling news feed at the bottom of the screen. No channel had any additional information.

"I can't believe we just saw her."

Jim rubbed my shoulder. "I know, it's creepy, isn't it?"

I stood and made my way to the nursery, which also doubled as our office. "I'm going to look her up."

Jim followed me. "Look up the staff at the French consulate while you're at it. That Jean-Luc Gruyère guy."

I laughed. "Gruyère is a cheese."

Jim dismissed my comment with a wave. "Gruyère, gouda, whatever."

"His name was Gaudet."

"He was cheesy all right," Jim said, ignoring me, "with his shirt unbuttoned. Give me a break."

"Maybe you should wear your shirt like that," I teased.

Jim laughed. "Bet you'd love that."

I smiled. "Just because you didn't care for the guy doesn't mean he has anything to do with Nancy Pickett's death."

"I'm not saying he killed her. I'm just sayin' to look him up."

I wiggled the mouse to bring my computer to life. Laurie cried from the other room. Jim went to fetch her from the bassinet as I typed *Nancy Pickett* into the database Galigani had given me access to. I found her driver's license number and noted the clean record. I jotted down her address. She lived in the Marina District. Why would a Marina resident go for a morning jog in Golden Gate Park? The two districts weren't close. Surely she would jog at the Marina Green.

I poked further into her record. There was a short bio for her that gelled with everything I already knew about her. She was divorced. Maybe she had friends that lived near Golden Gate Park and they all ran together. That would certainly explain a morning jog there. Except, then where were her friends when she was attacked?

What if she'd been killed somewhere else and just dumped in the park?

Jim returned to the nursery with Laurie in his arms. He proceeded to change her diaper. "Did you find anything?"

"Not really. Not yet. She lived in the Marina on Chestnut Street."

"Hmmm. What's she doing running in the park? Wouldn't she run the Presidio?"

"Or the Green."

"What did you find on Jean-Luc?"

"Nothing. I'm still looking into Nancy."

Jim finished changing Laurie's diaper and then handed her off to me. "I'll get his card."

"How am I supposed . . ." I turned to watch Jim leave the room. ". . . to work with Laurie in my lap?"

I typed with one hand and googled Nancy's address, then mapped it. It was literally three blocks from the Marina Green.

Jim returned and gave me Jean-Luc's card.

I typed his name into the database and drew a blank.

"He's a foreign diplomat. I don't think he's in the system."

Jim plucked Laurie out of my arms. She pedaled her feet as she dangled in front of him and let out a little giggle. "Yeah, ask Galigani. Something's up with that guy."

Laurie and I had a fitful night. We woke several times to nurse and just stare at each other in general. She seemed fine, no symptoms from the car accident had manifested so we were both settling down into our normal, nervous routine instead of the paranoia-on-steroids one from the last few days.

After rising and putting on a pot of coffee, I updated my to-do list:

To Do:

1. ✓ ~~Call Dr. Clement for appointment.~~

2. Call insurance AGAIN—what's the holdup?

3. Reschedule holiday photos—get Laurie's dress cleaned.

4. ✓ ~~Christmas tree,~~ cards, shopping, ~~decorating~~. 2 out of 4 = 50% done. Progress!

5. Find stupid kid that hit us so I can give him a piece of my mind!

6. ✓ ~~Finish background checks Galigani gave me.~~

7. Buy new car!

I dialed Galigani. He picked up on the first ring.

"Hey. I finished with the boring research you asked me to do."

"What do you mean boring? Research is the building blocks of all investigations, if you can't do that, kid—"

"Did you hear about the reporter from Channel Five?"

Galigani hadn't. I filled him in with as many details as I had.

When I finished, he grunted. "So what are you saying? Investigating the murder of a reporter is more interesting than doing background for me?"

"Slightly more interesting."

"Let me guess. You want me to poke around? Ask a few questions."

I laughed. "I would never suggest such a thing."

We hung up and I proceeded with my chores. I sorted the laundry and threw the whites in the machine. As I added bleach, the phone rang. I picked it up expecting Galigani—what could he have found out so soon?

Paula's voice filled the line. "Hey! You'll never guess what I just got in the mail!"

"A Christmas card?"

"Oh! You are good! Yes. A Christmas card with an invite to a Christmas party, but you have to guess from whom."

"I give up."

"You're no fun."

"I think you've told me that before."

Paula snorted. "The French consulate."

"What? How did you get invited to that?"

"I party in the right circles," Paula said.

I laughed. "Unless there's something you haven't been telling me—"

"Nah. We went to the consulate before we left for Paris last year. In case I ended up giving birth I wanted to know what to expect. We must have ended up on their mailing list. Any news from your insurance?"

"They're AWOL, but I have another development for you."

"What's that?" Paula asked.

"Did I tell you that Jim and I saw Nancy Pickett leaving the consulate the day we were there?"

Paula breathed in sharply. "Nancy Pickett? I saw on the news that she was found dead in Golden Gate Park."

"I know."

"Let's go to the party," Paula said, after a moment. "You can be my date."

"Jim will never go for it."

"Don't tell him."

"No. I'll tell him. Of course, I'm gonna tell him," I said.

"What am I going to wear? I don't have any fancy maternity clothes."

"I don't have any—"

"Oh. Shut up. I have zero sympathy for anyone who is *NOT* eight months pregnant, looking for a party dress."

I laughed. "Let's go shopping."

I folded laundry and stacked it on my bed while Laurie lay in the middle of it chewing on a board book.

Jim came into the bedroom and studied me.

"What?" I asked.

He picked up a T-shirt and fussed with it.

I could tell by the way he scrunched the shirt he wanted to tell me something. "What is it?"

"How are you feeling?"

"Fine."

"Do you feel, you know, strong?"

"What are you asking me?"

The phone rang, interrupting us. Jim answered and I could tell by his side of the conversation that it was our insurance adjustor finally calling us.

Jim balled up the shirt as he listened. Finally, he said, "That's ridiculous!"

Laurie kicked her legs and made a face. Suddenly, it struck me that having her in the middle of the bed with clean laundry might be a bad choice. I plucked her off the bed in time to intercept the spit-up partly with my blouse, the balance landing on the hardwood floor.

Jim tried to wipe my blouse with the T-shirt in his hand. I shook my head to stop him, but he was absorbed in his conversation and insisted on mopping up the floor with the clean shirt. "I can't believe this!" He paused. "Well, that's all fine and good, but where does it leave us?" He paused again, then said, "Great. I'll wait for your fax."

He hung up and tossed the now soiled shirt into the laundry basket. "Looks like I'm going to have to fight the insurance company for a new car."

"But we're not at fault," I said.

Jim sighed. "Jean-Luc Cheese-head isn't liable either. His license is issued by the Department of State and his insurance isn't cooperating because he has diplomatic immunity and basically they can't enforce anything on them."

"He wasn't driving. You think the kid has diplomatic immunity, too?"

Jim shrugged. "Does it matter? We don't even know who the kid is."

"Jean-Luc does. I'm sure of it."

"Look, honey, don't worry about it. I'll handle it," Jim said, seething.

Now didn't seem like the right time to mention the Christmas party.

Instead I said, "Before the phone rang, you wanted to ask me something."

Jim hung his head. "Oh yeah. If I needed . . . to take a trip—"

"Where do you want to go?"

I expected him to say he wanted to go to the neighborhood pub, drink some beers with David, Paula's husband,

and watch football. Instead, he sat on the bed next to Laurie and toppled one of my piles of laundry.

"Honey, I got an e-mail from Dirk Jonson. He's asking if I can do a trip to New York to pitch the Zenia account. Are you okay if I go?"

He looked pained.

"When?"

"Wednesday. I'd be gone until Sunday. I hate to leave you alone with Laurie. But your mom can help you, right? And Paula."

I tried to hide my smile. Jim would be out of town during the consulate party. I could go with Paula, try and track down the kid, and never even have to mention it to him . . .

CHAPTER FIVE

To Do:

1. Reschedule holiday photos.

2. Get Laurie's dress cleaned.

3. Christmas cards and shopping.

4. ✓ ~~Get dress for holiday party (need heels, purse, and wrap, too).~~

5. Find stupid kid that hit us at party—does he have insurance? Diplomatic immunity?

6. ~~Buy new car!~~ Research safest car.

Paula and I arrived at the consulate promptly at 6 P.M. We'd parked in a nearby lot and walked the few blocks to the party. Paula had scored a vintage red dress at one of the shops we had visited on Haight Street. It was a décolleté gown with the neck and shoulder bare. She had covered herself with a winter white shawl and looked the epitome of holiday cheer.

I was wearing a tiny black dress, the size of which had surprised me. I was sure it fit only because it cost a bundle. My theory is that designer dresses are cut large to make you feel slim as you drop a ton of money on them. Paula tried to assure me the reverse was true, but I didn't believe her.

I'd tied in the holiday colors by picking a pair of ridiculously high heels in a delicious red and matching them to a wrap. I loved the feel of my dress and heels as we walked toward the consulate. It was a cold evening and the silk wrap did practically nothing to protect me against the breeze; nevertheless I enjoyed the feeling of sophistication—how long had it been since I'd been dressed up?

And the purse! The purse was spectacular. A tiny little itty-bitty thing by Rafé New York. It was embossed snake leather and delicately beaded. Only room for my phone, lipstick, and some cash. No diapers, no wipes, no bottles, no pacifier, no baby booties, no baby anything. Oh! Oh! Oh! The joy of a solo outing with a girlfriend!

I happily glanced at Paula. Pregnant Paula . . . Okay, so babies were never quite out of my consciousness but still I loved the sound of my own high heels clicking on the cement—yes, focus on the heels.

Sophistication, finesse, grace.

Wow! These heels are really high . . .

In fact, the balls of my feet were beginning to burn a little. I glanced at Paula's feet clad in a pair of green patent leather ballet slippers that curiously made the same wonderful clippity-cloppity noise as my heels.

Why did I feel like I had to kill myself in high heels in order to feel elegant?

We approached the glass door of the consulate and a uniformed security guard held it open for us. He indicated a table for us to sign in.

As we passed him he left out a soft, "Oh la la."

I turned back to him and he raised an appreciative eyebrow at me.

I felt giddy again.

"Just when you were wondering why you bothered to wear high heels," Paula said with a smirk.

I poked her. "How did you know what I was thinking?"

Paula laughed. "You're starting to limp." She produced the invite to a woman who crossed-referenced the guest list.

"Yeah? Well at least I'm wearing 'em, loafer lady."

Paula stuck out a foot. "These are *not* loafers!"

"Practically."

Paula held back a laugh. "Are you going to rub in the fact that you're going to drink a cocktail now, too?"

Since Paula was pregnant and wouldn't be drinking she was our designated driver.

I smiled. "No."

Paula raised an eyebrow. "You're not going to rub it in, or you're not drinking?"

"Please. Of course, I'm drinking."

We made our way to the bar. I ordered a cosmopolitan for myself and a Perrier for Paula.

The ballroom was decked out in holiday trimmings, with a glowing Christmas tree in the center of the room, just below a staggering chandelier. The Christmas tree was made up of different size LED lightbulbs and gave off a soft white light and an annoying hum.

Paula and I exchanged looks.

She raised her perfectly arched brows at me. "Hi-tech. You think it's green?"

I smirked. "It's white."

She gave me her famous you're-not-funny look and said, "I mean, as in energy efficient."

I shrugged. "Well, they didn't kill a tree for it, but for all we know they're using up enough power to light up San Francisco for a day."

The bartender brought us our drinks and I slipped some cash into the tip jar for him.

A man with unruly curly hair stepped up to the bar and ordered, then he turned to Paula and I and in a French accent asked, "You like the tree?"

"It's blinding me," I answered.

Paula elbowed me. The man tried to suppress his grin.

"It's beautiful," Paula said.

"What?" I asked. "I can't hear you over the tree."

At that the gentleman gave an outright laugh, but Paula only frowned at me.

The bartender returned and handed the man his drink; without another word he slipped into the crowd.

"Where are your manners? I can't take you anywhere," Paula said.

I spotted Jean-Luc making his way around some guests and pointed him out to Paula just as a plate of Coquilles Saint-Jacques wafted by us.

Paula glanced at Jean-Luc, then flagged a waiter down. "I don't know what takes my breath away more—a handsome Frenchman or these hors d'oeuvres." She reached out and accepted a napkin from the waiter, then as delicately as I'd ever seen, proceeded to pop seven oyster fritters into her mouth. The waiter simply stood with the tray held out for her.

I cleared my throat and frowned. "Talk about manners."

With a mouthful of oysters, Paula said, "What? I'm eating for two!"

The waiter smiled and moved the tray closer to her. She picked up two additional oysters and put them on her napkin. "*Merci beaucoup.*"

The waiter gave a slight bow and retreated.

I watched Jean-Luc mingling. He touched almost everyone he greeted, a kiss here, a pat there, a squeeze, a handshake, a hug. Finally his eyes landed on mine with a generic welcome look. No recognition.

Maybe I looked a little different than the other day. After the hit-and-run and the trip to the emergency room I must have been even more disheveled than my normal self.

He squeezed Paula's free hand. "Welcome, *mademoiselle.*"

"Thank you for inviting us. Lovely party. Great hors d'oeuvres."

Jean-Luc laughed and pulled Paula closer, whispering something inaudible. Paula giggled.

He ignored me and proceeded on to another guest.

"What did he say?" I asked Paula.

"I don't know, he said it in French. But it gave me chills. Look!" She showed me her arm filled with goose bumps. "He's so sexy!"

I shrugged. "If you like that sort of thing."

Paula laughed and pushed my shoulder. "Every woman with a pulse likes that sort of thing! Jealous?"

"Pfft, he's a turkey. Besides, he's only giving the pregnant gal a little attention."

"God bless him," Paula said. "Someone has to."

From inside my purse my phone buzzed. I finished my cosmopolitan and placed it on the bar. Paula pinched my elbow as I reached inside my purse. "Look, I think that is the consul and his wife."

I glanced across the room as I pulled my cell phone out. A silver-haired gentleman was talking to an elegant woman more or less his age. I looked at the caller ID display. Jim.

Suddenly I missed him terribly.

What was I doing here? How angry would he be if I told him where I was?

"Honey!" I said, into the phone.

"Kate?"

"Yeah!"

"I can't really hear you. Where are you?"

"Hold on," I said. I left Paula in her place, oogling a waiter with a tray of escargot-stuffed mushrooms, and moved toward the exit. "Is this better?" I asked Jim.

"Sort of, yeah. Where are you?"

"I'm out with Paula."

"Good for you."

He was sincerely happy for me. Oh! The guilt!

"I was missing you and Laurie and wanted to check in with you, but I'll let you go. Have fun and call me when you get home," he said.

I promised to call him later and hung up.

I returned to Paula's side and found the waiter pleasantly parked in front of her with the tray of mushrooms.

She smiled and through a mouthful of food said, "These are so good! You have to try them."

I winked at the waiter. "I'm good, you can have mine," I said to Paula.

She beamed as she helped herself to another two mushrooms. The waiter bowed and retreated.

"I love this party," Paula said.

I laughed. "I'll bet."

The consul began to make his way toward us. All eyes were on him. He seemed to single me out and was suddenly by my side. "*Bonsoir, mademoiselle.* Wonderful to have you visiting the consulate. Please tell me, is everything to your liking?"

His gray eyes were on mine, a smile on his face. He was probably in his late sixties. Definitely a man who was used to getting his way.

"It's a lovely party." I smiled. "Thank you."

"And your interest in France is . . . ? Will you be visiting her soon?"

No! I was rear-ended by one of your vehicles with my infant in the car, am lucky to be standing here in front of your pompous arse, and some half-wit ran away from the scene and refuses to take responsibility!

Paula leaned in to save me. "I was in Paris for several months. *Très magnifique!*"

The consul seemed to grow an inch. "*Bravo!*"

A woman I presumed to be his wife, appeared at his side and laced her arm through his. She said something in French. He gave a slight nod to us and ushered her to the bar.

"What did she say?" I asked Paula.

Paula shrugged. "My French isn't that good. I think she wanted a drink or something."

I rolled my eyes. "I could guess that, I mean, they sidled up to the bar."

Paula tilted her head and waved her hand in a gesture of complete disregard, reminiscent of a French dismissal.

"What did you do all that time you were in France?" I asked.

Paula frowned. "What do you mean?"

"I thought you studied French. That you were at least conversational."

"I am conversational! I tramped all over Paris with Danny in tow. I know how to ask all sorts of kids' things. Like, *Où est les toilettes les plus proches de mon enfant vient de ramasser chien pooh.*"

"You're gonna make me ask, aren't you?"

"What?" Paula said, batting her eyelashes at me.

"I got the 'where's the toilet' part and something about dog pooh?"

Paula smirked. "It means, *Where's the nearest restroom— my kid just picked up dog pooh.*"

I laughed. "If you can say that, I'm sure you can understand what they're saying now." I shifted my eyes toward the consul and his wife at the bar.

A waiter shimmied past with Coquilles Saint-Jacques on his tray.

Paula's eyes were on the waiter instead of the consul. "They're talking too fast."

"Maybe if you focused on them instead of the food, you'd be able to catch it."

"No, I don't think so. But if I hurry I think I can catch him, it's the second time I've missed him," Paula said, following the waiter.

I laughed and watched her tap the waiter's shoulder and demurely accept his offer of Coquilles Saint-Jacques.

Across the room I spotted Kimberly Newman speaking with Jean-Luc. She seemed agitated. Her hands were moving frantically back and forth. Her gaze spanned the room and stopped just past me to where the consul stood with his wife. Their heads were bent toward each other and they seemed to be sharing a joke.

Kimberly grimaced.

From behind Kimberly, I spotted a ponytail. My breath caught.

Could it be him?

I jerked around to try to see past the people blocking my view.

It was him.

It was the boy who had driven the SUV right into Laurie and me. He looked a bit older than I'd thought initially, more like twenty-one or twenty-two.

A wave of anger surged through my body, jolting me into action.

I waved frantically at Paula to get her attention. She was busy talking to the waiter. I pressed through the crowd, bumping elbows and saying, *"Excuse-moi,"* to anyone who would listen, trying to get closer to her, my eyes still on the boy.

He was having a heated conversation with Jean-Luc. I had to reach him and I had to confront him or at the very least strangle him.

I grabbed Paula's elbow. "That's him."

Paula followed my gaze. "Oh! He's just a boy!"

I pulled her arm. "Come on."

We pushed through the crowd. The boy looked up momentarily and spotted me making my way toward him. His eyes widened in recognition and then he quickly looked around the room. He darted toward an exit on the right-hand side of the building and disappeared.

"Go without me, you'll be faster," Paula said.

"In these heels?"

Note to self: Do not wear ridiculously high heels if you are going to have to chase hit-and-run perpetrator. No matter how delicious the shoes!

·CHAPTER SIX·

The wind buffeted me as I exited the building. The door opened to a balcony. I peered over the railing: a narrow path led to a garden; off to the right was a staircase that descended to the path. The garden was dark and rather small. I could make out a row of bushes, probably rose-bushes. No one appeared to be hiding in the garden.

Where could he have gone?

I walked the length of the balcony. Although there were several strings of Christmas lights near the doorway, the main lights were off probably to encourage partygoers to stay indoors. The wind whipped around and I regretted only having a skimpy wrap.

When I reached the far end of the balcony I was in complete darkness. I guided myself by feeling along the wall. I felt a handle, it was a doorknob. I twisted it, but it was locked. The boy must have escaped through there.

I pulled my phone from my purse and used the light-up display to look around. Directly in front of me was an ivy trellis, which bordered the end of the balcony. Obviously, the boy hadn't gone in that direction, he must have gone through the door.

I punched Paula's number into my phone, although I was so angry my hands were shaking and I had to dial twice. I took a breath as the phone rang.

She picked up immediately. "Where are you? Did you get him?"

"No. I'm on the balcony. On the left side of the building, there's a door here that he must have used, but it's locked. Do me a favor and walk through the inside, see if you run into him."

"What do I do then?"

"I don't know. Entertain him a minute 'til I get there. I want to stay here in case he comes out again."

"Okay, well, I'm walking into the bowels of the consulate now. Oh. Red rope. Okay, let me just . . . get . . . over . . . whoa . . . pregnant lady almost capsizes. Don't worry, I'm okay."

"Good."

"I can't believe no one stopped me from walking back here. Ooooh . . ."

"What?" I asked.

"Beautiful statue."

"Paula focus. We're looking for a hit-and-run guy. Not statues."

"Um . . . yeah. Wow."

"What?"

"Oh. Never mind."

Suddenly, I heard voices at the other end of the balcony. I realized I'd been leaning against the door and with my black dress on and in the absence of lighting I was invisible to the parties that had just come through the main balcony doors.

I squinted. One figure was a large man. Definitely not the boy. And the other figure was feminine. I watched them embrace and kiss.

Paula's voiced filled my ear. "Well, I reached the end of the building. No sign of your perp."

The couple laughed. They didn't know I was there. The man said something in French and the voice . . .

It was the consul.

Uh . . . oh. Wasn't he married? His wife was in her sixties. I couldn't tell much about the lady he was with right now, but she definitely wasn't the wife.

I pressed myself into the wall. The last thing I needed was to encounter the wrath of a high-ranking official for witnessing his infidelity.

"I see the door," Paula said.

I froze. If she opened the door surely that would alert them to my presence. But what other escape would I have? I was already chilled to the bone, and waiting until they left could take forever. I'd glaciate!

No. Better to have Paula let me in. Even if the consul did see me, Paula and I could pop back into the party and disappear before he identified me.

"Hey!" A man's voice barked in the background of Paula's phone.

"Oops! Sorry," Paula said.

"Who's that?" I whispered to Paula.

"I didn't know anyone was here in the dark." I heard Paula's voice although at a bit of a distance as if she wasn't holding the phone to her ear.

"What are you doing here? No one is allowed back here.

The party's limited to the foyer," the man's voice said.

"Right. Sorry. I was looking for a restroom," I heard her say.

Did this mean she wasn't going to be able to open the door?

My teeth were chattering now. I glanced back at the consul. He had his hand inside the top of the woman's dress. The woman began to pull off his jacket.

Geez, they must really be hot for each other, because it was colder out here than the heart of a man who would smash into a woman and infant and leave them at the side of the road.

There was silence on the phone. I checked the digital display. The connection had dropped. Either Paula had hung up or . . .

What if she was in danger? Should I pound on the door? Were they even in this room? What if Paula was in a different room altogether? I had to get back to her.

Why would she be in danger? Stop getting ahead of yourself! Paula's probably fine, focus on catching the pinhead.

The consul and the woman descended the stairs and walked in the direction of the garden. Now was my chance to scoot down the balcony and get back inside the ballroom.

Suddenly the ivy trellis next to me began to vibrate.

Oh God! Ponytail had been hiding and now he was going to jump me.

Ire rose inside me. I pressed a button on my phone to make it light up and aimed it at the ivy. "Who's there?" I demanded.

The bush shook violently and then something shot out toward me.

I recoiled.

A huge hairy rat trampled across my feet.

I let out a bloodcurdling scream and involuntarily began to dance around, the heebie-jeebies taking over my brain and causing me to shout, stomp, and shudder repeatedly.

Footsteps pounded up the staircase, and the consul appeared by my side. *"Mademoiselle!* What it is? Are you all right?"

His hands grabbed at my arms in an effort to calm me down.

I gave another stomp and tried to shake off my disgust. "A rat," I said breathlessly. "I saw its beady little eyes."

Another round of willies shot up my spine, shaking my shoulders.

"A rat?" The consul let out a belly laugh. "Is that it? I thought you were being killed." He laughed again.

A mix of anger, adrenaline, and bravado surged through me. "It's not funny!"

The consul reined in his laughter and composed his features, putting a hand over his heart. *"Cherie,* I'm sorry. The screams, the noise, I thought there was a fight up here."

I squinted at him. "There could have been. I was following the driver who—"

The main door to the ballroom flew open, a swell of party laughter escaping.

The man with the unruly curly hair stepped out. "Eloi!"

The door closed, silencing the noise, and the consul bolted toward the man with me in tow.

"Ici," the consul said, steering me toward the man.

The man's eyes widened when he saw me.

The consul fired something off in French.

The man nodded at the consul and replied in rapid French. They seemed to come to an immediate understanding.

The man said, "*Mademoiselle*, please come back inside with me."

The consul straightened his jacket and retreated down the balcony toward the locked door and ivy trellis. He fished a set of keys from his pocket.

"No! Wait! One of your staff or whatever crashed into my car—"

The consul ignored me, inserted a key into the door, and disappeared.

I turned to the curly-haired man. "He's here tonight, a boy with a ponytail—"

The man dug into his sports coat and pulled out a brown wallet. From the wallet, he retrieved a card and handed it to me.

"I followed him out here—" I continued.

"Please, *mademoiselle*, come see me on Monday. This is my direct number." He opened the door to the ballroom. The din swept over us.

His hand was on the small of my back and he unequivocally thrust me inside. "Let's take a look at the Christmas tree."

I broke free from him, jerking away from his touch.

He frowned but I ignored him, scanning the crowd for Paula. I rushed toward the back of the building, guessing that she could still be there trying to figure out a way to break me in through the door.

But then wouldn't the consul have run into her? And if so, so what? They couldn't do anything worse to me than they'd already done by smashing into my car when my most valuable treasure was in it.

I scrambled over the red rope, clearly there to keep guests out of the area. My heel got hung up on the rope and I pitched forward, breaking my fall with my hands.

"Mrs. Connolly," a voice said from above me. "May I help you?"

Hands gripped my shoulders and righted me.

Jean-Luc.

He remembered me. Of course he did. His pretending earlier had just been a snub.

He spun me around. "No one is allowed back here except consulate personnel."

I shrugged his hands off me.

What was with these people touching me?

"Consulate personnel who run into women and infants and then flee the scene of the crime?"

Anger flashed across his face. "This is not the time nor the place to discuss your accusations!"

I squared off against him, my eyes boring into his. "I saw him. I saw the boy who hit me. Does he have diplomatic immunity, too? You were talking with him. You and the reporter Kimberly Newman. Does she know consulate personnel are in the habit of running into American citizens and then disappearing? Would that make a nice front-page headline?"

Jean-Luc's upper lip twitched into a sneer. "What is it you want? You want money? We can pay for your car."

"Your insurance is denying—"

Voices filled the corridor. I spun around to see a band in tuxedos emerge from one of the rooms with Paula in tow.

"Kate!" Paula laughed happily.

One of the band members handed Jean-Luc a glass of champagne. They exchanged pleasantries, and then Jean-Luc smiled over his shoulder at me as he walked with the band member toward the foyer. "You have my number, Mrs. Connolly."

I squinted at him. "I have your number, all right." On a whim, I followed him for a few steps and said, "Let me give you mine." I pressed my business card into his hand.

He snickered but gave it a cursory glance. His head whipped up. "You're a private investigator?" he said, his voice full of annoyance.

A gentleman standing apart from the crowd whipped his head in our direction. He had gray hair but a dark mustache and eyebrows. He watched the exchange between Jean-Luc and I with interest.

Now it was my turn to smile.

Playing games isn't reserved for the French.

Before Jean-Luc could say anything else, he was pushed toward the stage by a band member. He took the stage and grabbed a microphone. He made several remarks in French, which were greeted with cheers and whistles from the crowd.

I looked at Paula for a translation. She shrugged. "The usual, you know, *Ladies and gentlemen, thank you for coming, hope you're having a blah blah*—" Paula raised an eyebrow and said, "Oh!"

"What?"

"He just announced that the consul has been awarded the *Légion d'honneur*. That's a big deal. Huge."

I scanned the crowd for the consul. I found him making his way to the podium with his wife at his side.

What happened to Miss Hot and Heavy?

When I'd screamed, he'd come running, but what about her? Was she still outside in the garden?

The consul's hand swept through his hair. He laughed as he took the stage. To others the laugh probably came off as if he was happy about the award, but to me it played arrogant and cocky. He accepted the microphone from Jean-Luc.

Apparently, fidelity is not a requirement for the Legion of Honor.

Several reporters snapped pictures of the consul as he gave his speech. I thought of Nancy Pickett. Could the award have been the story she was working on? Maybe she'd gotten wind of his affair and was looking into it.

What about Kimberly? Was she working on the same story as Nancy? I searched around for her, but didn't see her.

"Where's the award?" I asked Paula.

Paula pulled her eyes off the consul and looked at me. "What?"

"Does he get a plaque or something, a trophy?"

Paula waved her hand in dismissal. "Oh, they'll have an official ceremony for him in France. I think they get a ribbon, you know, a badge."

As the consul droned on, I perused the crowd for the boy. No sight of him. However, I saw that the gentleman with the gray hair and dark eyebrows kept an eye on me.

Feeling a bit deflated, I asked Paula, "Are you ready to go? I didn't tell you but on the balcony I saw two rats."

Paula's eyes widened.

"One real, that attacked me from an ivy tower and another one who commits adultery but still gets the highest commendation in the land." I nodded toward the consul.

Paula made a disapproving face. "Jerk. Let's go."

As we walked toward the exit, a waiter materialized in front of Paula and knowingly waved his tray in front of her. She played coy for a moment, then gave up and popped a few more oyster fritters into her mouth.

"For the road," she said.

I felt a light touch on my arm.

I looked up and was surprised to see the man with gray

hair and black eyebrows that had been watching Jean-Luc and me.

"Did I overhear you say you're a private investigator?" he whispered urgently.

I nodded.

He pressed a cocktail napkin into my hand. "Please call me." He glanced around nervously and then sped toward the exit.

"Who was that?" Paula asked through a mouthful of oysters.

I wiggled my eyebrows at her. "My mystery man."

Paula snorted a laugh through her nose and then punched my arm. "Don't make me laugh with food in my mouth. You want me to choke?"

I rubbed my arm. "If I say you shouldn't talk with your mouth full then you're going to hit me again, right?"

"No, of course not," she said, casually linking her arm through mine and pinching my wrist.

"Ouch!"

She steered us toward the exit. "I was going to step on your foot, but I figured your feet were already sore enough."

I pushed open my front door and waved at Paula's car as she sped off. Before I could even greet my mom, I kicked off the high heels.

"Instruments of torture!" I said.

Mom laughed. "Nobody forced you to wear those."

She stood in my living room holding Laurie and slowly rocking her back and forth. Laurie's tiny face peeked out from the tight swaddle. She was sound asleep.

I threw my pocket-size Rafē New York purse onto the coffee table and took Laurie out of Mom's arms. I clutched her to me, feeling overwhelmed with gratitude and love for my little angel.

I held Laurie close so I could breathe in her scent, but instead all I could smell was Mom's face cream.

"Did you put her down at all?" I asked.

A guilty expression crossed Mom's face. "Yes," she said unconvincingly.

"No, you didn't," I countered. "She's smells exactly like you. I bet you held her the entire time, didn't you?"

"What's wrong with that?" Mom asked. "I don't get to see her very often."

"You're over here every day! And I don't care if you hold her the entire time, but just yesterday you were giving me a hard time about it, telling me that if I don't put her down to sleep, I'm going to spoil her."

"Well, that's true. *You* shouldn't hold her all the time. But I'm her grandmother, it's totally different."

Before I could object, Mom picked up my purse from the coffee table and asked, "What is *this*?"

"My purse."

"Well, no wonder your feet were hurting! Haven't I told you a million times? You need to have a purse big enough for an extra pair of shoes!"

Mom never left the house without a backup pair of shoes. If she wore high heels to a dinner, she always stashed a pair of flats in her bag. Even when she wore flats or tennis shoes she took along an extra pair, proclaiming proudly that if her shoes inadvertently got wet she had a backup plan.

My feet throbbed, but suddenly I didn't want to admit it. "Oh. The shoes weren't that bad."

Mom made a face. "You're limping!" She upturned my

purse on the coffee table. "What can you get in this thing, anyway?"

My cell phone, lipstick, and cash tumbled out along with the crumbled cocktail napkin.

"The necessities."

"No. You don't have the necessities! No backup shoes! And if you go without those then at least you have to have an emergency Band-Aid for the inevitable blister or *blisters* you're going to get." She picked up the crumpled cocktail napkin. "And what's this? You need to pack a handkerchief so you don't have to blow your nose on a napkin!"

"I didn't blow my nose on it—"

Mom opened the napkin to reveal the name *Chuck Vann* and his phone number in black marker. She gasped, "One night without Jim and—"

I laughed. "Don't be so melodramatic. I didn't pick up the guy—"

Mom talked over me. "Well, with the dress and heels and all . . . I hope you told him you were married with a baby."

"Oh, stop." I shook my head. "It's a lead. Someone interested in my services—"

Mom raised an eyebrow.

"I mean, you know, as a private investigator."

Mom squinted. "Why?"

"I'm not sure. He seemed nervous and rushed." I shrugged. "I'll call him in the morning."

Mom gathered her bag. "Did you find the guy who ran into you?"

With my free hand, I dug into the side zippered pocket where I had put a few of my own business cards along with the one the curly-haired gentleman had given me. I pulled it out now and examined it.

It read, *Christophe Benoit, Deputy Consul, Press Attaché*.

I showed the card to Mom. "Sort of, but I didn't get a chance to talk to him. Instead, I have to call this guy."

Mom nodded and stroked Laurie's cheek. "She was a dear, took her bottle at seven, just like you said." She kissed me on the cheek. "Will you need me to baby-sit tomorrow?"

"I don't think so. You have a hot date?"

She wiggled her eyebrows at me. "Yes."

"Which one?"

After being divorced and single for years, Mom had finally stepped into the dating scene and currently juggled two boyfriends: my boss, Galigani, and a pharmacist, Hank.

"Hank."

I smiled inwardly. Good. That meant that maybe Galigani would be available to meet with Mr. Vann and me.

Mom examined the heels I'd kicked into the corner. "Can I borrow these?"

CHAPTER SEVEN

To Do:

1. Reschedule holiday photos—get Laurie's dress cleaned.

2. Christmas cards and shopping.

3. Get Jim to follow up with insurance company.

4. Call Mr. Vann.

5. Call Christophe Benoit.

6. Decide on Christmas dinner recipes and practice (butternut squash soup?).

7. Pick up Jim from the airport.

In the morning I dialed Chuck Vann.

"Hello, Mr. Vann. This is Kate Connolly, the private investigator. We met briefly at the French consul's Christmas—"

"Mrs. Connolly. Thank you so much for calling me. I'd like to speak with you about retaining your services."

What could I tell the guy? I'd been dragged into a few investigations and gotten lucky?

I cleared my throat and sat up a little taller hoping that would make my voice sound more professional. "Certainly."

There was silence on the line.

Was he going to ask me something? Or should I say something?

"Uh . . . yeah. I do investigation work. Mostly for private parties. Sometimes for attorneys."

That much was true. Yes. I'd worked for both! Wow, now my little business was starting to really sound like something! Never mind that I didn't have a license! So what?

"I see," he said. "Have you been retained to look into the consul?"

Interesting! Why would I be looking into the consul?

"I have not been *officially* retained to look into the consul," I answered.

Boy, did I sound like a lawyer or what?

Mr. Vann said, "Can we meet at your office? I think I'd like to discuss hiring you to do just that."

Office?

Shoot! Here was the part where I couldn't help but sound unprofessional. No office! Could I rent one for a day?

"Mrs. Connolly?"

"Yes. Uh. My office is . . . uh . . . under construction right now." Okay, not a complete lie. It was under construction in my mind. Kind of like in the design phase. Visualization phase to be honest. "Why don't we meet at—"

"Not in public. Can you come here? I live on Lake Street."

Why didn't he want to meet in public?

He gave me the specifics as I jotted them down in my notebook. I tried to schedule the meeting for Monday when Jim would be back, but Mr. Vann sounded so distraught that I reluctantly agreed to meet him that afternoon. With Mom on a date, that left Paula for baby-sitting. I dialed her immediately, but she didn't pick up.

I sent her a text message, then called Galigani.

"I have a problem. Someone wants to meet me to maybe hire me as a PI and I've got a baby in tow."

"You got several problems then," Galigani said.

"Yeah? How so."

"Number one, you need a sitter for the meeting."

"That's why I'm calling you."

"So I can baby-sit?"

"Was that fear in your voice?" I asked.

"No!"

"What was it then? Your voice cracked. You scared of a three-month-old?"

He was silent for a moment, then cleared his throat. "Just a frog. I was going to say your second problem is that you're not a PI."

"That's never bothered me before."

"I thought *that* was why you were calling me, about the PI stuff, not to baby-sit."

"Look, in one instance you're baby-sitting me and in the other it's Laurie. Take your pick."

He laughed. "You want me to go to the meeting with you?"

"What? So you can steal my client?"

"I wouldn't do that. What time's the meeting? You can tell the guy I'm the nanny. I have nothing better to do today anyway—your mom's busy."

"Meeting's at three on Lake Street. I'll swing by and pick you up at two."

I hung up before he could say anything else. I dreaded him asking me where Mom was. I had no idea what she'd told him about Hank and I didn't want to be put in the middle.

After hanging up with him, I called the mall photo place and forced them to pencil Laurie in for a holiday photo shoot on Monday at eleven. Then I packed Laurie and sped to the grocery store. I had tons of Christmas shopping to do, but a Saturday in December didn't seem like a smart time to do it. I could shop on Monday while waiting for Laurie's photos to be printed.

Oooh! I was getting smart and time conscious! After all, shopping on a Monday was one of the benefits of being master of your own schedule. No time clock to punch Monday at 9 A.M. like in the corporate world.

I was just feeling smug about my time management when I realized I was running late. Grocery shopping with an infant takes so much more time than flying solo! I'd stopped in every aisle to either check on her, wipe her, or tickle her. I considered myself lucky that she'd been in a good mood and extremely patient.

I'd particularly lost a lot of time in the infant section, after fighting with myself on whether or not to buy formula. I'd finally succumbed, thinking that if I took on the case Mr. Vann wanted to discuss I might be out of the house when Laurie needed food.

As I put several cans into the basket, I felt a huge ball of ash in my stomach, as though I was a terrible mom.

Couldn't I just produce enough milk for Laurie via the

*pump? If I put time and effort into it . . . or if I didn't take
the case . . .*

No! Breastfeeding didn't make the measure of the mom,
I reasoned as I pushed the cart out of the aisle in scarcely
enough time not to second-guess myself.

At home, I hurriedly put the groceries in the refrigerator and then fed Laurie. I changed her into a fresh diaper
and jumper then put her back into the car to pick up Galigani.

I filled him in on the party at the consulate. Galigani
listened in silence. As I searched for parking, he surprised
me.

"So what do you know about this guy?"

"Who? The boy from the hit-and-run?"

"No. Mr. Vann."

"I don't know anything about him. Just that I saw him
at the party and he wants to hire a PI."

Galigani squinted at me. "What's he want to hire a PI
for?"

I shrugged. "I thought that's what he was going to tell
us now."

Galigani put his hand on my wrist. "Never go into a
meeting blind. Never. That's how you get hurt."

I blinked at him.

I should have run Vann's name through the database.

I parked the car. "What do we do now?"

Galigani took a deep breath and reached into his pocket.
"It's a good thing I'm baby-sitting."

He handed me a folded sheet of paper. Chuck Vann's
background report. I scanned it quickly. No criminal con-
victions, good credit, and an advanced degree in engineer-
ing from UC–Berkeley.

I nodded at Galigani. "Okay. So there's nothing to worry

about. The guy looks nice enough on paper and even in person—"

"There is something to worry about."

"Uh. Oh. What?"

"He's Nancy Pickett's ex. He's the prime suspect in her murder. McNearny pulled him in for questioning yesterday."

McNearny was Galigani's former SFPD partner and he'd worked the two homicides I'd investigated. He wasn't necessarily a fan of mine.

"Why didn't you tell me?" I asked.

"I'm telling you now," Galigani said.

"Yeah, but we have Laurie with us!"

"Vann's not going to do anything. He probably wants you to help him clear him somehow."

"What did McNearny say? Does Vann have an alibi?"

"Well, an alibi is always nice. Nancy was last seen alive Thursday morning and she wasn't found until Friday."

"What's her time of death?"

"ME's putting it around Thursday morning between six and nine." Galigani glanced at his watch. "Why don't we talk to the man ourselves?"

I took Laurie's car seat bucket out of the car and trailed Galigani to Mr. Vann's doorstep.

Mr. Vann appeared in a white button-down shirt and gray corduroy pants, looking quite professorial. Judging by the circles under his eyes, he clearly hadn't slept much the night before.

He seemed surprised to see me with Laurie and Galigani in tow.

"Mr. Vann, this is senior investigator Galigani and our secretary, Laurie," I said.

Mr. Vann laughed and extended his hand to Galigani. "Pleased to meet you. Call me Chuck. Come in."

He ushered us into a comfortable living room. The room was lined with bookshelves that were filled from floor to ceiling.

"Can I offer either one of you anything to drink?" he asked.

Galigani and I both declined, seating ourselves on the sofa. Chuck nervously cleared his throat and then picked up a manila folder from a side table. He pulled a chair toward the coffee table and faced us.

He opened the folder and spoke into it more than to us. "I need to hire someone to look into the murder of Nancy Pickett." He glanced up, checking us for recognition. He nodded when he realized both Galigani and I knew who Nancy was.

"Nancy and I were married fifteen years. She was found dead in Golden Gate Park, last Thursday morning. I think she was killed because of a story she was working on. I can't prove it, though." He laughed bitterly. "If I could prove it, I wouldn't need you, right?"

"What about the police?" Galigani asked.

Anger flashed in Chuck's eyes. "They're looking into it, of course. We all know how much they care about justice," he said, his voice thick with sarcasm.

Galigani fumed next to me. "Well, let me say right off the bat—"

"You're a former cop," Chuck finished dryly. "Anyone could see that a mile away: It's written across your forehead." His eyes flashed to me. "That's why I thought . . . I thought Kate . . ."

Laurie kicked her feet in delight and cooed to Chuck as

if appreciating him appreciating me. Chuck smiled. "She's darling."

Galigani squirmed next to me. I glared at him. "Believe me, Mr. Vann, we understand the need for private investigators," I said.

He studied me. "I thought you might."

"Why don't you tell us what you know?" Galigani asked.

"Will it be confidential?"

At the same time as I said, "Of course," Galigani stood and said, "If you want confidentiality, go see an attorney."

I'd never seen Galigani mad and I didn't know what to do. Seemed, since he was my boss, I should stand with him and share his indignation. Yet, I wanted to stay to hear out Chuck. After all, Chuck was a potential client. If I landed him, maybe I'd be able to afford a down payment on a new car, regardless of how long my insurance company dragged its feet.

Galigani frowned at me when he saw I was still seated. He grumbled, "May I use your bathroom, Mr. Vann?"

Chuck stood. "Down the hall on your left."

Galigani nodded and headed down the hallway. I figured he was trying to save face after standing, but the idea of him slipping into other rooms and snooping amused me.

As soon as Galigani left the room, Chuck leaned in toward me in a conspiratorial fashion. "What were you doing at the consul's Christmas party last night? Are you already investigating them?"

I knew my reasons had probably nothing to do with his but I nodded anyway.

He nodded back at me. "Nancy was looking into the Legion of Honor requirements."

"Looking into it? You mean she was reporting on it?" I asked.

"She was concerned about the validity of the award."
Chucked opened the file on his lap. "She'd been meeting
with the consul the day before she was killed. He claimed
he didn't know why he was up for the commendation."

I recalled her leaving the consulate that day. "Was she
working with Kimberly Newman?"

Chuck's head jerked up in surprise. "Kimberly? No.
They were friends, but as far as I know Nancy was working alone. Why do you ask?"

"I was at the consulate on Wednesday and I saw them
leaving together."

Chuck chewed on his lip. "He handed me the folder. I
have a list of people for you to start with. Kimberly's not
on the list, but maybe she should be."

I opened the folder and perused the list. William Clarkson and Mindy Burnfield. I recognized them from a news
story I'd read the other night. They had found Nancy.
I said as much to Chuck and he nodded. "Already did
your homework."

I cringed. I hadn't done as much homework as I should
have. Galigani still hadn't returned from the restroom. Where
was he?

My phone buzzed from the depth of the diaper bag.

"Excuse me one second," I said, retrieving the bag and
bumping Laurie's car seat at the same time. Laurie cooed
and flailed an arm at me as I dug into the bag.

I read the display, a text message from Galigani: Keep
him busy.

Uh oh. I'd been right. He was snooping.

I pressed the button to delete the text and said to Chuck,
"I'd like to review the list with you. Who is Karen Nolan?"

"That's Nancy's boss. I called several times, but she's
on vacation, what with the holidays and all."

I rubbed Laurie's little arm. "Okay, what about the others?"

"Gordon is Nancy's father, her mother's deceased, and Elliot is her brother. I spoke to Elliot when Nancy's body was found in the park. I don't think he or Gordon know anything, but I thought it might be helpful for you if I put their names down."

I nodded. "Who's Ramon?"

Chuck grimaced. "The boyfriend."

"Want to tell me about him?"

Chuck rolled his eyes. "Obviously, I don't care for him. He came between Nancy and I, but do I think he killed her? No. You should talk to him though, because I don't want to and he may know something."

"Okay. I can talk to him, no problem. What about yourself, Mr. Vann? I understand you met with Officer McNearny. Is there anything you want to share with me?"

He looked at his hands. "I teach a class in Palo Alto on Thursday mornings. I've been doing it for the last twenty years. But we didn't have class last Thursday because the semester ended on Wednesday."

Uh no.

We sat in an uncomfortable silence. Finally I asked, "What about the award? Tell me, why was Nancy concerned about it?"

Chuck glanced around the room as if suddenly noticing that Galigani hadn't returned. He turned toward me, a confused look on his face.

"He's got a . . . condition," I whispered.

Chuck nodded and shook his head, as if forgiving Galigani for popping a cork earlier.

"Nancy called me Wednesday night. This wasn't unusual.

We talked regularly and we were still pretty friendly. She told me she was looking into it and had found some irregularities in the vetting process." He indicated the folder. "I printed out some stuff for you I found online about the consul. Anyway, she told me she was frightened. I didn't think anything of it. I guess I thought she meant she was worried about her job. She was very ambitious. Wanted an anchor job and always thought if she could break a big enough story it might make Karen wake up and see her. But . . ." He shook his head and sighed.

An uneasiness settled over me. If Nancy had stirred up something big enough to get herself killed, did I really want to poke my nose into it?

My eyes landed on Laurie. She was wide awake and staring right back at me.

Galigani materialized in the doorway. He eyed me and nodded.

I rose. "Mr. Vann. I'll study the documents you gave me and get back to you soon."

Chuck stood, disappointment on his face. "Um. Do you have a contract or something for me to sign?"

I glanced at Galigani. "I need to evaluate the firm's current obligations before taking on another case."

Galigani bowed his head to hide a smirk.

In the car, Galigani said, "What was that about the firm's obligations?"

I shrugged and put the car in gear. "I don't know. You didn't seem to like the guy and . . ."

"You're lost without me?"

I snorted. "He thinks Nancy was killed because of the

story she was working on. If that's true, why do I need to get involved? Someone from the consulate already ran me down and that was an accident."

Galigani fiddled with the heater in my car. "Was it?"

"Oh come on, are you trying to make me more paranoid than I already am?"

Galigani laughed. "You're looking into them anyway, so why not get paid?"

"I'm not looking into them. I was trying to find the guy responsible for smashing into Laurie and me."

Galigani nodded. "It's doubtful she was killed because of the story. Do you know stats on homicide cases where the ex is the killer?

"Over sixty percent," I said.

Galigani smiled. "Okay, you did some research, huh?"

I shrugged. "Google's a good friend, and I remember the number from the last case."

"The guy have an alibi?"

I shook my head. Galigani sighed.

We drove in silence for the next few minutes, then I pulled into Galigani's driveway. "You think he's making up the story angle? Reporter pokes into a hornet's nest and gets stung?"

Galigani shrugged. "If he is, we'll find out." He climbed out of my car, then leaned back in and handed me something.

It was a flash drive. "What's this for?"

"I copied Chuck's e-mail file and Internet history. Do you know how to import a .pst file?"

"What a hack you are! I would have never thought you'd do that!"

Galigani laughed. "Why not? You think I was born yesterday? Or is it the opposite, you think I'm too old to—?"

"I didn't think you were the type," I said.

"I'm the type to figure things out."

"He wants to hire us. I don't think he's hiding information from us."

Galigani made a face. "Well, this way we'll know. If Nancy Pickett was scared or thought the consul is hiding something, you may find some leads here." He straightened, closed the car door, then waved at Laurie in the backseat before retreating into his house.

CHAPTER EIGHT

That evening, I snuggled into bed with Laurie. She was nestled on my arm asleep as I perused the file Chuck had given me. Inside I found a who's-who directory printout of the consulate personnel.

My heart stopped. Staring up at me from the pages was Armand Remy, assistant in cultural services, aka hit-and-run driver. The listing was complete with e-mail and phone number.

On a whim, I grabbed my cell phone and dialed. I got his voice mail. What could I say?

Would it do any good to leave a message?

I hung up, frustrated with myself. Why did I chicken out? As I looked at the square-inch picture of him, I felt like strangling him.

How could he have left Laurie and me stranded at the

side of the road? The accident I could forgive, I suppose. Accidents happen, but what kind of a man leaves a mom and infant? He'd known about Laurie, too. After the accident, when I'd locked eyes with him as he sped off, I knew he'd seen her in the car seat.

I placed Laurie into her bassinet and took the flash drive Galigani had given me over to the computer. How would I import the .pst file without overriding my own data? Just as I was getting frustrated with the whole process my phone rang.

Jim's voice filled the line. "Honey, how are you?"

A sense of peace and security flooded me. "We're good. I miss you. I found him."

"Him, who?" Jim asked.

"The hit-and-run driver."

"How?"

I hadn't thought this conversation through. If I mentioned Chuck Vann, I'd have to tell him about the Christmas party, wouldn't I? Better to save that conversation until he was home. "Long story," I stalled. "I can't wait until tomorrow."

"I know, me, too. We landed the account!"

"Oh Jim! That's great."

"Yeah. It's going to be big for us. Lots of work in the New Year."

My phone beeped to notify me of a call waiting.

"I'm so happy for you. Honey, I have a call coming through, but I'll pick you up from the airport." I blew kisses through the phone and then clicked over to the new call.

"Kate? What are you doing? I haven't seen you at the café for ages."

It was my neighbor, Kenny. He was a gifted seventeen-year-old who'd graduated recently from the School of the Arts. He'd landed a spot as a substitute trombone player for the San Francisco Opera, but because he'd been helping me out of a jam, he had basically blown his shot to play. Now he was out auditioning again.

I moved to my front window and peeked out. Kenny, with his spiky green hair, waved at me.

"What are you doing out so late?" I asked.

"It's seven."

"That's it?" I was so exhausted from running around all day it felt much later. "In that case, what are you doing home on a Saturday night?"

"I'm not home. I'm over here." He pounded up my front steps. "You got anything to eat?"

I swung open the door. "Laurie's asleep," I said.

Kenny put his finger to his lips. "I'll be quiet," he whispered.

I smiled. "You don't have to whisper, just don't yell."

He stepped inside and jumped on my couch in such a way that he was immediately reclined.

"Get your shoes off my couch."

He kicked his Skechers off.

"I actually meant for you to sit up, you hooligan."

Kenny laughed and propped his head up with a pillow. "I'm too weak. I need to eat. Whatdya got?"

"What's wrong with your place?"

"My parents are visiting my aunt in Washington."

"Didn't your mom leave you any food?"

Kenny made a face. "Come on, Kate, they're vegans. She left me bean curry."

"That sounds good," I said.

"No it doesn't. No part of it sounds good. Not the bean part and not the curry part."

I laughed.

"Where's Jim?" Kenny asked. "Is he grilling anything?"

"He's on a trip."

Kenny pressed his lips together. "It's a good thing I came by then."

"Why?"

"So you and Laurie can have a man around. To, you know, feel safe."

I kept the thoughts to myself that a) he was not a *man* yet and b) I hadn't been feeling unsafe at all.

"What do you want to eat?" I asked.

"I really want some steak, but hey, I'll take whatever you got."

Because I'd actually gone shopping, I had a full refrigerator for a change, but the thought of cooking anything elaborate fatigued me.

"I got steaks."

He sat upright. "Yes!"

"But I'm not doing anything fancy. Just a quick grill on the stovetop," I warned.

"No problem. I'll do the sides."

We moved into the kitchen. As I prepared the steaks, Kenny cut some fresh green beans and sautéed them.

While we ate, I brought him up to speed on the events of the last week. Kenny offered to import the .pst file for me. It took him about three seconds.

If this keeps up I'm going to have to invest in a remedial computer course! Another thing to add to my to-do list.

Kenny hovered over my shoulder as I absently clicked

through Chuck's e-mails, sorting by the ones sent from Nancy. By the tone of the notes, they were obviously still very close. She seemed to depend on him for moral support and encouragement.

Laurie cried out from my bedroom.

"I'll get her," Kenny said happily.

He went to fetch Laurie out of the bassinet and returned shortly with her in his arms. "Uh . . . I think she's wet."

I nodded toward the diaper-changing table.

Kenny looked frightened and held Laurie out to me.

"You don't know how to change a diaper?"

"Yeah. I know how. Sure. I know how."

I nodded again toward the changing table. "I just grilled you a steak. The least you can do is a diaper change."

Kenny sulked over to the changing station.

"Be sure to hold on to her. She's very squirmy," I said.

"How do I change her with only one hand?" he whined.

I ignored him and continued to review the e-mails. I found one long exchange about the consul, and could see why Chuck had been concerned, but it didn't give me much to go on.

Am working on a story about the French consul, Eloi Leppard. He's to receive the highest honor from the French government—the *Légion d'honneur*, only something is strange about it. I got a call on it today. I'm going to look into it.

And about a week later:

Things with the consul are turning grim. I went to the consulate today and I think I was actually threatened. I'm not liking this one bit, but if I'm scared I'm probably on the right path, right?

A string of frantic replies from Chuck followed, asking who threatened her and why she was scared, but as far as I could tell his messages had gone unanswered.

Now I had a strong desire to hack into Nancy's computer. The police would certainly have her computer in custody. Who else would Nancy have confided in? Her boss, her boyfriend?

Kenny had bundled Laurie into a blanket and was seated in the living room with her in his lap while he channel surfed. I took advantage of his baby-sitting and continued to work.

I looked over the list of contacts Chuck had given me and began dialing. I left messages for Nancy's father and brother, but got nowhere with the news station. I spoke briefly with her boyfriend, Ramon. He agreed to see me the following day in the afternoon. In the morning, I needed to pick Jim up from the airport. He'd be able to watch Laurie while I met with Ramon.

When Ramon gave me his address a chill tickled my spine. He lived in the Richmond district, which bordered Golden Gate Park. His apartment was just off the 41st Avenue park entrance, not far from where Nancy's body had been discovered.

As soon as I hung up I did a cursory background check on him in the database Galigani had given me access to. He'd declared bankruptcy and lost the house he'd been living in a few years ago, but other than the financial troubles everything looked in order. There were no outstanding warrants or judgments on him. He seemed pretty clean.

I poked around online and scoured the news from the past few days. I knew Nancy had gone missing on Thursday morning, the day after Jim and I had seen her. I read that her body had been found by a couple walking in Golden Gate Park on Friday: William Clarkson and Mindy Burnfield.

According to the article, they lived in the Sunset District, which was my neighborhood and also bordered Golden Gate Park. They lived about ten minutes away from us. They were on Mr. Vann's list of people to talk to so I copied their address into my notebook.

Man, this investigation business was starting to get so busy that I'd need an assistant myself. I laughed. If I was an "intern" for Galigani and I needed help, where was I gonna find an intern for an intern?

I checked on Kenny and Laurie. She was asleep in his lap. With his feet propped up on my coffee table he was watching a rerun of a reality show.

"Nowhere better to be on a Saturday night?" I asked, as I took Laurie out of his arms.

Kenny shrugged. "There's a new girl working at the café."

I raised an eyebrow. "Yeah?"

"Hot butterfly tattoo on her shoulder."

"So, why don't you ask her out?"

"Pfft. You have to have money to take a girl out." He rose. "Thanks for dinner. I better get home and practice. I have an audition next week."

I let him out, then nursed Laurie. Before putting her down for the night, I laid her on the changing table to give her a clean diaper. I had the best laugh I'd had in weeks as I found that Kenny had put her diaper on backward.

I put Laurie down, then fell into an exhausted sleep.

I dreamt I'd caught Armand Remy on the balcony at the consulate. After a heated exchange, my hands had wrapped around his neck. I squeezed and squeezed. I woke with a start and noticed I had the sheets gripped tightly in my hands. I released the sheets and fell directly back asleep.

CHAPTER NINE

To Do:

1. ✓ ~~Reschedule holiday photos.~~

2. Get Laurie's dress cleaned.

3. Christmas cards and shopping.

4. ✓ ~~Find kid~~ Armand Remy!—does he have insurance?

5. ✓ ~~Call Mr. Vann.~~ Prepare contract!

6. Call Christophe Benoit.

7. Computer class?

I awoke with a start as I heard our front door open. Someone was in the house!

I jumped out of bed and looked around for the phone or a shoe or anything to hit an intruder with. Luckily, before I could grab anything I heard Jim's voice call out.

I rushed to the living room and jumped into his arms. "What are you doing here?"

He squeezed me. "I caught another flight, didn't you get my text?"

"No! When did you send it?" I kissed him all over his face. "I missed you."

"Me, too. I'm glad I'm home."

"You scared me though. You're lucky I didn't rush out here with a weapon and bash you—"

He laughed. "It wouldn't be the first time."

He put his fingers in my hair and kissed my lips. A wail escaped from our bedroom.

"Uh oh," I said.

"Peanut!" he said, taking off down the hall.

He scooped her up in his arms and cradled her. She stopped crying immediately and curled up like a little sow bug on his shoulder.

It was 6 A.M., still dark out, but feeding time for Laurie.

"Are you hungry?" I asked Jim. "I can make you breakfast after . . ."

"No," he yawned. "Let's go to sleep."

Later in the morning, I prepared Mr. Vann's contract. I had to spend some precious extra time fighting with our printer, not only reprinting, but shutting our temperamental computer system down and then booting it up again, hoping a new connection to the printer would help. A new printer was probably in order, or maybe a whole new system; either way, it spelled time and expense!

In the afternoon, I filled Jim in on the case and then left Laurie with him watching some football. I first drove by Mr. Vann's house and dropped the contract in his mailbox, then took off for my appointment with Ramon. I stood outside his place and rang the bell. I was starting to feel good about taking on the case.

Ramon answered the door wearing khaki pants, a white T-shirt, and black apron. He was about five feet ten inches tall and tan with smooth, even facial features. He had full lips and high cheekbones. His hair was jet black and piled high with some sort of gel. He wiped his hand on the apron and gave me a smile.

"Kate? Come in. I hope you brought your appetite."

Although I never left home without it, I'd promised myself I wouldn't eat anything prepared by a suspect ever again. The last time I'd eaten at the widower's place I'd landed myself in the emergency room to get my stomach pumped and it had all been due to my paranoia. Not worth eating here.

As soon as I stepped into his apartment the smell of frying onions hit me. I breathed it in—certainly that couldn't hurt.

"Come to the kitchen, we can talk there," Ramon said.

I followed him down a narrow hallway to the brightly lit kitchen.

"I'm making pollo adobo, a traditional Mexican dish. Have you tried it?"

I nodded. "Delicious."

I watched as he expertly mixed in a puree with some chicken that was browning. When he put the dish on simmer, the timer on the stove beeped, and he opened the oven door to reveal a glass pan of cheesy enchiladas.

Using an oven mitt he extracted the pan. "Sit," he said, "I'll get you a plate."

There was a small table with a window bench. Some mail was on the table alongside several covered hot dishes.

My mouth watered as I seated myself. "None for me thanks, I just ate," I lied.

Ramon looked hurt. "Oh." He glanced from the pan to me. "They aren't very big. Won't you have just one?" He smiled. "I have a nice red sauce, not too spicy. My secret is I mix fire-roasted tomatoes with sundried." He brought his fingers to his lips and kissed them, indicating a mouth-watering, delectable sensation.

I busied myself pulling out my notebook and pen, something else to focus on rather than melted cheese and frying onions. "No, thank you," I muttered into my bag.

Ramon put the glass pan down on a trivet. "Well, it should cool a minute anyway. It's okay to change your mind."

I nodded. "As you know, I've been hired by Chuck Vann to investigate the murder of Nancy Pickett."

Ramon's face darkened. "Do you think I need an attorney?"

NOTE to self: Do not sit in the farthest corner of apartment with suspect between you and the exit!

I swallowed a dry lump in my throat. "Why do you think you need an attorney?"

"Chuck hired you to investigate me, right? He thinks I killed Nancy? The cops asked me a bunch of questions around the same line. I can't prove that she actually left my house and then, God, she was found only a couple blocks from here." He pinched his lips together as if trying to suppress his emotions.

My palms were moist and for some inexplicable reason, I rose. Maybe I figured I'd feel less vulnerable standing if he was standing.

"I wasn't hired to investigate you, per se. I'm sorry if I gave you that impression."

He licked his lips and sized me up. "I'm on everybody's short list. Doesn't take a genius to see that, but I didn't do it and I'll help however I can. What do you need?"

He pushed the pile of mail to the side to make room for my notebook. I noticed the top envelope looked like a cell phone bill.

I opened my notebook. "What can you tell me about your relationship with Nancy?"

He returned to the stovetop to stir the pollo abodo. "We'd been dating for about six months. The night before she disappeared she was here with me. I think I was the last person to see her alive. Well, I mean, you know, the last person who didn't kill her . . . I mean . . ."

I nodded. "I understand, go ahead."

"We weren't living together, but we spent a lot of time together. Or . . ." He looked up from his stirring. "A lot of nights together. Nancy worked a lot, and I really never saw her during the day. Mostly she'd come over for dinner. I like to cook. Well, I *love* to cook. I'd give anything to have my own catering business." He nodded toward the enchilada dish. "Are you sure you don't want to try?"

It took every ounce of willpower I had to decline again. I love Mexican cuisine and his cooking looked and smelled authentic and traditional, yet I could tell he was clever about putting his own twist on recipes.

Ramon pouted and sprinkled salt into the adobo. "Anyway, with Nancy we'd watch a movie, drink wine, and, you know. She'd usually spend the night, so that morning was really no different. She always got up super early. I'm not a morning person. I don't know how she did it, but she'd get up early, still dark out, you know? Have on her workout clothes and just go. I wouldn't see her again until dinnertime."

"When she was here did she run in the park?"

Ramon looked up from the pot. "No. She had a membership at Club Zen, do you know it?"

I shook my head.

"It's new." Ramon continued, "It's a fancy fitness center in the Embarcadero. Near the station. So, she'd go there, work out, shower, and then go over to work."

So, maybe she'd never made it to her destination.

"Did you tell the police this?"

He put down the spoon and slowly nodded.

So either Nancy had been picked up outside his house, killed, and dumped in the park, or . . .

I pushed the thought of Ramon as a suspect out of my mind. If I focused on that I'd never make it through the interview.

I eyed the cell phone bill on the table. Certainly the police had access to all that. I was always one step behind.

I indicated the phone bill. "You didn't happen to have a family plan with Nancy, did you?"

Ramon crossed to the table. "We did! Free to call each other, you know?"

He handed me the bill and my fingers virtually zinged. I was going to get inside information! I ripped open the bill. "Can you help me identify the calls?"

We sat together at the table and I gave Ramon my pen. Meticulously he began to write names next to the numbers. After a moment he sprang up.

"What is it?" I asked.

"My adobo!"

I laughed. "I thought you found something!"

For the first time since I'd walked into his apartment he laughed, too. It lit up his face and relaxed him. "Sorry. I can't let the adobo burn. It's for the . . ." He sighed and his shoulders drooped. Any cheer that had just been on his face vanished. "We're having the services tomorrow."

He suddenly moved with fury over the adobo, throwing in spices, stirring, and whipping the mixture in a frenzy. I looked over the bill in my hand; most numbers had names next to them. The same names appeared repeatedly: "me," "Dad," "Elliot," and "Station." I'd be able to look up the others in a reverse directory at home.

"Did Nancy ever talk to you about work?"

Ramon shrugged. "The usual complaints. Disliked her boss, wanted more money, and thought her coworkers took her for granted."

"Do you know any of the stories she was working on? Like one, maybe on the French consul?"

"No."

"Chuck thought that maybe a story she was working on might have gotten her in trouble."

Ramon stared at me. "Is that what Chuck told you?"

I nodded.

Ramon shrugged again. "I thought for sure he'd tell you to look into me."

My stomach flip-flopped. "Anything about you I should know?"

Ramon laughed. "What? Like you don't know my history?"

I stood up straight, feeling a nervousness in my stomach. After being scolded by Galigani for not checking out

Chuck Vann, I'd run Ramon, Nancy's dad, her brother, and even her boss through the database. I'd found nothing—other than Ramon's financial troubles.

"I don't."

Ramon eyed me. "Oh. I didn't mean it to sound like anything . . . I just thought you might have looked me up."

Now I felt like I was being tested.

"I did look you up, Ramon. I didn't find a criminal history."

Why not challenge him?

"Have you gone by a different name?" I pressed. "Ever been convicted—"

"Nothing like that," Ramon said.

"What then?"

All I needed for him to say now was that his previous girlfriend had been found dead in his house. Again, without being able to control myself, my thoughts turned to escape. Maybe I could grab the boiling adobo and throw it at him then rush out of the apartment.

As if reading my mind, Ramon turned off the heat beneath the pot and pushed it to the back burner. He wiped his hands on his apron.

"I don't have a criminal history, but I thought Chuck would try to poison you and the police against me. Chuck was always telling Nancy I was out for her money."

I thought about the bankruptcy in Ramon's past. Maybe Nancy had told Chuck about that and it'd made him over-protective toward her.

I placed the cell phone bill in my bag. "Thank you for sharing this with me."

Ramon chewed on his thumbnail. "Sorry, sometimes I feel like everyone's out to get me."

"Is there anything else I can do to help you?"

"You got a key to her apartment?"

Ramon smiled. "Yes! I do." He retreated down the hallway. I waited in the kitchen and, unable to contain myself, peeked under a lid to one of the pots on the stove. A chocolate-sauce scent wafted up.

Molé.

Ramon returned with a key in his hand along with a piece of paper. "Kate, I don't know if it's important. I found this in the back pocket of Nancy's jeans, but only after I washed them."

He handed me the key along with a dried, crinkled paper. I unfolded it carefully and read it.

"It's an address," Ramon said. "But I don't know whose. I thought it was just a work thing . . ."

I pocketed the paper. "I'll look into it. Thank you."

When I arrived home the house was empty. My breasts were burning and I either needed to feed Laurie or pump. It seemed a miracle to me how Laurie and I had fallen into a schedule; my body was completely aligned with her needs. I texted Jim and hoped he would respond quickly. Even though I'd only been gone a short while, I was missing him and Laurie like crazy.

While I waited for a response I dove into research to distract myself. I pulled up the reverse directory database I had access to and was not entirely stunned to see that Nancy had made calls to the French consulate and Kimberly Newman. What surprised me was to find that she had phoned Armand Remy. Granted he was an assistant at the consulate, so maybe she needed him to set up an appointment or something.

Time to find out. I dialed Armand. This time I didn't chicken out when I got his voice mail. I left a message as my front door creaked open.

I leaned into the hallway to get a view of the door. Jim entered holding Laurie's car seat bucket followed by David, Paula's husband.

I rose from the computer and greeted them at the entrance. "Hey. I was wondering where you'd gone."

Jim laughed. "You weren't wondering that hard, because you didn't even call me."

I kissed him and pulled the handle of Laurie's car seat out of this hand. "I just got home a few minutes ago and, yes, I did call. I sent you a text."

Jim pulled the phone out of his pocket. "Oh yeah. There it is. It was loud at the bar."

I released Laurie from the car seat. She was dressed in an outfit that would have been great if we were Eskimos. Complete with a fur-rimmed hat. Her cheeks were flushed and her hair was matted against her forehead. "Oh no! Chicken Little is too warm. Look at her!"

"Is that why she's been crying?" David asked.

Jim glared at David. David laughed and leaned over to kiss my cheek. "Only kidding, Kate. She was an angel. Never even made a peep."

I clutched Laurie to me. "Is this how you all treat my baby when I'm not here?"

"I didn't want her to be cold," Jim said.

"Where'd you take her, Antarctica?"

David sat on my couch. "No. We took her down the street for beers. She loved it, didn't she, Jim?"

Jim smiled. "She was a big hit: People loved her almost as much as the game."

I rolled my eyes and left the room to change Laurie. When I returned to the living room they were sprawled about watching the fourth quarter.

"She's in a new rabbit suit," I said, proudly showing Laurie off.

Jim and David absently nodded to me, their eyes glued to the TV.

"What's up with Paula?" I asked David. "Any news?"

David didn't even look up from the game. "She's at her sister's with Danny. No baby yet. No contractions. Nada."

Jim looked up. "Oh, we couldn't figure out how to collapse the stroller. It's in our driveway."

I stared at them dumbfounded. "Between the two of you, you couldn't figure it out?"

They ignored me.

"There's a red lever near the back wheels . . ."

I was talking to glazed eyes.

"Never mind," I said. "I'll go down and get it in a minute."

I headed to the bedroom to nurse Laurie. They didn't even notice that I'd left the room.

My thoughts turned back to the case. Was it a coincidence that Nancy had called Armand? I had definitely been in the wrong place at the wrong time when Armand crashed into me, but did he know something about Nancy's death?

I hadn't been able to figure out who lived at the address Ramon had given me, only that it was on Bush Street, near the consulate. I wanted to drive by but . . .

I studied Laurie's beautiful face, her tiny chin and the long lashes that seemed to just get longer and longer each day.

She was the reason I was working from home, but that

didn't mean I had to run out on her all the time. I resolved to think about nothing but her for the rest of the day. After all, it was Sunday. Family day. Okay, so Jim was engrossed in the game, but we were all still together.

I could investigate further tomorrow. On a Monday, like a normal working mom.

CHAPTER TEN

To Do:

1. Christmas cards and shopping.

2. ✓ ~~Contact Armand Remy. Does he have insurance?~~ Left a message—now what?

3. Research safest car.

4. ✓ ~~Prepare contract for Mr. Vann.~~

5. Call Christophe Benoit.

6. Why isn't Laurie flipping over? Am failure as a mom.

7. Christmas recipes! What am I going to make for Christmas dinner?

8. ~~Computer class.~~

Due to the street-cleaning schedule and San Francisco draconian enforcement efforts, I had to park several blocks away from the building on Bush Street. It was early, 8 A.M. on a Monday morning. I'd left Jim and Laurie at home asleep. Being out while they slept made me feel productive. I wasn't taking any time away from my family. And, it made me feel professional, handling things during office hours. Of course, there was that added benefit that I'd hope to find the occupant home before leaving for work.

The address was a Victorian flat. One residential unit on top of the other. I needed the top one.

I examined the house for a mailbox and found two. Both mailboxes fed into a covered, secured garage.

I absently wondered about what I would say to the occupant when he or she opened the door. How about, "Hi, I'm a PI—who are you?" Would that work?

I climbed the stairs and caught my breath at the top of the landing. Man, that was a lot of stairs, and they were steep, too. I had a good view of downtown San Francisco from the top.

I pressed my finger to the doorbell and noticed cracked wood near the doorjamb. My stomach dropped. I pressed gently on the door. It opened, ominously inviting me in.

Uh oh.

"Hello?" I called out.

A chill swept me from head to toe and I couldn't suppress the shudder. Obviously there had been a break-in. Hopefully, that was all it was. If I entered would I find the place ransacked?

"Hello," I called again. "Anyone home?"

I leaned in just a bit. I could make out a corner of the living space. It looked immaculate, a bit barren, but nothing strewn about.

"Don't go in, don't go in, DON'T go in," the voice in my head screamed.

What should I do? Call the cops? Call Jim? Ring the downstairs neighbor's doorbell?

I retreated down the stairs. No way was I going in there alone.

About halfway down the staircase, I knew I was kidding myself. It's like that piece of warm devil's food cake staring up at you from your dessert plate, with the thick dark frosting, maybe a little strawberry goo swirl on top, and vanilla ice cream on the side. You know you shouldn't, but you want just one little bite.

I ran back up the stairs and pushed the front door wide open. I promised myself I was only taking one step to see around the living room corner.

"Heeeell-oooo?" I called out. I was frozen at the doorway with one foot in and one foot out. I could now see into the living room. Everything was wrong with nothing being amiss. Visually, there was nothing upturned in the room or kiddiwampus. It was sparsely furnished, like a college-student setup.

Everything was silent but even the air seemed charged somehow. I could see an open doorway to the left, presumably to the rest of the flat. I strained to see around it, but couldn't unless I stepped completely inside.

I picked up my back foot from outside and pulled it in. Then, like in a game of Simon Says, I took one small step forward and leaned my whole upper body in so I could see into the doorway. And finally, just like I do with the cake—ignoring any warning system I may have in my head or body—I dive in with complete abandon.

Once inside, I could see down the short hallway to the

bathroom. The door to the bathroom was open and I could see an arm dangling out of the tub.

Red stained the tile floor and I swallowed back my dread.

I crossed the small hallway and stood in the bathroom doorway. A gasp escaped me.

Armand lay dead in the tub, soaking in bloodred water. I covered my mouth and prayed silently. Frozen in place, I stared at him, willing him to pick up his head. He was just a boy!

I'd wanted to find him so badly, but I hadn't wanted this. I thought if I'd found him, it would be hard not to want to strangle him. After all, hadn't I even dreamt about it? But seeing him dead only brought me grief.

It looked like suicide. His forearms were slit about two-thirds of the way up his arms and his face was completely white, all the blood and life drained from his body.

My heart went out to his mother. The most horrendous news a mom could fear and now she'd receive it in the face of the holidays.

I fumbled for my cell phone, my hands suddenly shaking uncontrollably. I dialed Galigani as quickly as I could.

He picked up on the first ring.

I closed my eyes, but Armand's image was burned into my brain. "I shouldn't have come inside," I said into the phone.

You can't unsee things in your mind.

"Kate? Where are you?" Galigani asked. "Are you all right? Inside where?"

I explained the situation to him. He told me to retrace my steps and wait for him and the homicide cops on the front stoop.

Homicide.

Surely he would call McNearny. They were old partners. I dreaded another encounter with McNearny.

"You don't need to call homicide, I think it was a suicide!" I said, instantly regretting the words.

"Suicide?" Galigani screamed. "Why the hell was the door broken in? The guy breaks into his own place to kill himself?"

While waiting on the front stoop I prayed.

Please let Galigani get here first. Please let Galigani get here first and NOT McNearny.

Suddenly, I caught myself. How selfish! I was more worried about my fate than poor Armand. I said a prayer for him and his family and after several moments realized that my worry about McNearny was a defensive mechanism employed by my small mind, so as not to face the real issue—mortality.

I fidgeted on the stoop.

Yes. I would have to discipline my mind.

Meditation was supposed to be good for that. I would add that to my to-do list. In the meantime, what would I say to McNearny if he arrived before Galigani?

Simple. Just explain the truth.

Yes. The truth.

And that would be . . . what exactly? That I couldn't resist sticking my nose inside the door?

Mercifully, I watched Galigani's familiar form walk down the block. When he reached me, instead of scolding me he embraced me. "Kid. You can't do stuff like that! You put yourself in unnecessary danger."

I clutched him hard, relieved to feel another person's

touch. One that was alive and warm. "There was no danger," I choked. "He's dead."

Galigani tsked at me. "You're in shock. We'll have to talk later."

He was right. I had a strange adrenaline working in my system, keeping all my pieces glued together. If I thought too much about Armand, I knew I would come apart at the seams.

An unmarked vehicle parked in front of the building and homicide inspectors McNearny and Jones stepped out.

With a simple nod of acknowledgment to Galigani, McNearny said, "Thank you for finding us more work, Mrs. Connolly."

Jones shook Galigani's hand and raised his eyebrows at me.

McNearny examined the front door. "Go ahead and tell us how you broke in, Mrs. Connolly."

"I didn't break in!" I protested.

"Oh? You live here?" McNearny said.

"I mean, I didn't do that," I said, pointing to the busted doorknob.

McNearny let his eyes roll back in complete disdain for me. "Did you enter the premises this morning, Mrs. Connolly?"

"Yes. I pushed the door open, but just a little and took a tiny peek, you know, just a little tiny peek," I said, nervously. The three pairs of homicide-experienced eyes bore down heavily on me. "I didn't know he was dead! I called out and no one answered. What if he needed help?"

"If he'd needed help, don't you think he'd have answered your calls?" McNearny suddenly screamed in my face.

"Not if he was unconscious!" I shouted back at him.

Galigani's eyes went wide as I yelled at McNearny.

McNearny waved his hand in a gesture of "enough" and said to Jones, "Book her! Breaking and entering. Interfering with an investigation."

Jones opened his mouth to protest but a look from McNearny shut him down before he could get any words out.

Galigani frowned. "Come on, Mac. You don't need to do this. The kid's on our side."

McNearny's face turned beet red. "She is *not* on my side. Maybe she's on your side, I don't know. *We* used to be on the same side! The only thing she is—is a *thorn* in my side." He turned from us and barreled into the flat.

Why did he always have to be so mean?

Jones stood silently a moment. "You heard him, Kate. I'm sorry."

"You're not arresting her!" Galigani said.

Jones held up his hands and gave a hopeless shrug.

"It won't hold up. It's just a paperwork nightmare and he's only trying to inconvenience Mrs. Connolly," Galigani protested.

Jones nodded. "I know, but he's the senior guy. I don't need any more hassles."

Galigani put a hand on my shoulder. "Go with him and I'll call Jim and then Barramendi."

Jones grimaced. "Barramendi? You're going to call that guy?"

Barramendi was a high-powered criminal defense attorney. I had worked with him last month on another case.

Galigani and I exchanged glances. "He's a fan of Kate's."

Jones waved us off. "Forget it. You're right, it'll be a paperwork nightmare." He pushed open the front door of the flat and yelled into McNearny, "They're going to call Barramendi."

There was silence from inside.

We all stared at each other and waited. Finally, McNearny called from the interior, "I hate Barramendi. Forget it."

I realized I'd been holding my breath.

Jones leaned close to us and said, "You better go home."

McNearny shouted from the inside, "Tell Connolly to get in here!"

Jones sighed and motioned me inside the flat.

McNearny was standing in the doorway of the bathroom in the exact spot I'd stood. "Did you touch anything Connolly?"

"No. Just the front door when I pushed it open."

"Do you know the vic?"

I swallowed past the dry section in my throat, but didn't feel I could speak. "Mmm hmm."

McNearny stared at me. "You *know* the guy?" Before I could answer, McNearny swore under his breath. "Jesus H. Christ, of course you know the guy. You know everyone in the damn city. Everyone who ends up dead."

"I only sort of know him," I said in my defense.

I looked at Armand's face. It was puffy and swollen. His long hair stuck to his shoulders and I noticed a bruising around his neck for the first time.

I filled in McNearny and Jones on the hit-and-run, the party at the consulate, and my visits with Chuck and Ramon. McNearny held his head as I spoke, occasionally looking up but mostly he seemed to keep his eyes on Jones and Galigani instead of me. If he'd been a cartoon someone would have drawn smoke coming out of his ears.

Finally when I finished McNearny looked at me. "You

cover a lot of ground, huh? Jesus, I'd hate to see what kind of trouble you'd get into if you didn't have an infant slowing you down!"

I cringed and felt my face flush.

He was right! I should be home with Laurie.

Wait.

Why should I feel like I was supposed to do nothing else but be at home with her?

Her blue eyes, little eyelashes, and tiny face flashed before me and I couldn't deny the pang I felt and the outright desire to hold her to me.

"What else do you know about the murder of Nancy Pickett?" Jones asked.

"Not much; her ex thinks she was killed because of a story she was working on about the French consulate."

Galigani coughed into his hand.

Was there some part of the story I was supposed to suppress?

Maybe the part about him hacking into Mr. Vann's e-mail.

"Hello?" a voice called from the front door. It was Nick Dowling, the San Francisco Medical Examiner, who I'd met during the previous two cases I'd worked on.

"Back here," McNearny barked.

We were crowded in the hallway. Nick Dowling peeked around and said, "Whoa! Full house."

McNearny ushered us into the living room. "All yours, Nick."

I glanced around the living room, hoping for something obvious. There was a dusty bookcase filled with small model cars and a table nearby with stacks of paper on it. In the center of the table was an empty spot as though a stack had been moved.

No suicide note, no huge muddy footprint, no dead ringer.

McNearny turned to Galigani. "You have anything you want to get off your chest?"

Galigani scratched his head and played dumb. "I don't think so."

McNearny nodded, seemingly satisfied for the moment.

"Okay, either of you come across anything, notify me immediately, or I will arrest you and I don't give a damn about Barramendi."

CHAPTER ELEVEN

I gripped Galigani's arm as we climbed down the steep stairs. "There is something."

Galigani wiggled his eyebrows. "There always is."

"Well, I didn't mean to hold it back. I only thought about it now and I don't even know if it's important."

"Spit it out."

"When I was at the consul's Christmas party, the consul slipped out on the balcony with a lady who wasn't his wife."

Galigani eyed me. "He's having an affair? With who?"

"I don't know. Do you think that outing the affair was Nancy's story?"

"Let's find out." Galigani steered me in the direction of the consulate.

"How?"

"Let's ask around."

• • •

At the consulate it seemed business as usual. There was a slight hustle and bustle as people formed a line at the red marble counter waiting for their passports or visas. The receptionist was the same lady who had attended Jim and me the other day. I wondered if she'd remember me.

"Who are we going to ask? The receptionist?"

Galigani shrugged. "That's a start."

I frowned. "You're just gonna come right out and ask her?"

Galigani laughed. "If the opportunity presents itself."

I pulled Christophe's card from my purse and showed it to Galigani. "Should we start with him? I met him at the party and I was supposed to talk to him today anyway about the accident."

It was finally our turn at the counter and Galigani asked for the consul instead.

The receptionist smiled and immediately deferred us to one of his assistants. I silently prayed it wouldn't be Jean-Luc.

We waited in the reception area. After several minutes a woman with a long face and red polka-dotted scarf wrapped tight around her neck appeared. Even though she was tall, she was still sporting four-inch heels. She hovered over both Galigani and I.

Galigani flashed his credentials. "Miss, I'm a investigator looking into the death of Nancy Pickett. Can we speak privately somewhere?"

The woman's mouth turned down. "I'm afraid I do not know Miss Pickett. Was she a French citizen?"

"No. American reporter."

The woman cocked her head to the side. "Perhaps you

would like to speak with Christophe in our press and communications department. He works with the American journalists."

Galigani and I exchanged looks.

"That would be fine," Galigani said.

We followed the woman down a hallway. My cell phone buzzed. Galigani nodded to me indicating that I should attend to my phone. I glanced at the caller ID. It was home.

I answered expecting Jim, but Mom's voice filled the line. "Where are you? We're late for the photo shoot."

Laurie's Christmas photos!

My heart plunged.

I'd forgotten the photo appointment! I'd thought I'd been so smart to schedule her photos during workweek hours to avoid the crowds, but that was before I decided that I should hold normal work hours and, of course, before I'd found Armand dead.

The woman stopped in front of an office and looked at me.

"Mom, something's come up. Let me call you back."

I hung up. The woman nodded at me, then knocked on the office door. She introduced Galigani and me to Christophe Benoit.

Christophe stood, his expression serious, as though he expected trouble from us. He greeted us and then invited us to sit across from his desk.

His rumpled curly hair was so endearing and I found myself liking him regardless of my vow to dislike everyone associated with the place.

Galigani filled Christophe in on Nancy Pickett's death and Mr. Vann retaining us.

Christophe's face filled with sadness. "I knew Nancy,"

he tsked. "I provided her with data for a story she was working on."

"Which story?" I asked, leaning in.

"It was a human interest story on France's foreign aid to Sudan."

"I saw her leaving the consulate the day before she was killed. Had she been meeting with you that day?"

Christophe wiggled the mouse on his computer and took a moment to look at his online calendar. "No. I hadn't met with her for some time. The last time was in November."

"She was with Kimberly Newman, another reporter. Were you meeting with Kimberly?"

Christophe's eyes darted right. He clenched a fist and shifted his body toward his computer so that his face was concealed by the monitor. "Kimberly Newman? No. I have not met her."

Well that didn't seem right. Surely he was lying. But why?

What had Kimberly been doing at the consulate?

I sighed at Galigani. The case seemed to be moving faster than I could. I should have already spoken with Kimberly—but when?

I probably shouldn't have taken yesterday off.

A feeling of guilt rushed through me as I realized that Armand was most likely killed yesterday. What if I had visited him then? Would I have run into the killer? And was his killer the same person as Nancy's?

I doodled in my notebook and wrote Armand's name in the margin. When Galigani glanced at me I pointed to the name.

Galigani took a breath.

"Can you tell us about Armand . . ."

"Armand Remy," I finished.

Christophe looked puzzled. "Armand? He is an assistant here. Would you like to speak with him?"

I opened my mouth to speak, but Galigani's hand shot out and touched my arm. "No need. I think we are done for today." He stood.

I stood alongside him as we were about to exit. Galigani turned back to Christophe. "So the consul got a big fancy award, huh?"

Christophe beamed. "Yes! The *Légion d'honneur*; it's a great accomplishment. And today, we got word from the San Francisco Board of Supervisors that they intend to give the consul a resolution commending him for his success serving and building Franco-American relations among the residents of the city and county of San Francisco, and—"

Galigani nodded, cutting off Christophe's proud rampage. "Is he here today?"

Christophe laughed. "Oh, *non, non, non.* He doesn't come in on Monday mornings."

"Probably was out celebrating . . ." Galigani's eyes locked on Christophe's." . . . celebrating with the *wife* at a nice dinner."

Christophe blushed slightly. After a moment, he said, "Probably."

As soon as we left his office, I turned to Galigani. "I wanted to talk to him about the hit-and-run. Why did you wave me off?"

"There'll be time for that. Let the authorities notify the next of kin. After that, you can clear up the insurance matters."

I sighed and dialed home as we exited the building. Galigani continued to walk next to me in silence. Jim picked up on the third ring.

"Honey! I'm so sorry I blew it!"

"What?"

"The photo thing with Laurie. Now I'll have to re-schedule. Unless they can squeeze us in tomorrow, I don't see how I can get the Christmas cards printed and out in time. Maybe we'll have to do New Year's cards instead."

"Oh, don't worry about it. Your mom took her."

"What? Mom took her where?"

"To the mall for the photos. Listen, I'm sorry, I have to go. Dirk Jonson is calling through on the other line. Are you on your way home?"

My chest constricted. Mom had taken Laurie?

I should be happy, right? I'd have Christmas cards in time.

My baby was getting her first Christmas photos taken and I wasn't there!

"No," I said to Jim.

"Huh?"

"I'm not coming straight home. I'm going to the mall."

"Okay. I gotta go. Call me later." Jim hung up.

Galigani watched me, a frown on his face. "Why are you crying?"

I wiped the tears streaming down my face. "I'm not crying. I'm late and I'm parked about a mile away!"

Late.

I'd been too late to save Armand.

Galigani pointed to his car. "I'm parked right here. I'll take you wherever you want to go."

• • •

Any hope I'd had of making it in time was dashed when I saw Mom, who was wearing a headband with reindeer ears glued to it, pushing Laurie's stroller out of the photo shop. The ears flopped as Mom walked and her eyes lit up when she saw me, but her face turned serious when she spotted Galigani.

"Kate! Don't worry about a thing. We got the job done," Mom said.

Laurie was decked out in a beautiful green crushed velvet dress. She had on a little Santa hat and gave a cheerful baby coo when she saw me. As I got closer she kicked her feet and got progressively noisier, indicating a desire for me to get her out of the stroller.

I pulled her out and hugged her close. I glared at Mom. "How could you do this?"

"Do what?" Mom asked.

"I wanted to do it," I snapped.

Mom looked at Galigani for an explanation. Galigani shrugged. "We found the kid that hit Kate. He's dead. She's upset."

Mom sighed. "Oh! Darling—"

"What? No," I said to Galigani. "That's not it. I wanted to be the one to get her pictures taken. *I'm* her mother. She's *my* baby!" I choked back a sob. "It's her first Christmas! I . . . , this isn't even the right dress!"

Mom looked at me as though I was an alien. "Well, the red one you picked out was dirty from the accident. I got her this one from Macy's."

"Maybe I can treat you beautiful ladies to lunch," Galigani said.

Mom looked panicked. "Oh, Albert, isn't that sweet of you. But no, we couldn't. We have to get Laurie home."

Galigani blinked.

"Maybe tomorrow?" Mom asked.

Something seemed wrong, but I was so upset about missing Laurie's photos that I couldn't pick out what it was until I saw a man approaching us.

Hank!

Mom's other gentleman friend.

My brain was stuck in some kind of mental sludge. I should say something, make something up, do something, but the mental fog was too great. All I could do was sort of clear my throat to try to get Mom's attention. Mom looked at me, the reindeer ears swinging back and forth, a frown creasing her brow.

It was too late . . . a hand reached for her shoulder.

"Hello, Vera!" Hank said, planting a kiss on her cheek and laughing. "Or should I say, deer! And look, it's Santa's little helper!" He reached across and grabbed one of Laurie's feet. He tugged at it and she gurgled happily at him. "Hello, Kate," he said.

I looked at Galigani, his lips set in a line. Not disappointment, not upset, more like mild curiosity. He stuck his hand out. "I'm Albert Galigani."

Hank smiled and shook his hand.

"Hank," I said. "Mr. Galigani is my boss."

Galigani flashed me a look but I couldn't make it out because Mom was shooting me her own panicked look.

Hank wrapped an arm protectively across Mom's shoulder. "Will you all be joining us for lunch?"

Galigani licked his lips and squinted at Hank.

He knew. He had to know.

"I . . . uh . . ." I muttered.

What could I say? Couldn't my phone ring? Or Laurie start to fuss? Instead, she laughed. She swung her feet in the air and giggled.

Great fat lot of help she was.

"I couldn't possibly," Galigani said. "But thank you for the offer." He nodded to Mom and smiled, then turned on his heel and spun around.

"Wait! You're my ride!" I said. "We have work to do."

And suddenly, I realized I couldn't go with him and take Laurie. He didn't have an infant seat in his car. I was stuck with Mom and Hank.

He turned back to me, looking at me with eyes that said I was a traitor. "Nah, kid, don't worry about it, take the afternoon off."

CHAPTER TWELVE

How I got through lunch, I'll never know. I tried to focus on Laurie and keep my mind off the sticky sweetness of Hank's affection for Mom. That he was devoted to her there was no doubt. Did he suspect Mom had been dating Galigani for the last month? Seemed unlikely. He'd brought more vacation brochures for her to peruse, ranging from an African safari to gold mining in the high country.

Mom giggled and clucked at him.

To keep from pulling my hair out, I evaluated the proofs of the Christmas photos. It was a black-and-white printout of thumbnail photos of Laurie. Laurie in her green dress on a sled with a white winter scene background, Laurie with the Santa hat propped on pillows with a Christmas tree in the background and fake presents around her, and finally Laurie looking like a little angel wrapped in a sheet with an aluminum halo stuck to her head.

I hated the angel photos. Not that there's anything wrong with angels, but dressing her up as an imitation of something struck me the wrong way. Plus, she seemed upset in those shots, like she was cold in the sheet. I was glad that Mom had picked one of the sled photos for the cards. The prints were supposed to be ready in one hour. It seemed like an eternity.

I texted Jim and asked him to pick Laurie and me up. I figured by the time he arrived I'd have the prints in hand and be ready to escape.

I should have been putting together my Christmas list and a plan of attack on the stores. After all, since I was in the mall I should take advantage and knock out my shopping, but I only picked at the salad I'd ordered and thought about the day. What a disaster—from finding Armand to missing the photo shoot to witnessing the Galigani-Mom-Hank debacle—and it was only lunchtime?

Mercifully, my phone buzzed. Jim was five minutes away. Plenty of time for me to swing by the portrait place, pick up the prints, and meet him in the parking garage.

I buckled Laurie into the stroller, thanked Hank for lunch, and waved to Mom. Mom wiggled her fingers at me and mouthed, "Call me."

Yeah. Right. It'd be the first thing I'd do when Laurie turned twenty-one!

"I don't get why you're mad at your mom," Jim said.

We were driving home and I'd filled him in on the day's events. His statement made me even angrier.

"I'm mad at you, too."

"Me? Why?"

"Why did you let Mom take Laurie to the Christmas photo shoot?"

He looked dumbfounded. "I thought you'd be happy about it. One less thing for you to do."

"One less thing? Like it's a burden? Being with her, doing the mom things I'm supposed to do with her, that's not a burden!"

"No. That's not what I meant." He looked at me, concern in his eyes. "She was trying to help. Why don't we take a nap when we get home?"

I grumbled and leaned my head against the headrest. "If she wants to help, she can do the laundry, go grocery shopping, cook dinner, do all the boring, mundane chores. She doesn't have to take the fun mommy stuff away from me."

Jim guffawed. "She does that stuff for you, too! You're absolutely spoiled rotten by her. You can't possibly be upset that she took Laurie to get some pictures taken."

I made a face at him. "Well, I am. I'm mad at her about that and I'm mad at her for putting me in the middle of her two boyfriends."

Jim pulled into our garage. "Geez. Talk about selfish. What do you care what she does with her boyfriends. Think about poor Galigani."

"Yeah. He's gonna be mad at me, too."

Jim parked the car. "Hope he doesn't fire you."

"He can't fire me. I found the client on my own."

Jim raised an eyebrow. "Well, he can stop helping you and that would . . ."

"What? That would be what?"

Jim scratched at his nose. "Nothing. I didn't mean anything."

"That would be what? Poor Kate, can't figure anything out on her own, she needs Galigani to work things out for her? Or her mommy, otherwise she can't even function. Is that what you were going to say?"

"No. I was going to say I love you."

"Yeah, right."

He got out of the car and pulled Laurie out with him. "I do love you. And I'll love you even more after you take a nap and leave this mood behind you."

I sat in the car stewing for a while, until I heard Laurie's hunger cries. Then I had to suck it up and get back to mothering. While I nursed her, I came to terms with the missed photo shoot and vowed to take her back to the mall for a photo on Santa's lap.

In order to work out some frustrated energy I decided to try my hand at making fudge. Since I was so remiss with Christmas shopping, maybe I could give out goodie baskets.

I searched online for a simple recipe that only included ingredients I had on hand. I found a mouthwatering one for raspberry truffle fudge. While I melted the chocolate chips and mixed in the condensed milk I thought about Armand.

Suddenly everything I'd been fretting about this afternoon with Mom seemed so silly. Jim was right: I was a spoiled brat.

Poor Armand and Nancy would have no Christmas. Their families were in mourning. Thank God, Laurie and I had walked away from the accident. I had so much to be grateful for.

I quickly added heavy whipping cream and raspberry

liqueur to the chocolate mixture and poured it out on a pan to cool. I put the pan in the fridge, wiped my hands on my apron, and took it off.

Tomorrow I would pick up the case again, talk to Kimberly, go to Nancy's house, but for right now I'd focus on being a wife and a mom.

I searched the house for Jim. I found him napping with Laurie in our bedroom. I lay next to them and felt a mixture of grief and distress shudder through my body. I sobbed and held Laurie; after a moment I felt Jim's hand on my forehead.

"Everything's going to be okay, honey. It's not your fault the kid is dead."

I held on to his arm. Laurie, who was nestled between us, reached her small hand up in sleep and grabbed onto my necklace. I was surrounded by love and support. I took a deep breath and felt a measure of relief as I slipped into a deep sleep.

CHAPTER THIRTEEN

To Do:

1. Mail Christmas cards.

2. Christmas shopping and recipes (need to buy baskets to fill).

3. Buy NEW car!

4. Talk to Kimberly Newman.

5. Check out Nancy's apartment.

6. Interview Nancy's dad and brother.

7. Meditate.

I stood in front of Kimberly Newman's Mediterranean-style house. She had gorgeous windows with a front and center view of the bay. There were sailboats docked directly in front of her house, across from the Marina Green. They rocked back and forth as the wind pushed through them.

While I was admiring her view, a Mercedes pulled into the driveway. The tinted window rolled down and Kimberly appeared behind it.

"Can I help you?" she asked politely.

I didn't know whether or not to stick my hand out—after all, she was in a car. Was it professional to stick my hand in her face?

"I'm Kate Connolly, a private investigator looking into the death of Mrs. Pickett. Do you have time to answer a few questions?"

Kimberly's face saddened. "Oh, yes. Of course. Give me a minute."

The garage door automatically opened and she drove inside. A few moments passed before she poked her head around the garage corner. "Come inside," she said.

She pulled scores of shopping bags out of her trunk. Handing me a few, she smiled. "Do you mind?"

I smiled back. "Not at all."

I took the bags from her. They were from Neiman Marcus and Saks Fifth Avenue. I was dying to rip them open and peek, but maintained enough composure not to.

"Follow me," she said. She hit a button on the wall and the garage door closed behind us.

I followed her up the interior staircase to the main landing.

"This way," she said over her shoulder.

We went up another staircase, which led to a master suite. There were glass doors to a balcony, where a small table and some chairs sat. In the center of the bedroom was an enormous white bed and a Mission-style side table and dresser. The coverlet of the bed had a beautiful Waterford pattern. She flopped the bags on the coverlet. "You can drop them here," she said.

I placed the bags next to the others.

Man. What an incredible room, spacious, light, feminine!

"I had myself a little shopping spree." She giggled.

"Christmas is just around the corner," I said, cringing at the thought of all the shopping I still had to do.

She laughed. "I know, but this stuff is for me. I have a big party . . . well, you might know. My boyfriend is Calvin Rabara, the San Francisco supervisor. And his annual Christmas-slash-fundraiser-slash-re-election party is this Friday at the Merchants Exchange Building. I had NOTHING to wear."

"Mmmm," I mumbled trying to sound agreeable instead of bitter.

I'm sure her closet was barren.

Pangs of jealously hit me. *Socialite, size what? Four? Six? Skinny witch.*

I pushed the feeling away. *She didn't have a tiny little pumpkin, like me. I had been a size six at one time! And the time wasn't that long ago, only about a year.*

No regrets. I'd trade all the fancy parties in the world to have my Laurie. But that didn't excuse being out of shape. I had to put exercise back on top of the priority list.

Kimberly's face changed from perky to serious. "What's this business about investigating Nancy's death?"

I explained to her about Mr. Vann hiring me. I left out the part about finding Armand. I didn't know if their deaths were connected and Galigani had warned me about spreading the word if the next of kin had not been notified yet.

"Anything you can tell me about Nancy or what you might even know about her death could help," I pressed.

Kimberly puffed her cheeks with air and remained silent, thinking. She took a seat on the bed and motioned me to take a high wingback chair that was adjacent.

"I met Nancy a few years ago. We work at the same station. You know that, right?"

I nodded.

"We didn't work on the same stories or anything, but the crew is small and we were friendly. We went out to lunch together occasionally and shopped. Did you know that she lived a few blocks from here?"

I nodded again. The key Ramon had given me to her house was burning a hole in my pocket.

"Sometimes, we'd run together on the Green. Maybe two mornings a week."

"Were you scheduled to run together on the morning of her death?"

Kimberly shook her head. "No."

"I heard that maybe she was heading downtown to a gym near your office?"

Kimberly frowned. "Really? I assumed she'd decided to run in the park . . . isn't that where they found . . ."

I waited for her to continue.

"She didn't like the gym. Maybe you should talk to some of the members or staff there, but I don't think she went all that often. I thought . . . I thought she went running in the park that morning . . . her new boyfriend . . ." She made a face, then completed her thought with her eyes closed. "Her new boyfriend, Ramon, lives near the park. She'd starting running on a trail near his house. That's where they found her."

She sat in silence with her eyes closed momentarily,

giving me the perfect opportunity to study her face. She was beautiful in the classical sense: her nose was large and angular but it suited her sharp jaw and cheekbones.

Her eyes fluttered open, dark blue with ultralong black lashes that were, I'm sure, aided by expensive mascara. "I miss her. We weren't super close, but I always knew she was nearby if I needed someone to lean on."

"When's the last time you saw her?" I asked.

"Monday at the station."

An alarm went off in my head. I had seen them together at the consulate on Wednesday. Had she forgotten about that? She didn't know, of course, that I'd been there.

I looked down at my fingernails, giving her time to reconsider her answer. I was surprised to find my nails in such bad repair. Kimberly's nails were filed into even blunt squares and she had on a pretty pink polish.

Get a manicure, Kate, quick!

I waited for her to say something. She didn't.

I looked up at her. She was fingering one of the bags on her bed.

"What do you think happened to Nancy? Do you think it was a random act of violence?"

Kimberly pressed her lips together. "I think, and this may be an unpopular opinion at the station, but I think Ramon is behind it."

"Why?"

"I never liked him. Nancy was a little different around him, which happens, I suppose, with some women when they fall in love, but . . ." She straightened and took a breath. "I didn't like him for her."

"Why is that an unpopular opinion at the station?"

She laughed bitterly. "Everyone loves him, because he'd cook this incredible, delicious fatty food and bring it to the station. God, talk about pigs at the trough. Give the station folk some food, it could be anything really, and they throw themselves at it. So, they loved Ramon because he'd make a big spread for them. They won't hear of any bad talk about him—he's the darling Mexican chef."

She seemed incredibly jealous, but I wasn't sure of what. Was she jealous because people were eating food she regularly denied herself? Or jealous because they liked Ramon?

"What do you think Ramon's reason to hurt Nancy would be?"

She shrugged. "Do people even need a reason anymore? The whole world is out of control." She pulled her legs up under her on the bed and sat cross-legged. She hugged herself. "Maybe Nancy was breaking up with him or something."

"Had she said anything to you about leaving him?"

"No, but I don't know. Like I said, we weren't super close."

"Do you know who was?"

Kimberly shook her head. "She was friendly with people at the station, but didn't spend much time with any of them. I think mostly it was Ramon."

"Do you know anything about a story she was working on that might have ruffled some feathers?"

Kimberly frowned. "Like what? Are you saying she might have been killed because of a story?"

"Nancy's ex-husband, Chuck, thinks that might be the case."

Kimberly's face showed disbelief. "I doubt it. Like what? What story?"

"I was hoping you could tell me."

She shrugged. "Sorry."

"The consul was given the Legion of Honor and a commendation from the Board of Supervisors . . ."

She stared at me blankly. "So?"

"Could that have been what Nancy was working on? The award? The commendation?"

Kimberly shrugged. "I don't know what stories she was working on, and even if I did, I wouldn't be at liberty to tell you. You'd have to ask Karen Nolan at KNCR."

She gave me a threatening look as if warning me about something.

Did she think I was going to steal Nancy's story and make headlines with it? Gimme a break.

"Any idea why Nancy would be phoning an intern from the consulate and have his address on her?"

Her face paled, but she collected herself quickly.

"Any number of reasons. As reporters we're constantly reaching out to people."

Okay. So most likely he'd been a source, but what is it that Kimberly didn't want me to know?

Even though every ounce of me wanted to tell her about Armand's death and see her reaction, I refrained. Galigani had reminded me several times to wait until the next of kin had been notified and I didn't know if that had happened yet or not. I certainly had not read any news reports on it this morning, when I scoured the Internet.

I stood. "Right. Thank you for your time."

She unfolded her legs, dropped them to the floor, and stood. "Sure."

"One more thing," I said. "What were you and Nancy doing at the French consulate on Wednesday?"

Kimberly's legs seemed to buckle under her and she collapsed onto the bed.

CHAPTER FOURTEEN

Her face was a mask of disbelief. "What do you mean?" She shook her head back and forth. "I wasn't . . . we weren't . . . what are you implying?"

Her anger was building, so I did my best to downplay it. "I thought you and Nancy were at the French consulate on Wednesday."

"Who told you that? Christophe? Or the receptionist, Marie?" She bit her lip. "I don't know if Nancy was there or not. Maybe she was. I can't say about her, but I was definitely not there. I wasn't there."

Christophe? Hadn't he told me he didn't know Kimberly?

"I didn't mean to upset you, I'm only trying to retrace Nancy's steps and figure out what happened to her."

Kimberly's head turned sharply to the floor. "I'm not upset."

"I thought maybe that's what Nancy was doing at the consulate. You know, interviewing the consul on his thoughts about the award, that sort of thing."

Kimberly's face turned up to me; she stared at me a moment, then squinted. "How do you even know about the award? Our station didn't run the story. It got bumped because of gang violence in the mission. The story's supposed to run tonight. Filler."

She said the final word as though it left a bad taste in her mouth.

"They announced it at the Christmas party," I said.

I watched her face carefully, her eyes darting to the right and back again. Her expression unchanged.

I'd also seen her at the party.

Was she going to deny being there, too?

"Oh yes," she whispered.

"You were there, weren't you? At the Christmas party."

Kimberly swallowed. "Yes. I cover big social parties like that for the station." Her eyes flicked across me, up and down. "What were you doing there?"

I smiled at the implication.

Indeed, what were the likes of a rumpled new mom, turned PI, doing at a party hosted by a foreign diplomat?

"Friends in high places," I said.

She sniffed but said nothing.

I handed her my business card. "If you can think of anything that might help me out, please contact me."

She took it from me and crushed it in her hand. "Certainly," she said.

Outside, I wondered why Kimberly had denied being at the consulate last Wednesday. There was definitely a strange connection between Nancy, Kimberly, and the consul—I just needed to figure it out. Maybe Paula and I could crash the supervisor party at the Merchants Exchange Building on Friday. I'd have to ask Paula to snoop out the details.

And what about Armand? What was his role in all this? Was his death even related? And if so, how?

Since my car was legally parked, I walked the short distance to Nancy's apartment. I glanced at my watch. I had only three hours between feedings. I'd left home over an hour ago. I'd have to hustle if I wanted to be back in time.

Nancy had lived in a four-unit building on Chestnut. Although the neighborhood was the same as Kimberly's, the residences could not have been more different. Nancy's apartment house had chipped paint and dirty windows. It looked like it was in desperate need of some TLC. The roof sagged and the iron gate was rusted.

I tried the key Ramon had given me and entered the dirty foyer. The marble steps led up two levels where I found apartment number four with bright yellow police crime-scene tape across the front door.

Darn! Certainly I was not supposed to enter.

I looked down the hall. The other unit on the floor was silent. Grabbing my cell phone out of my bag, I dialed the one person I knew would egg me on.

"Yeah?" Paula said into the line.

"Any news?"

"I had my visit with my OB this morning. She laughed when I asked how soon. No contractions, no effacement, no dilation, no nothing! I'm in the Great Wait phase."

"Hmmm," I said.

"Only I'm feeling like a great white! Wait. Is that a shark? I mean, whale. Is there a great white whale?"

"Ummm."

"Never mind, I can tell by your hmmm and your ummm that you don't care. So why don't—"

"Of course, I care!"

Paula laughed. "Why don't you get to the real purpose of your call?"

I took a deep breath. "I'm in front of Nancy Pickett's apartment door, with a key mind you, but there's police tape blocking it."

"Bummer."

"I should just leave, right? That would be the *right* thing to do?"

"What? Leave? You said you had a key!"

"I do."

"Well, untape and retape, stupid."

"But McNearny almost arrested me yesterday for breaking and entering."

"What?"

I quickly filled Paula in on finding Armand.

"That was different, you found a dead guy and *had* to call him. He should have thanked you, by the way. When would they have found him if it hadn't been for you? We know Nancy's not in the apartment, so it's not like you're going to have to call him."

"Okay."

"Call me back and let me know what you find," Paula said.

"Wait, before you hang up. I have a favor."

"Shoot," Paula said.

"See if you can find a way to get us into Calvin Rabara's party on Friday night."

"Ooh, now you're talking. That's a good distraction from the Great Wait. Where's the party?"

"Merchants Exchange Building."

"I'm on it. What am I going to wear?"

I laughed. "We'll shop. I have to finish my Christmas list anyway." I glanced down the hallway again. Still no one in sight. "I gotta go."

I hung up, moved the police tape, and held my breath as I inserted the key into the lock. It turned smoothly and within a second I was standing inside the late Nancy Pickett's apartment.

The interior couldn't have contrasted more with the exterior of the building. It was brightly painted in cream and burgundy tones. The décor was sophisticated with heavy, sturdy furniture. The sofa and love seat had solid oak wood frames, giving the impression that the owner had been a no-nonsense gal. Stable, dependable, secure.

The only indication that anything was wrong was the smell. The apartment smelled musty. Like it hadn't been aired out in a few weeks. Like no one was currently living here. Which was the case.

For some odd reason, the smell made me sad. I knew, of course, that Nancy was dead, but the scent caused by her absence affected me.

I was standing in the main living area. To the right, there was an opening to the kitchen with the counter in between the two rooms doubling as a bar/eating area. Two bar stools were pushed up against the counter.

On the left were two doorways. I crossed the room and peeked in the first. A small bedroom that Nancy had been using as an office. The second was a larger bedroom—Nancy's room—and between them was a shared bath. From the looks of things she had obviously been living alone.

I peeked into her closet. Tailored suits in all colors of the rainbow hung neatly side by side like soldiers in a row.

What could I possibly learn by being here? That she was meticulous? Yes, that much was clear.

I took a breath and glanced around the room. It seemed impossible to find anything the police may have missed.

I walked through the bathroom into the office. There were extension cords, a monitor, and printer, but her computer was gone. On the wall there was a bulletin board. Pinned to it was a "bring a friend" coupon for Club Zen and a yoga class schedule.

I opened a drawer on her desk. My heart sank as I looked at all the pens lined up, the paperclips and staples. She was definitely organized. No hidden diary jumped out at me, no false drawer, no hidden key to the mystery. No lead period.

I looked through the rest of the desk. She had a filing cabinet dedicated to financial matters and another filled with more supplies, like blank greeting and thank-you cards.

All the juicy stories she had been working on were probably at her station desk. I closed the drawer and headed to her bookcase.

It was filled with classic novels and a few finance and journalism books.

Dejected, I walked to the kitchen. I aimlessly opened a few cabinets. No money or secret notes stuffed in a cookie jar.

I dialed Paula. "This was a waste of time."

"You didn't find anything?"

"No."

"Her computer?"

"Gone."

"No note saying, 'If I die soon, so-and-so did it?' "

I refrained from smiling. "It's not a joke."

Paula laughed. "Sorry. How about a talking cat or something? A canary?"

"I'm hanging up now."

Just as I closed the phone, I heard a key slip into the front door lock. My heart stopped as I watched the door open.

A man in a tan work suit with a carpenter's belt on stood in front of the door. He clasped his hand to his chest as he saw me standing in the kitchen.

"Whoa! Sorry! I didn't knock. I didn't think . . ."

"It's okay," I said. "I . . . I'm . . ."

What was I supposed to say? "I'm not supposed to be here. I'm trespassing. Clearly I crossed the police tape" . . . Wait a minute—so had he.

"You a friend of Nancy?" he asked without waiting for an answer. "I'm Carl, the building super. I got a call from the police today, telling me it was okay to remove the tape. You got the same call?"

Better not to answer.

"I'm a private investigator. I was hired by Nancy's ex-husband . . ."

Carl's eyes widened and he stroked his mustache. "Oh. Yeah. Sad about Nancy. She was really great."

"Did you know her well?"

Carl worked his mouth in a little circle. "I felt like I did, because I watched her every night on the news, you know. But no, not well. She lived here a long time though. Since her divorce a few years back. She was friendly and—" He shrugged his shoulders. "—just genuinely a nice person."

"Did you ever meet her current boyfriend?"

Carl smiled. "Ramon? Sure. Great guy. He must be very upset."

I sighed and on an impulse asked, "What do you think happened to Nancy, Carl? Random act of violence—"

"No!" His passion surprised me. "She was obviously targeted. I'd just changed the lock on this apartment." He looked at me puzzled. "Someone broke in here." He gestured to the office. "Stole her computer."

My breath caught. "Her place was broken into? When?"

He shrugged. "Week before last. I think it was a Wednesday. Yeah, Wednesday, because I had to call a locksmith that night and the missus got upset. It's her knitting class night, and I couldn't watch the grandkids so she had to stay home," Carl said.

I got the chills.

Wednesday, the day of my hit-and-run. The same day I saw Nancy and Kimberly.

Why hadn't Ramon mentioned a break-in? He must have known. How else would he have the new key?

"Any idea who it was?" I asked.

Carl shook his head. "She reported it to the police. I don't know if they have any leads."

My phone buzzed. I glanced at the text message display.

L & I miss u. When r u coming hm? L is hungry. Formula?

Ah! I had to get home soon or Jim would give Laurie formula and I'd be stuck bonding with the breast pump instead of my petunia!

"Thanks, Carl. You've been a great help." I handed him my card. "If you can think of anything that might help us find out what happened to Nancy, please call me."

·CHAPTER FIFTEEN·

To Do:

1. Get Santa photo taken.

2. Mail Christmas cards.

4. Christmas shopping and recipes. (Need baskets to fill.)

5. Buy NEW car!

6. ✓ ~~Talk to Kimberly Newman.~~

7. ✓ ~~Check out Nancy's apartment.~~

8. Interview Nancy's dad and brother.

9. Talk to Nancy's boss (Karen Nolan).

10. Shop for supervisor party!!! Crash party.

11. Meditate.

The following morning, I reviewed my ever-growing to-do list while I nursed Laurie. The good thing about adjusting to breastfeeding was that I could actually do other things now while feeding Laurie. Something I could have never dreamed about the first few weeks postpartum. But now a few months later, breastfeeding seemed so easy I wondered what had been so difficult about it the first month.

And it had been difficult. I was so stressed out about it all: about whether or not she was getting enough milk, if we were doing the "latch" thing right, if we were on schedule. I don't know how I managed to stay with it.

Now, I combed her hair with my fingers and whispered to her, "You and I are going to solve this thing out, right, little monkey?"

She blinked up at me and kicked her feet. I grabbed a foot and tugged at her leg. She reached up for my face and tangled her hand in my necklace instead.

I picked up the phone and dialed Galigani. I got his voice mail and left a brief message wondering if he was still upset about yesterday. I'd received a return call from Nancy's brother and dialed him back, only to leave a message. I subsequently ran through a string of calls to Nancy's boss, and then the people who'd found her body. I left messages and hung up, frustrated.

Honestly, why couldn't anyone ever pick up their phones?

Caller ID was great in some instances, but now I felt like everyone was screening my calls and deciding not to answer an unknown number.

I burped Laurie then propped her up with some pillows. She goggled at me, delighted to be sitting up on her own. I smiled at her, marveling how much she had developed in the last month. Suddenly, she pitched her head forward and collapsed abruptly out of her seated position.

She let out a pitiful complaining wail, which I took as admonishment for trying anything new with her. I picked her up and took her to our nursery/office and set her down in the crib. Jim was hunched over the printer swearing.

"What's going on?" I asked.

He tugged at a sheet of paper. "Printer jam."

I flipped the release at the back of the printer.

"I tried that," Jim said.

I pulled at the paper, tearing it. It was even harder to remove when all that was left was a stub. "Downside to home office," I said.

Jim laughed. "Yeah we can't call the maintenance department."

"This is the third time it's jammed this week. I hate to break the news to you, honey, but I think it's time for a new printer," I said.

Jim nodded solemnly as if I was suggesting the execution of a dear friend. "Want to go to Office Depot?"

"Office Depot! No. I want to go Christmas shopping."

Jim laughed. "You can buy me a new printer for Christmas."

"I want to go to Union Square, but I want to see the tree and Christmas decorations, not reams of paper and office supplies," I whined.

Laurie kicked her legs at the mention of Union Square as though she knew she'd be in for a treat. I tried to use it to my advantage. "Even the baby wants to go Christmas shopping."

Jim plucked Laurie out of the crib and raised her high in the air. "Monkey! Don't you know what fun buying office equipment is?"

Laurie's little face scrunched up, her lips formed a circle but no sound escaped for a moment. Jim and I stared at her as if she had been stuck in a freeze-frame. Finally, a pitiful and somewhat staccato wail escaped her mouth.

I laughed. "Bug! What is it?"

"Obviously, she wants to go Christmas shopping with you and not office-supply shopping with me."

She let out a series of little breaths as though she were ready to hyperventilate. I took her from Jim and pressed her to my chest. "I know, peanut. I feel the same way."

I stashed her in her crib and said over my shoulder to Jim, "I'm going to shower and get ready for Union Square. You are free to join us. And if you want to peel off and go to the—" I wrinkled my nose. "—office place, that's fine."

Jim laughed. "Okay. We'll do it. Family day at Union Square. You guys can buy ice cream, chocolates, and shoes or whatever. I'll get a new printer."

"Great because I need a dress for Calvin Rabara's party."

Jim frowned. "Calvin Rabara? The supervisor?"

I nodded.

"How did we get invited to that? I didn't know we were going."

I pointed to him and me. "We're not. Unless, I mean, you want to go. I was going to crash it with Paula be-cause—"

Jim held out his hand. "I don't need to know. Do I need to know?"

I laughed. "Not really." I headed down the hall as the phone rang. "Can you get it?" I said, over my shoulder. "Otherwise, we'll never leave."

"You're just avoiding your mom," he said.

I grimaced to myself, knowing he was probably right.

I ran the water before stepping into the shower, not only waiting for the hot water, but also trying to overhear the conversation Jim was having. I couldn't make out who he was speaking to, only that it was a hurried conversation and then silence.

I stepped into the shower and tried to let the water put some sort of inspiration into my head. Union Square was a few blocks from the consulate. Should I pop over there and see . . . what? What was I hoping to see? Something suspicious?

I could visit Armand's downstairs neighbors—maybe they had seen something or heard something on Sunday night. After all, his apartment had been broken into. What did that have to do with Nancy? Anything?

When it was clear that the shower was not going to provide an *aha* moment, I turned the water off and stepped out.

I toweled off and retreated to my bedroom. I pulled a cardigan off a hanger and proceeded to ready myself for the outing. After a few minutes, Jim came into the bedroom holding Laurie.

He'd put her in a red wooly footed outfit that had a picture of a snowman on the front.

"Awww. She's so cute," I said. "Even in that hideous outfit!"

Jim laughed. "You don't like it?"

I smiled. "I wanted to take a Santa photo today." I scanned my closet for something warm. "Where did it come from?"

Jim shrugged. "I don't know. I thought you got it for her. It was in her drawer and it looked cozy." He hugged Laurie protectively. "I don't want her to catch a chill. Where's her hat?"

"Jim, we live in San Francisco, not Nebraska."

"Just because you refuse to wear hats doesn't mean Laurie shouldn't wear one."

"Um hmm," I replied from deep in the closet. I didn't bother to tell him that I didn't refuse to wear hats, I just never seemed to remember them.

"Dress warm, honey, and wear good walking shoes."

I nodded. "Who called?"

"Paula. She's joining us."

Jim, Laurie, and I rode the streetcar to Powell Street. We walked to Union Square and waited for Paula by the Christmas tree. She emerged from the underground tunnel and waddled over to us, one hand on her belly and the other swinging furiously to give her walking some momentum.

"Laurie's so cute! But what's she wearing?" she asked.

"It mysteriously appeared in one of her drawers. I suspect the crazy grandmother," I said.

Paula squatted next to the stroller and stroked Laurie's check. Laurie was sound asleep, no doubt from being bundled so warmly. "Don't worry, honey. Auntie Paula will be in charge of wardrobe decisions today. I'm gonna buy you a stupendous getup!"

Jim kissed me. "I'll leave you all to it then. Should we meet back here in, say, two hours?" He glanced at his watch. "We can get lunch together."

Paula patted him. "Don't worry. I'll make sure we're not late."

Jim nodded and headed toward Office Depot on 3rd Street. Paula, Laurie, and I drooled over the dresses in the Dior windows.

Paula said, "Let's go to Nordstrom, I can't fit into anything here."

I laughed. "Well, I probably can't either, and if by some miracle I do—the price tag is—"

"Prohibitive. Tell me about it." Paula sighed.

She pushed Laurie's stroller.

"I got it," I said, trying to pull the handles away from her.

She gripped the handles. "Stop it. I need to lean."

We laughed.

"If you need to rest, just say so," I said, pushing open the door to the San Francisco Centre for her and Laurie.

She nodded. "How about a cup of coffee and sitting under the dome?"

I desperately needed to make the most of my time here, grab a dress suitable for the supervisor's party, and purchase as many Christmas gifts as I could possibly carry, but I smiled despite myself.

The dome was the 102-foot-wide historic "Emporium" dome that had recently turned one hundred years old. Grabbing a cup of coffee, sitting under the huge skylight, and people watching was a favorite pastime for Paula and me.

I nodded. "Of course."

We ordered two cups of decaf and took our steaming mugs to a table.

Paula propped her swollen feet on the empty chair opposite her. "I shouldn't have come shopping with you. I'm slowing you down. Sorry."

"Don't be silly. I don't mind sitting down awhile," I said.

"I just had to get out of the house. David's mom came to watch Danny and I needed a break."

As soon as I took my seat, I surveyed the crowd. I saw a tall man with curly hair scamper away. He seemed familiar. I jolted up and said to Paula, "Stay here with Laurie."

I followed the man, who was now moving so quickly

away from me that he was getting annoyed looks from the crowd as he bumped shopping bags aside.

He jumped onto an escalator. The construction of the Centre was such that the escalators were in the middle of the mall, so I moved in the opposite direction to see if I could catch his face.

That unruly curly hair could only be . . .

Yes!

It was Christophe, the press liaison from the French consulate.

What was he doing here?

Certainly the consulate was only a few blocks from the Centre, so it was conceivable that he was using his lunch break to shop, but then why run when he saw me?

Chills went up and down my spine. Had he been following me? He bolted as soon as I saw him . . .

I returned to the café table under the dome and told Paula about Christophe.

She frowned. "You don't think it was a coincidence?"

"He was clearly running from me."

"Do you think he recognized you?"

I pushed away my coffee. "I'm sure of it."

"Why do you think he ran?"

"He obviously didn't want to talk to me. Could he have been following me?"

Paula looked confused. "Why would he be following you? And from where? Surely not your house. You took the streetcar, didn't you?"

I nodded.

"Did you see him on the streetcar?"

I shook my head.

Paula gave a dismissive hand wave. "Nah, he wasn't

following you. Maybe he just saw you and wanted to know if it was you."

"Why though? And why would he run from me?"

Paula shrugged. "I dunno. Why don't you ask him?"

I stared at her blankly. "Because he's not here, is he?"

"You should have gone after him."

I laughed. "And then what?"

Paula sipped her coffee. "Do, you know, your usual nosy thing." She bobbed her head back and forth from shoulder to shoulder and gave an exaggerated blinky eye routine "So, Christophe, what are you doing at the Centre? Were you wondering what to buy me for Christmas?"

I covered my face with my hands. "I don't blink like that and I don't sound like that either."

Paula laughed. "Yes, you do. You just don't know it."

I shook my head in complete denial.

"Why don't you run up to the consulate?" she asked.

"And do what? Do that ridiculous head bob and stupid question routine you just proposed? Besides, what about the Christmas shopping?"

She waved her hand at me. "Oh. I've been done for ages."

"Figures."

Paula played with her mug. "I'm happy to sit here with Laurie if you want to take a little stroll."

I couldn't imagine confronting Christophe at the consulate, but I could ask Armand's neighbors a few questions . . .

I walked the short blocks to Armand's flat. The skies threatened a downpour. The clouds looked as heavy as my stomach felt. I couldn't shake the idea that Armand's and Nancy's murders were related. But how?

Both their apartments had been broken into. Could that be the connection? Was someone looking for something? And if so, what was so important that it could lead to two murders?

I stood in front of his flat and rapped on the front door of the downstairs neighbor. A woman, who looked to be in her early twenties, if that, answered the door. She seemed surprised to see me there. She may have been expecting someone else. She had long blonde straight hair and was wearing jeans and a green holiday sweater with a cowl neck that dipped down to reveal lace-trimmed cleavage. Her feet were bare and she squished her bright pink toenails against the carpet as I introduced myself.

When I asked her about Armand, her face creased. "Oh. Armand," she whispered.

"You knew him, then?" I asked.

It wouldn't be surprising to find she hadn't associated with him at all. Neighbors are funny in San Francisco. Some can be best friends and others act like they've never seen you before.

I felt a raindrop on my hand and automatically turned my palm over to evaluate the rain.

The woman's eyes turned to the sky. She pulled the door opened wider. "Come on in, before it lets loose."

I stepped into the downstairs version of Armand's flat. The units were identical in terms of layout, except this one had an extra room at the front, whereas in the upper unit the space was taken up by the staircase. From the looks of it she used the extra room as a sewing area.

She noticed me eyeing the room and said, "I make costumes." She smiled and led me to the main living area. I stood at her front window and looked down the street to the French consulate, feeling as though it was the epicenter of my case.

"Costumes for what?" I asked.

"The opera, the symphony, whatever client I can get. Right now I'm repairing some costumes from the Renaissance Faire."

I thought of my neighbor, Kenny.

"Do you know Kenny Greer?" I asked.

She looked thoughtful. "No . . . I don't think so."

If she'd met him, she might not remember him, but I was certain he wouldn't have forgotten her with her shiny hair and bright toenails.

"He's my neighbor. He's a sub for the opera."

Her mouth formed a round *O* and she smiled. "I don't usually get to interact with the casts. I'm only a low-level seamstress. My name is Kyra, by the way."

I smiled. "It's nice to meet you, Kyra. San Francisco's such a small town that I had to ask."

She laughed. "I'm from a small town. San Francisco is nothing like it, but oddly enough I know what you mean. I seem to run into people I know here more often than I ever did at home!"

"Did you know Armand was killed?" I asked.

She gasped, then covered her mouth. "He was killed?" she asked after a moment.

I nodded.

"I thought he . . . I thought I'd heard he killed himself . . . that he was found with his wrists . . ."

"His house had been broken into. His front door lock was busted."

She frowned, but before she could reply a cell phone buzzed from the coffee table. She jumped as if it were the call of a lifetime. "Excuse me. I have to get that."

She pressed at the phone and smiled excitedly as she put it to her ear. She moved away from me and toward the front door. "Sorry," she said over her shoulder. "I get such bad reception inside. Make yourself at home." She gave me a little wave.

In someone older I would have thought it rude, but she was so cute and excited for her call that I found it hard to be offended. Besides, with her outside, it gave me a chance to poke around.

I walked to the end of the apartment. The bathroom door was straight ahead of me and her bedroom on the right-hand side, directly below Armand's room. Images of Armand's lifeless body in his tub hovered at the back of my mind, but I refused to let them come to the forefront. Inside, I peeked inside Kyra's bedroom. There was a glass door to a small deck and garden. I hadn't recalled Armand having a back deck. I pulled open the door and stepped onto the deck.

The downpour that had been threatening had still not manifested, but it was starting to drizzle, an annoying drizzle, the kind that forces you to wipe your face after a moment.

There was a small patch of land that could pass for a garden if anyone had taken an interest. As it was now, it was merely dry weeds that had been tamped down by winter. I looked up at Armand's flat. I had been right—no deck or door to the garden, but there was a fire escape.

I touched the metal bars, now wet and slippery from the drizzle. I tested the first rung. It seemed stable enough so I climbed onto the narrow staircase and hiked up the short distance to Armand's bedroom window.

My breath caught as I tried the window. It was unlocked and I had full access to his flat. But my thoughts were on Kyra. What if she came back and found me hanging out on the fire escape?

What was I doing anyway? So what about the fire escape?

Kyra didn't have a motive to kill Armand and, besides, the front door had been broken into.

I climbed down the fire escape and wiped my hands on my jeans. As I straightened I let out a tight gasp and covered my wildly beating heart. Kyra was directly in front of me.

"Oh! I'm sorry. I didn't mean to scare you," she said.

How nice of her to apologize to me when I was the one sneaking all over her property.

I let go of my chest. "No. I'm sorry. I . . ."

"Come back inside," she said. "It's going to start pouring any second."

I followed her into her bedroom then back down the short hallway to the living area. We sat down on the couch.

"Sorry. I shouldn't have left you alone. That was rude. But my reception is terrible in here and that was . . ." She smiled. "Well, my new boyfriend, I guess." She shrugged. "It's all so new; I don't know what he is . . . But I definitely didn't want to miss his call." She wiggled her eyebrows at me.

I nodded, waiting for the inevitable question, "What the hell were you doing snooping around my place?" But it didn't come.

She let out a little high-pitched cheer. "Ooooh . . . and

he's so hot. Hot, hot, hot I tell you. He worked with Armand." She cast her eyes downward as if giving Armand a moment of silence but quickly resumed her enthusiasm for her new beau. "That's how we met, through Armand. He's coming over in a few minutes. He wanted to meet you."

My mouth went dry.

He wanted to meet me?

She laughed. "Don't look so scared! He doesn't bite. It's just that I told him you were here and he works across the street." She motioned to the window. Reflexively I glanced out: The French consulate loomed.

I was certain I hadn't seen her at the Christmas party, but there had been a lot of people in attendance; she could have been there and I might not have noticed.

Could she be the woman who had been with the consul on the balcony at the party? No. That was absurd. If she was the other woman, the consul certainly wouldn't be running over to meet me. And Kyra had said the guy was hot. It was hard to imagine her describing the over-sixty-year-old consul as hot.

But who was I to say?

Hot is definitely in the eye of the beholder.

Who else could be her boyfriend?

"He's concerned about Armand," she continued, her eyes landing on her feet. She squished her toes into the carpet again. "Well, you know, the body and everything. I think they're going to send his remains back to France. It's really terrible, isn't it? I mean, he was so young. My age, you know? He was upset about a car accident he'd been in, but . . ." She shook her head. "A girlfriend of mine killed herself, too. Senior year in high school." She sighed sadly. "I don't get it." She straightened as if suddenly recalling something. "You said, maybe it wasn't suicide?"

Car accident!

That was me. He'd hit Laurie and me. Could he have been so upset by it as to kill himself?

No. It couldn't be.

The doorbell rang and I practically jumped off the couch. Why was I so skittish?

Who cared about her boyfriend? It could be anyone over at the consulate.

What if it was Christophe, with his handsome face and dark curly hair? He could be dating Kyra. They would look cute together.

What would I say to him? *"Hey, weren't you just at the San Francisco Centre? Why did you take off?"*

Or what if she was dating Jean-Luc?

Hot.

Yes. Jean-Luc was definitely hot, but his arrogant face was the last one I'd wanted to see right now.

Kyra pulled the front door open and jumped into Jean-Luc's arms. She wrapped her skinny legs around his waist and let out another high-pitched squeal.

"Hi, baby!" she said, planting a kiss on his lips.

He returned her kiss, a little too passionately. He held onto her bottom as she straightened her legs and let her pink toenails dangle inches away from the carpet. She ran her hand across his chest, letting her fingers get tangled in the hair.

When their embrace/kiss was over, Jean-Luc released her and glanced at me with a self-satisfied smirk, I'm sure expressly designed to make me feel uncomfortable.

Well, forget it. I could fight fire with fire.

I smiled at him. "Wow. Imagine seeing you here."

Kyra glanced from Jean-Luc to me. "Do you two know each other?"

Jean-Luc stepped toward me.

"I've had the *pleasure*. Yes," I said my voice thick with sarcasm.

Jean-Luc laughed, but Kyra tilted her head and looked puzzled.

"Are you *investigating* Armand's death?" His eyebrows went up on the word *investigating* and his tone implied I could no more carry out an investigation than tie my own shoes.

I smiled and licked my lips, preparing for attack, but before I could answer he whipped around toward Kyra.

"*Ma cherie*, can you make me a cup of coffee? Strong. Like you do so well?"

Kyra looked nervously at us, afraid, I'm sure, to leave us alone.

I tried my best to give her a reassuring look, but didn't trust myself not to pop Jean-Luc in the face if she wasn't present.

Kyra spun on a heel and left the room. Jean-Luc closed the distance between us, his head jutting toward me like an angry turkey. "What are you doing here! Get out of my business!" he said in a fierce whisper.

I pressed my fists to my sides to keep from pummeling his arrogant face. "Someone broke into Armand's place. He was killed—"

"Armand killed himself! It's tragic, but none of your business. The San Francisco Police are investigating and his parents are due in tomorrow. The last thing we need is you poking your big nose into—"

"He didn't kill himself," I said through gritted teeth.

Jean-Luc's eyes flashed and he looked as if he wanted to strangle me. "I am a man of little patience. I don't suffer fools. Armand slit his wrists; no one broke into his place—"

"But they did. I found him." Calmness returned to me like a wave washing over my body. I unclenched my fists. "I found him, and when I found him, his front door was busted."

I gave Jean-Luc my best, "Elementary, dear Watson," look.

For his part Jean-Luc looked generally perplexed. He frowned and shook his head back and forth.

I did my best to take advantage of his confusion. "Why was he speaking with Nancy Pickett? Don't you have an official press guy to work with reporters?"

Something I couldn't make out flashed across Jean-Luc's face. Fear? Anger?

His hand jerked up in an aggressive way. "What are you asking?"

"Nancy Pickett was murdered. Strangled and left dead in Golden Gate Park. A couple days later, Armand is found dead. Why were they talking to each other? What's the connection?"

Jean-Luc squinted. "What proof do you have that they even knew each other?"

Proof?

I did have proof. Sort of.

I knew Nancy had called Armand and she'd either visited him or was planning to, if she had his address.

And what kind of person asks for proof anyway? Was he challenging me? Clearly he hadn't denied that they may have met or at least spoken.

Kyra stood in the doorway. She was holding a dainty cup on a saucer and looked as if she was assessing the situation. I wasn't sure how much of our exchange she had seen or overheard. Jean-Luc backed away from me and smiled at her.

I turned to Kyra. "Were you home on Sunday night?"

She looked like a deer caught in highlights. She quickly glanced at Jean-Luc for direction, but he was staring at me practicing his bully body language. Kyra nodded.

"Did you happen to hear anything? Or see anyone going up to Armand's place?"

She shook her head.

"When did you see him last?"

She glanced again at Jean-Luc; this time he gave her a curt nod. She muttered, "I don't remember."

She crossed the room and handed him the coffee. He gave her a satisfied smile. She positioned herself exactly next to him so that they both stood in front of me.

Completely aligned.

That was it.

I was stonewalled.

No more niceties from Kyra; no more answers from either one of them.

CHAPTER SIXTEEN

On the walk back to Union Square I texted Paula. She was already sitting with Jim and Laurie for lunch at Kuleto's. Kuleto's serves Northern Italian food and is in the heart of Union Square.

I mentally thanked Jim for not picking a French restaurant. Not that I don't love French food, but right now I needed a serious break from the case.

I hightailed it down Powell Street, feeling guilty that I'd taken time away from my family and friends and for what? For another confrontation with hairy/cheesy man?

I pulled open the heavy wooden doors to the restaurant. Kuleto's, with high-vaulted ceilings, genuine Italian marble floors, and wrought-iron and copper railings made me feel immediately at ease.

Jim, Paula, and Laurie were seated at the forty-foot-long, intricately carved Brunswick bar made in England, with garlands of garlic, dried peppers, sausages, and herbs hanging over it.

Jim stood and smiled widely when he saw me approach. He kissed me and rubbed my back. "You look stressed out."

"Thank you for picking *Italian*." I smiled.

He laughed and pulled the bar stool out for me. I seated myself.

Laurie's stroller was parked in a corner with what appeared to be our new printer in it and dangling on the handle was a suit bag. Laurie was seated happily on Paula's lap drooling over a bread stick clasped in her sticky hand.

"What are you guys doing?" I demanded, pulling the bread stick out of Laurie's hand.

Paula and Jim exchanged looks. "What?"

The tip of the bread stick was gone, the balance of it melting with drool. Laurie smiled at me, a piece of the stick in her mouth. I flicked it out and she cried.

"She's not supposed to be eating bread," I said.

"She liked it," Jim said.

"Well, of course, she likes it. But she could choke," I said.

Laurie continued to cry. Paula grabbed another stick out of the basket. "Oh please, you are so mean. Denying the poor little thing a piece of bread. It's dissolving in her mouth, she's not going to choke!"

Laurie grasped the bread stick Paula offered her and immediately stuck it in her mouth.

"I thought she wasn't supposed to have solids until six months."

Paula flicked her hand at me. "That's what they told me with Danny, but I started him at four months. They're too hungry otherwise."

I watched Laurie as she sucked and devoured the bread. Her first bread stick. Another first that I had almost missed!

A waiter appeared and placed an antipasto dish in front of us. Thinly sliced prosciutto ham, shaved artichokes, and Frisee Parmesan. My mouth watered and I dove into the plate with delight.

Jim popped some prosciutto into his mouth. "Did you find anything out?"

"Mr. Cheesy Jean-Luc is dating the girl that lives in the flat under Armand."

Paula made a face. "That'd make sneaking upstairs to kill him pretty convenient."

Jim raised an eyebrow. "Only Armand's place was broken into, right, Kate?"

I nodded, eating an artichoke. "Yeah. But I did notice Jean-Luc seemed kind of surprised when I mentioned that."

Jim made a face. "You can't trust that guy, he's too squirrelly."

My phone buzzed from inside my jacket. I pulled at it frantically, hoping it was a return call from earlier. Instead Mom's number showed on the display.

I felt a pang of guilt as I pressed the send-to-voice-mail button, but it wasn't before Jim saw the display.

He squinted at me curiously, but chose not say anything.

Laurie continued to drool on her stick, leaving more in Paula's lap and on the floor than in her mouth. The waiter returned with our main dishes.

"I ordered for you," Jim said as the waiter placed a veal scaloppini dish with capers, garlic, spinach, and lemon in white wine sauce in front of me.

"One of the many reasons I love you."

Paula handed Laurie to Jim and dug into her lunch: a wild mushroom–stuffed chicken breast with Madeira cream sauce.

Jim looked from Laurie to the printer-occupied stroller as the waiter placed his lunch—grilled filet mignon, gorgonzola tortelloni, spicy escarole, and garlic confit—in front of him.

I laughed. "Let me scarf this down, then I'll hold her."

Jim leaned forward to inhale his dish. "No worries. I'll enjoy the aroma while you eat. Take your time."

"I got you a dress for the party," Paula said in between bites.

"You did?"

"Gold, Ann Taylor, little bitty number, you're gonna love it."

After lunch, Jim and I said good-bye to Paula and waited in line for about an hour and a half to get Laurie's picture taken with Santa. She was asleep by the time our turn finally rolled around and we weren't able to rouse her long enough to have open eyes in the photo. The end result was nevertheless still adorable with Laurie sucking on her thumb, her beautiful long lashes surrounding her closed little peepers. Even Santa seemed smitten with her.

At home, I nursed Laurie and put her down for the night. I searched the entire house for my to-do list and finally gave up and started a new one.

To Do:

1. Mail Christmas cards and CATCH UP on all Christmas items!!!

2. Interview Nancy's dad and brother.

3. Talk to Nancy's boss (Karen Nolan).

4. Is Armand's death related?

5. Decide on Art Exploration class for Laurie (they start in January).

The following morning, I connected with Mindy, the woman who had found Nancy's body in the park. We made arrangements to meet and I left Laurie in Jim's capable hands.

I parked on Irving Street, one block from the entrance to the park where Nancy's body had been found, and noted the thirty-minute limit on the meter. When had the city changed out all the meters from two hours to thirty minutes?

I was already rushed with the three-hour turnaround time to get back to Laurie and now I'd have to complete my interview and return to my car in half an hour.

I'll have to voice my opinion at the supervisor party on Friday!

I laughed to myself, as if they would care at all what I had to say about the state of parking in San Francisco.

As I climbed the stairs to the Inner Sunset flat the front door opened before I hit the top. A woman about six feet tall stood at the door. Her straight dark hair was pulled into a ponytail and she had a thin scar that ran across the length of her chin.

"Hi, I'm Mindy. You must be Kate?"

I shook her hand and stepped inside the apartment. It was crowded with boxes piled high against the far wall.

"I'm moving," she said as way of explanation.

I nodded. "Glad I was able to catch up with you."

She nodded, although the side of her mouth twitched and she didn't look glad about it at all. "Sorry that Will's not here. He said he would be but . . ." She shrugged. "You never know with him."

As if on queue a key slipped into the door and then the knob clicked. The door opened and a man equally as tall as Mindy stepped in. He was wearing a green tie-dye shirt and holding a small brown paper bag.

"Hey, girl, got your favorite." He put an arm around Mindy's waist, kissed her check, and handed her the paper bag.

She let him kiss her, although her face remained blank and her shoulders seemed to tense. She clutched the brown bag and glanced around the room for a place to set it.

"I'm Will Clarkson," the man said extending his hand. "You the PI?"

I shook his hand as I watched Mindy find a box and stuff the bag inside. She pressed her hands against the lid and gave me a nervous look. I smiled reassuringly.

Will pushed aside some clothes that were piled on the sofa and motioned for me to sit. I looked skeptically at the small space he'd made for me. Could I take a seat and not topple the stack of clothes next to it? I sat gingerly.

No part of my body touched the stack! Oh my God, I must be getting smaller! The workout regimen of deep squats with Laurie in the baby carrier every morning was working! Okay, not every morning, but every morning I thought about it. Imagine what size I'd be if I was very diligent about my mini workout—I'd be at my prepregnancy shape in no time.

Mindy stood by the box she'd stuffed the bag inside of. She looked as if she was guarding the box.

"I wanted to ask you a couple questions about Nancy Pickett," I said.

Will ran his fingers through his full hair. "Sure. Yeah. No problem. Shoot." He crossed the room and put an arm on Mindy's shoulder. Mindy swallowed and looked down.

"Can you tell me about it? About finding her?" I asked.

"We were walking in the park and we found her there, facedown." He glanced at Mindy. "That's right, isn't it, babe?" He gave her shoulder a squeeze.

Mindy took a deep breath and fingered the scar on her chin. "Yeah. We told that to the cops already. Why are you asking us again?"

No way did I want to let up that I wasn't privy to cop inside information. It made me so second citizen.

"I just want to get an idea about it." When I had spoken with her on the phone, she'd seemed eager to help me, now she was annoyed. "Was Nancy on a path? Hidden? Clothed?"

"She had on running clothes. Shorts, tennis shoes," Will said.

Mindy covered her face. "Tell her about the coyotes."

Will's face darkened. His eyes narrowed and he shook his head as if trying to dispel a bad memory. "I think the coyotes had nibbled off her eyelids. Her face was . . ."

Coyotes! In Golden Gate Park!

"What coyotes?" I asked, trying to keep my voice calm.

"Guessing they come over the bridge from Marin," Will said.

Good God!

Another great reason to put off running until I'm in better shape. Not only could you get mugged and killed in the park, but you had to be able to outrun a pack of coyotes.

Will gave Mindy's shoulder another squeeze. "Right, babe?"

Mindy shrugged.

"Was she in plain sight?" I asked.

"No, she was off the path. The killer didn't do a great job of concealing the body. I mean, she wasn't in a clearing or anything and she wasn't covered up. I saw her right away."

"Could you tell how she was killed?"

Mindy straightened and threw her shoulders back, causing Will to release her. "She was strangled."

Will nodded. "Well, it's not like we know forensics or anything, but her throat was . . ." His hand instinctually went to his own throat.

"Red and raw, bruised even," Mindy finished for him.

An image of Armand in the tub flashed before me. His neck had also been bruised.

"You said she was off the path . . ."

Will nodded.

"How did you find her then? I mean, if she was off the path . . . ?"

He smiled. "We were hunting mushrooms."

I recalled the bag he'd given Mindy. Probably more mushrooms. Was mushroom hunting legal? She certainly seemed eager to hide them. Either they were violating some regulation or they didn't want to share their booty with me.

"Did you see anyone else on the path? On your way in or out?"

Will shook his head. "No, how about you, babe?" He rubbed her back.

She shrugged. "No."

Of course, Nancy had probably been killed the day before they found her anyway. That's what Galigani said the

ME thought and how else could the coyotes have gotten to her?

I fought the disappointment and worse, the feeling of having wasted my time. What had I learned? Besides that I could now have another excuse for not working out.

I stood. "Do you remember anything else?"

The both shook their heads.

I needed to get back to Laurie, not to mention a ticking parking meter. I pulled Laurie's diaper bag, which also doubled as my purse, onto my shoulder and a pain stabbed at my neck. My hand reflexively shot out to grip it. The whiplash from the accident had more or less faded, except at the most unexpected moments.

"Are you okay?" Mindy asked, grabbing my elbow.

"Oh. I'm fine," I said, a little embarrassed by her concern. I hate the feeling of being fussed over by strangers. I much prefer to feel in charge of something although that rarely happens.

"I was in a hit-and-run last week . . . Well, I mean, they hit me. A kid from the French consulate. Turns out they have diplomatic immunity so they aren't stepping up to pay for anything and—"

"French consulate?" Will asked.

"Yeah," I replied, glad for the interruption. Otherwise, I might have gone on to blurt out that poor Armand had been killed.

"That's funny. I saw an SUV with the front bashed up the other day. Sort of a coincidence, isn't it? I only noticed it because the vehicle was so new and then I saw the diplomat plates. I hadn't seen their fleet before—"

"When was this?" I asked, a sudden feeling of excitement building in my gut.

"I assumed they were going to Max's, the auto body shop down the street," he continued. "Sorry, what?"

"When? Do you remember when you saw it?"

Mindy pressed at her eyes. "It was last Thursday, wasn't it? The day before we found the lady."

Will squinted, then nodded. "Yeah. I think that's right."

"Did you manage to see the driver? Was he young with long hair?" I asked.

Will shook his head. "I didn't see the driver."

Images of Armand dumping Nancy's body in the park flooded my mind. Kyra said Armand might have felt bad about hitting Laurie and I, but that didn't seem like enough to make him commit suicide. How would he feel about murder? Would guilt over that make him take his own life?

"Thank you, you've been very helpful."

I left their apartment and walked down the street to the auto body shop. The garage was wide open and a red convertible Lexus was propped up on jacks as it was being worked on. The passenger side was smashed in and I silently prayed that side had been vacant at the time of impact.

I quickly eyed the shop. No SUV was in the queue to be worked on.

A mechanic appeared from under the convertible. He saw me and pulled himself up from the ground. He had on greasy coveralls and wiped his hands on a rag hanging from his back pocket. "Can I help you?" he asked, approaching me.

I gave him my best smile. "Anyone bring in a French consulate vehicle, an SUV, to have some front-end repair done?"

He pursed his lips, his blue eyes narrowing a bit. "When? Like recently, like today?"

"Last week."

He shook his head. "No. I work on a lot of cars, but I haven't worked on a consulate vehicle. I would have remembered that coming into the shop."

The car hadn't been here. Whatever the SUV had been doing in this neighborhood, so far from the consulate and so close to where Nancy's body had been found in the park, didn't have anything to do with this shop.

So what had it been doing here and who'd been driving it?

•CHAPTER SEVENTEEN•

To Do:

1. Exercise.

2. Get facial for supervisor party.

3. Call Karen Nolan again.

4. Call Mom?

5. CHRISTMAS!!! Ahhhhh!

The following morning I had a hard time dragging myself out of bed. I cuddled with Laurie until about 9 A.M. then finally rolled out of bed to find Jim.

He was installing the new printer and could barely be bothered with reading the instructions.

As I was preparing to read the manual for him, the phone rang. It was finally a return call from KNCR. Karen Nolan would meet with me today.

"Oh. I have to get ready!" I said, as soon as I hung up the phone.

Jim barely looked up. "Where are you going now?"

"Embarcadero, KNCR. I'll be back in time for the next feeding, don't worry."

Jim looked up from the printer, confused. "You don't have to rush back. Why don't you finish your shopping at the Embarcadero? I can just give Laurie a bottle."

Mom guilt burned at me. But he was right, rushing back made no sense.

I stood at the security desk at KNCR, the station where Nancy had worked, waiting for the producer of her news show. After a few moments a woman in her mid-twenties with kinky, short blonde hair pushed open the swing door that divided the lobby and the rest of the building.

She looked at me and smiled. "Are you Kate?"

I nodded and extended my hand.

She shook it and introduced herself as Ellie Schulze. She led me through a long corridor past a few green rooms. I peeked in on the way past and spotted Stan, the weather guy. He was about my height with dark hair and a perpetual grin. I never realized how short he was. I suppose TV can make you believe just about anything.

Ellie stopped at a door and knocked. "Ms. Nolan? Mrs. Connolly's here to see you."

The door squeaked open. Karen was seated in a desk chair with rolling wheels. The office was so small she could remain seated and still open the door. Her auburn hair was held back with several barrettes and fell to her shoulders. She thanked Ellie and motioned me in.

The space was cramped with lots of photos on the walls. Karen was captured with just about every TV personality I could imagine. I searched for one with Nancy and found it off to the left. It looked like a company picnic somewhere with green grass and trees in the background. Both women were wearing ball caps with the station logo on them and smiling into the camera.

Karen glanced around the room, her nose wrinkling. "Is this okay? We can grab a conference room."

"No need. I just have a few questions. Thanks for meeting with me."

She nodded. There was a folding chair in the corner and she motioned me to it. "What can I tell you that will help?"

I seated myself. "I've been hired by Chuck Vann. He's Nancy's ex-husband."

Karen nodded again.

"He's under the impression that Nancy might have been working on a story about the French consulate and that the story might have pushed some buttons."

Karen's brows drew close together. "Really?" She sat in silence, rocking back in her chair. After a moment she said, "The consulate? I think she was working on the award the consul received. Nancy was covering the story. I can't imagine there would be crossed-up feelings."

A soft rap sounded on her door. Karen looked annoyed. "Sorry. It's always something."

She pulled the door open. The lead anchorman, Jake Spencer, stood in the doorway. He hovered over us. If I had to guess I'd say he was six and a half feet tall, but it seemed like was seven feet tall. He filled the doorway with his broad frame and I feared he'd bump his head. For all his height he didn't stoop at all, just stood rigid in the doorway.

How had I never noticed this man's height on TV? Granted he was always seated but this was ridiculous!

Jake looked from Karen to me. "Oh. Am I interrupting?"

Karen introduced me then asked, "Do you know anything about the story Nancy was working on about the French consul?"

Jake sighed. "Poor Nancy. No. I wish I could help. Maybe Ellie?"

The last was said as almost an afterthought.

Karen frowned. "Who's Ellie?"

Jake smiled and his muscular jawline became almost cartoonish. "Our news intern."

Karen's mouth pressed into a line. She looked upset that Jake would even suggest someone else might have information that she didn't, much less an intern. She shook her head absently and waved at Jake. "Of course Kate is free to speak with her but . . ."

Jake caught my eye and gave me a discreet nod, which I took to mean I'd better have a word with Ellie.

The phone on Karen's desk lit up and rang. She sighed and grabbed the receiver. She spoke into the phone at the same time as she rummaged around her desk. She put the party on hold, located a business card, and handed it to me. "Let me know if I can be of any further assistance."

Further assistance?

I nodded. "Thank you for your time."

Jake waited for me to leave Karen's office and pulled the door closed behind me. "Ellie will need to sign you out. You can ask her about any news stories Nancy was working on. If anyone's on the pulse of this place it's her."

We walked toward the exit, passing the green room. A tray of hot food had been delivered in the short time I'd been in Karen's office. I peeked over at the tray—cheesy enchiladas.

Could it be a coincidence?

I pointed to the tray. "Who does the catering?" I asked.

Jake looked surprised. "Oh. Sorry, would you like some?"

I laughed. "No. No, thank you. I'm just curious who the caterer is."

Jake picked up a card peeking out from under the tray and handed it to me. *It read Ramon, the Brave Gourmet: Traditional Mexican Dishes with an Untraditional Flare.*

"Thanks," I muttered.

"I wish I could help you. Losing Nancy was a great shock to us. She was a wonderful lady."

Ellie materialized in the doorway to the green room. "Do you need me to sign you out now?" she asked.

I nodded and followed her down the hallway.

Jake called, "Good luck," after me.

"Ellie, do you know anything about the French consul story Nancy was working on?"

Ellie stopped walking and turned to face me. "The bio-tech story?"

"Biotech?"

Ellie looked past me down the hall. I turned. No one was behind me. I faced her. She waved for me to follow her outside. We walked the rest of the corridor in silence. She pushed on the exit door and we stepped out into the lobby. The security guard glanced up at us from his computer, looking about as interested in us as if we were chopped liver. As soon as we passed him his attention went back to his monitor.

Ellie asked, "Where are you parked?"

"In the lot across the street."

"I'll walk with you."

We exited the building; the breeze from the bay was whirling my hair around and making my scalp feel cold. Jim was right: I needed to get into the habit of wearing a hat, the last thing I needed was pneumonia.

Ellie moved closer to me, so no one could overhear us or so I could block the wind, I couldn't decide.

"I didn't think of it until you mentioned the consul, but we got a call . . ." She squinted and then looked up toward the sky. ". . . I don't know, probably a couple weeks before Nancy died. It was a guy from a biotech company in South City. He mentioned something about the consul. I transferred him to Nancy."

"Do you remember his name or the company?"

She shook her head. "I don't. I know it wasn't Genetech. Because that's pretty much the only one I know, but I associated it in my mind with Genetech. I'd forgotten about it until now."

"Why did you transfer him to Nancy?"

"She liked that sort of thing. She was our best investigative journalist . . ."

"What about Kimberly Newman?"

Ellie looked surprised. "Kimberly?"

"Was she . . . is she working on any story involving the consul?"

"No. Well, wait. I take that back. She did go to their Christmas party. That's her regular type of story."

"Was she scheduled for that even before Nancy's death?"

Ellie swallowed hard as if I had just suggested Kimberly was responsible for Nancy's death.

Had I just suggested that?

We crossed the street and entered the parking lot where I'd left my car earlier.

Ellie scratched at her chin. "I think Kimberly must have already been assigned . . . I don't really know though. I know Nancy was handling everything consulate related. So, it could be we would have sent Nancy instead of Kimberly."

Could Kimberly have been jealous that Nancy had been assigned to the story she thought should be hers?

"Who's in charge of the assignments?" I asked.

"Karen," Ellie answered in almost a whisper.

I nodded.

"Is it important?" Ellie asked.

I shrugged. "I don't know at this point."

"Well, if you talk to her again, please don't tell her, you know, that I said anything." A frown creased her forehead. "I don't want her to think I'm talking about station stuff if I'm not supposed to be."

"Don't worry," I said.

Ellie looked semi-soothed although the frown line didn't disappear.

I thought about Nancy's apartment and the stolen computer. "Can you tell me if any of Nancy's things are here at the station? Her computer, notes, that sort of thing?"

"The police took her computer and I just finished boxing all the rest of her things and gave them to her father yesterday."

We reached my car. I showed her the catering card. "Is this Ramon the same guy that was dating Nancy?"

She smiled. "Yeah! Isn't he hunky?" Suddenly she seemed to realize that drooling over a guy who'd so recently lost his girlfriend might not be appropriate because she grabbed my arm and looked serious. "I mean . . ."

"It's okay. So, it is him?"

She nodded. "He was always bringing us snacks when Nancy was . . . when she was working. Then when she passed, he stopped coming around. We missed him. We decided to hire him."

"Who decided?" I asked.

"Karen," she admitted.

I opened my car door and climbed in. "Thanks, Ellie, you've been a big help."

·CHAPTER EIGHTEEN·

Any plan I'd had to shop vanished when my phone buzzed.
I pulled the key from the engine and picked up the phone.
I found myself secretly hoping it was Mom or Galigani,
but I didn't recognize the caller ID.

It turned out to be Nancy's brother, Elliot. He and his
father were at his father's home on the peninsula, could I
meet with them?

I hung up and texted Jim.

Pull out the formula. Need to go for a ride to the
peninsula.

The drive took about thirty minutes without traffic and
thankfully since it was the middle of the day I didn't have
any to fight.

When I arrived, Nancy's father greeted me at the door.

He was wearing a gray sweater that seemed to draw out gray flecks in his blue eyes. He smiled sadly at me and showed me into a large, bright family room. Elliot was seated on a leather ottoman, but rose when we came into the room.

Elliot was tall with long skinny legs and a long skinny face to match. He had a man's classic receding hairline, which only gave the impression that his face was longer.

"Thank you for helping us find out what happened to Nancy," he said, shaking my hand. "Dad, do we have any eggnog left over from the reception? Maybe Kate would like a cup."

"Oh, no, I . . ."

"Please," Elliot insisted. "At any rate, I think I'd like a cup."

Gordon Pickett nodded and left the room, looking relieved to have something to do.

"I don't like him to think about Nancy's death . . . about her being hurt . . ." He shrugged.

"I understand. I know this is difficult for you."

Elliot moved across the room and patted an office file box. "After I got your message, I saved this for you. I don't know if it will help you, but when Chuck told me he suspected Nancy had been killed due to a story she was working, and then her office called telling me to pick up her stuff, seemed like I should go through it. So, I did, but I don't even know what I'm looking for."

I tried not to feel giddy about it. But any chance at real information could help me solve this case.

"Thank you. If it's okay with you I'll review it at home . . . uh, I mean my office. My *home office* and then return it to you," I said.

Yes. Home office made it sound better. Saying "home" sounded altogether unprofessional.

"Absolutely. Take your time with it. All that matters is finding out what happened to Nancy."

Nancy's father returned with three mugs of steaming eggnog. Elliot crossed the room and fetched a bottle of brandy. He held it out to me.

"No. Thank you. I have to drive."

He nodded, and then proceeded to pour a hefty amount into his own and his father's mugs.

Gordon picked up the mug and seated himself on the couch. "What can we tell you that will help?"

"Did either of you know that Nancy's apartment had been broken into?"

Anger flashed across Elliot's face and his head whipped toward his father. "Dad?"

"No! When was this? Was Nancy there when it happened?" Nancy's father asked.

"I don't think so. Her apartment was broken into a few days before her disappearance. Her computer was taken," I said.

"Her computer? Is that what made Chuck think she was targeted? So, it wasn't just a random attack in the park, was it?" Elliot asked.

"I don't think it was random. No. Did she talk with either of you about the French consul, Eloi Leppard?" I asked.

They shook their heads.

"How about Armand Remy? Did she speak with you about him? Mention his name? I found she made several calls to him and she had his address."

Elliot shook his head and looked at his father.

"I found Armand dead on Sunday."

"Good lord!" Gordon said. "Do you think his death has anything to do with Nancy?"

Elliot's face flushed. "How can that be? How can they be related at all?"

"I don't know that they are related. I thought that if Nancy uncovered something about the consul, and she found it out from Armand—"

"Then they killed the stool pigeon?" Elliot asked.

Gordon's eyes grew wide.

I shrugged. "I don't know anything for sure. It's just a theory."

"How do we find out?" Elliot asked.

I glanced at the office file box. "I'll start with that."

Elliot picked up the box. "I can take it out for you."

Nancy's father rose, his eyes welling with tears. "Thank you for helping us."

"One more thing. What about Ramon?"

Elliot and his father exchanged glances. "What about him?" Elliot asked.

"Do you know him? Do you like him? Trust him?"

Nancy's father sipped his eggnog and kept quiet. I looked to Elliot.

Elliot shrugged. "Sure. We liked him, right, Dad?"

Nancy's father nodded and swirled the remaining eggnog in his mug. "Yes. He cooked so many nice things for the service . . ."

"You don't think . . . Ramon?" Elliot asked.

I gave my best reassuring smile. "I've really only begun my investigation. I met with Ramon, he was very helpful."

Elliot let out a sigh. "Right. He's a good guy. I think he cared for Nancy a lot."

He cared about getting a catering gig at her place of employment, too.

I wonder how deep Ramon's loyalties ran.

Elliot walked me to Jim's car and placed the office file box in the trunk. He cleared his throat. "Uh. About Ramon. I didn't want to say anything in front of Dad, but I never trusted the guy."

"Why?" I asked.

Elliot sat on the bumper of Jim's car. "I don't know, he was kind of a male gold digger, if that makes sense. My sister was very successful. After the breakup with Chuck, she could have been with anyone. I didn't get the whole Ramon choice. It's obvious the guy didn't have a lot to offer."

"What about his catering business?"

Elliot made a face. "What catering business?"

"He's catering dishes for the station," I said.

"Since when?" Elliot asked.

"I don't know. I was just there—he was catering for them."

Elliot scratched his chin.

"How long had they been dating?" I asked.

"A few months," Elliot said.

"Why did she and Chuck split up?" I asked.

He shrugged. "Why does anyone break up? It just wasn't working for them anymore. Probably more on her side then his. He was always in love with Nancy. But he's fifteen years older than her and as his age started to slow him down I think Nancy started to pull away." He gave a cynical laugh. "Nancy, well, she could be kind of superficial." He fingered his receding hairline. "Every time she saw me, she gave me the name of a guy who does hair plugs."

I covered my face, trying to suppress a giggle. Elliot laughed outright.

"This is San Francisco, right? Not LA. And it's not like

I'm on TV," he said. "But, in terms of Chuck and Nancy, you could probably ask Chuck. He's a good guy. He'd never hurt Nancy and he'll tell you anything you want to know.

At home Jim was working on the computer and Laurie was napping. I took advantage of the downtime to dig into Nancy's office file box. There were framed photos of Nancy and Ramon, a stack of business cards, and several yellow legal pads. There were also a lot of file folders. Like Nancy's apartment, her records were neatly labeled and organized.

She'd been in the habit of dating everything, which for my purposes was extremely helpful. I put everything in chronological order and began reading the most current items. On one of the pads I found notes about the consul. If I was reconstructing the notes correctly, she'd received a call from Kevin Gibson at Reparation Research.

Reparation Research must have been the biotech company Ellie had told me about. Kevin had told Nancy that he'd had concerns about the consul placing several French scientists at Reparation Research. Apparently, it was rumored that some trade secrets and formulas may have been leaked to the French company *L'éternelle Jeunesse*. Could the consul be concerned this rumor could hit the newspapers? Would word getting out have affected his award?

I dialed the number listed for Kevin Gibson. I got the Reparation Research general voice option tree, so I punched the option for the operator. When I asked her to put me through to Kevin Gibson, she told me he was on vacation in the Bahamas, returning after the New Year.

Must be nice.

Jim looked up from his computer long enough to tell me two packages had arrived in the mail for me. He handed me a bubbled manila envelope with no return address and a larger box with my brother's address on it.

I tore into the larger box. Inside were three smaller packages wrapped in Christmas paper. I pulled them out and placed them under the tree. I eyed the box with my name on it.

"Can I open mine now?" I called to Jim.

He left the office and joined me in the living room. "What are you, a child? Can't wait until Christmas?"

Before he could even finish the sentence I had already torn into the box. It was a baby sling in a beautiful bright blue fabric with pink roses on it. This was the very sling I'd seen other mothers wear so effortlessly.

This was perfect. I could use this and nurse Laurie in it and not have to worry about waking her when she inevitably fell asleep in it. I loved the BabyBjörn that I carried her in, but getting her out of the contraption while she was asleep and not waking her was next to impossible.

The sling came with an instructional video that I placed on top of the TV. I put the sling around my shoulder and stuffed a sofa pillow inside it, then adjusted the ring.

Jim eyed the sling, then the video. "Are you going to watch that?"

I rocked the pillow around. "I'm sure I can figure it out."

Jim handed me the manila envelope. I ripped it open and frowned. I'm not much of a techie, but it looked like a raw computer part.

"Do you know what this is?" I asked Jim.

He squinted at it and shrugged. "I don't know. A hard drive?"

"Why would somebody send me a hard drive?"

Jim shrugged. "Who sent it?"

I showed him the blank envelope. Jim frowned. "Call Kenny. I'm sure he'll know exactly what it is and what to do with it."

Laurie began to stir from her nap. I plucked her from the crib before she could cry. During the day she napped in the crib, but overnight she still slept in the bassinet by my bedside. Now, she was getting so big that soon she would outgrow her bassinet and would have to sleep in the crib overnight. That meant out of our room.

I cradled her and whispered. "You don't need to grow so fast, you know."

She kicked her feet and moved her legs in a circular fashion as if riding a bicycle in midair.

"Are you trying to outrun me?" I asked.

I slipped her into the new sling, yet unlike the pillow, she was squirmy. I fussed with the material, the ring, and readjusting Laurie for over twenty minutes, by which time she was restless and wanted out.

That's what I get for not watching the instructional video!

I grabbed my keys and the diaper bag and closed the front door behind me. The café was within walking distance and I hoped Laurie would settle down during the walk.

Kenny was sitting in our usual spot in the café. A cappuccino cup in front him. All that was left was the foam. His headphones were firmly in place with only his tapping foot revealing that music was on.

I slide in across from him. It was actually difficult to fit into the chair at the small café table with Laurie in the sling.

Kenny nodded to the barista. "Tracy," he said with a lovelorn look on his face.

"Butterfly?"

He nodded and sighed.

I handed him some money. "Why don't you get me a decaf latte and get yourself whatever."

I fiddled with Laurie in the sling while Kenny flirted with Butterfly. How did other moms look so natural with the sling? I felt like at any moment Laurie would slide out.

Kenny appeared with a warm apple scone for us to split, a cappuccino for himself, and my latte. After he seated himself I handed him the package.

"What's this?" he asked.

"I'm hoping you can tell me."

He peeked inside the package. "A hard drive? Your computer crashed?"

"Someone sent it to me. Do you think you can make it work?"

"It depends. It doesn't look too banged up. I can try."

I sipped my latte and felt Laurie squirm in the sling. Why had I even thought to bring her in this sling? I reshuffled her. She let out a little protest cry.

The barista aka Butterfly made it to our table. "Aw. A little baby."

I pulled aside the sling fabric and let Butterfly peek in on Laurie. As she leaned in to look at Laurie I spotted the tattoo. I smiled to myself. Kenny was practically drooling. She seemed like a good fit for him.

"So, you're Ken's boss?" Butterfly asked.

Kenny shot me a look. I scratched my nose to keep from laughing.

He told her he worked for me? How sweet! And what

was the deal with "Ken." I hadn't known anyone to ever call him that.

"It must be superexciting. I wish I had a job like that. Working in a coffee shop, well, I mean, it's okay. But it's not like I do stakeouts and catch murderers or anything."

Kenny tugged nervously at his green hair.

"I couldn't do it without Ken," I said.

A couple walked into the café and Butterfly slipped back behind the counter, not before shooting Kenny an appreciative look. She liked him.

Laurie completely wormed her way out of the sling and began to wail. I tried to stick her back inside, but before I could do it, the ring at the top came loose and I was left holding the beautiful blue fabric in my hands.

I should have brought the stroller. Now I'd have to walk home holding Laurie instead and carrying the sling.

I downed the rest of my latte. "All right, tech support, I'm heading home. Let me know if you can bring the hard drive to life."

Kenny smiled. "Thanks, Kate."

"No problem, *Ken*."

Kenny ducked his head and tucked his headphones back in place. I figured he would stay until closing. Good for him.

· CHAPTER NINETEEN ·

To Do:

1. Watch sling DVD.

2. Enroll Laurie in art class.

3. Why isn't Galigani returning my calls?

4. Call Mom.

5. CHRISTMAS!!! Ahhhhh!

6. When do we get insurance check?

The next morning I lounged in bed staring at Laurie. Technically, she was "sleeping through the night" but "the night" only constituted six hours. Certainly not my definition of a night, but an improvement over last month.

Still, I was exhausted this morning and happy to spend my time daydreaming next to her until I was roused out of bed by the phone.

Paula's voice filled the line. "I'm so excited about the party tonight! I hope Mr. Supervisor puts out as good a spread as the French."

"I don't know about that, but at least we won't have to talk over an electronic tree."

Paula laughed. "Do you like the dress I picked out for you?"

Guilt-ridden, I stared into the closet at the plastic suit bag. I'd gotten home so exhausted from that shopping trip that I'd placed the bag into the closet and completely forgotten about the dress.

"I love it." And to avoid being quizzed about it I decided to change the subject. "What are you going to wear?"

"A potato sack. It's lovely. You'll be amazed at the things I can pull off. I'll pick you up at 5:30."

In the kitchen I found that Jim had brewed a fresh pot of coffee and left me a note. He'd gone for a run. I poured myself a cup of coffee and meandered to the bathroom to slather on a face mask.

If I didn't have time for a proper facial, then the least I could do was get rid of dry skin before rubbing elbows with the San Francisco elite.

I took my coffee to the office and sat in front of the computer thinking. Galigani still hadn't returned my phone calls. Fearing that he'd changed my password, I tentatively tried to log in to the background check database. I was able to get in without an issue, so that either meant he wasn't mad at me or he hadn't gotten around to terminating my access. I hoped it was the former.

Once past the initial screens, I typed in *Kevin Gibson, Reparation Research*. Kevin had never been arrested, had no open warrants for his arrest, and had good credit. He lived outside of San Francisco, on the peninsula in one of my favorite towns, San Carlos.

The database lookup got me nowhere nearer to knowing why he had contacted Nancy. I googled Kevin and found that he was a Harvard graduate with a degree in chemistry. His current position at Reparation Research was "Research Scientist II."

I saw that he had a Facebook account. Something my brother and his wife kept e-mailing me about. They were pestering me to create an account and upload a gazillion pictures of Laurie. I clicked on the Facebook link and saw that Kevin was "friends" with a bunch of people I didn't know and he seemed to like Celtic music bands.

I hit the "Send Kevin a message" link, which immediately brought me to a sign-up page. I reluctantly filled in all my information and created my own account. Then I was able to send Kevin a message.

I typed.

Hope you are well. I'm a private investigator in San Francisco, working on a case involving the murder of KNCR reporter Nancy Pickett. I understand that you may have contacted Ms. Pickett. Is there any way you can kindly share with me your communication with Ms. Pickett? I further understand from your office that you are on vacation in the Bahamas. I hope this is not too much of an intrusion on your time.

I hit SEND and then proceeded to start adding my own friends. Out of curiosity I entered every name I could remember from the consulate: Jean-Luc, Christophe, Armand, even the consul himself, Eloi Leppard. I didn't find any of them.

Oh well, what good would it do anyhow? Tell me what kind of music they liked?

I found my brother, Paula, and even Kenny, and noticed that they all had their pages marked as "private." I figured if I was going to upload a bunch of pictures of Laurie then I should do the same.

I poked around the privacy settings and adjusted them as I felt my mask getting tight. Better go wash it off before I had to peel it off.

Once I scrubbed the last bit of green from my face, I decided it was time to try the dress. Mentally I was already compiling a list of backup options before I even had the dress out of the bag.

I pulled the plastic bag up an inch to reveal the hem of the dress. It was gold with tiny red flowers on it. So far, so good. Paula had great taste, I knew that. I just hoped it would fit. I unveiled the rest to reveal a classically cut simple dress. V-neck, short sleeves, looked promising.

I slipped it over my head and got my arms stuck. I couldn't get the dress on.

Shoot!

What was I going to do now?

Served me right for procrastinating!

I fought the urge to cry. I took off the dress, disgusted, and threw it in a heap on the floor.

Wait a minute.

I picked the dress up again and examined the side.

What an idiot! I unzipped the hidden zip and slipped

the dress on over my head again, this time chanting, "Please fit, please fit, please fit."

I took a breath and yanked on the zipper. It closed seamlessly. I stared at my reflection. The dress fit like a glove.

I looked sophisticated. I looked slim. I looked . . . I looked like I could belong at an SF supervisor party.

I let out a whoop of happiness and ended up waking Laurie.

She wailed from the bassinet.

I leaned over her. She stopped crying as if suddenly calmed by the shimmer of my dress. "You like Mommy's new dress?"

She pedaled her feet and reached out to me.

"Wait! Before I pick you up, you monkey, let me change because you'll probably use me as a spit-up rag!"

Paula and I pulled up to valet parking at the Merchants Exchange Building and walked into the building. The street-level lobby had a gorgeous barrel-vaulted ceiling sparkling with marble, gold leaf, and bronze.

Both Paula and I immediately looked up to appreciate the glittery beauty.

"I only take you to the finest establishments," Paula joked.

I smiled. "It matches my dress!"

Paula laughed. "I planned that."

She was wearing a new simple black maternity dress with some green piping that she'd added herself for holiday cheer.

"Just promise you aren't planning to go into labor tonight," I said.

She smiled. "I can't promise. I can only hope."

She wasn't due for another few weeks, but it already looked like the baby had dropped.

In the elevator we were pressed up against other party-goers. We followed them to the ballroom and were happy to see that no one was at the door requesting invitations.

We slipped into the ballroom, which had a wonderful curved mahogany bar, a twenty-foot fireplace of creamy stone, and a honeycombed ceiling of mahogany octagonals.

We immediately spotted Kimberly. She was at the bar on the arm of Calvin Rabara, the city supervisor. The party was a thank-you to all his supporters. The mayor was standing next to Calvin, laughing and leaning into Kimberly's face.

She giggled at his joke and tossed her head to the side. As soon as she did our eyes connected. Her head jolted upright and then she seemed to suddenly shrink into herself. She adjusted the way she was standing so that Calvin blocked my view of her.

That was strange. Was she trying to avoid me?
Why?

Paula pulled me to the buffet table. "No dancing wait-ers this time," she huffed.

On the center of the buffet table was a chocolate fountain.

"We can hardly complain," I said, grabbing a plate and piling some cheese, bread, and chocolate onto it.

Someone bumped my arm. I looked up to find Christophe Benoit.

I tried to hide my shock. What was the press and communication liaison for the consulate doing at a fundraiser for Calvin Rabara?

Well, I suppose staff schmoozing is what gets consuls commendations and awards and whatnot?

"Mrs. Connolly!" he said, his hand on my arm. "What a pleasure to see you here."

"Christophe! Yes. I didn't know consulate personnel attended this sort of thing."

He laughed and grabbed a plate. "What sort of thing? A party? Of course, why not?"

What did this party have to do with French business though?

I immediately scanned the room for Jean-Luc.

"I guess you have to keep up with San Francisco politics," I said.

"How else are they going to get commendations," Paula muttered to me.

"Is the consul here?" I asked.

"Oh, *non, non, non*," Christophe said.

Kimberly broke away from Calvin and the mayor, then marched toward us.

"Wow," Paula said. "You're in trouble now."

"Kate! What are you doing here?" she said, trying to burn a hole through my head with her stare.

"She's my date," Paula said.

Kimberly looked from Paula to me. She seemed uncertain as to what to say. Her eyes shifted back to Paula, momentarily evaluating her, trying to determine if Paula could be a huge contributor to her boyfriend's campaign. If that was the case, she certainly wouldn't want to risk saying anything to alienate her.

She turned back to me and seemed to try to swallow a bit of her anger. "Is there something I can help you with?"

"I don't know. *Is* there something you can help me with?" I asked.

She glared at me. "Like what?"

I took a stab in the dark. "Did you send me anything in the mail?"

For her part, Kimberly looked genuinely confused. "What?"

I glanced at Christophe; he was more interested in the buffet than our conversation, but when I looked back at Kimberly she was gesturing toward the fireplace hearth. I followed her.

She didn't want to talk in front of him.

Interesting.

Christophe had told me he didn't know Kimberly, but now that seemed unlikely.

We approached the fireplace, the warmth from the fire penetrating the room. "What are you talking about?" she asked.

"I received a package yesterday in the mail. I was wondering if you sent it."

"No. What was it? Why do you think I sent it? Did it have to do with Nancy?"

"It was a computer hard drive."

Kimberly squinted. "Whose? What did it have on it?"

I'd been so caught up with my mini facial and trying on my dress this morning that I'd forgotten to check in with Kenny.

"I don't know. I was hoping you could tell me," I said.

Kimberly shrugged. "How would I know?"

"Why didn't you want to talk to me in front of Christophe?"

Kimberly's hand shot up to her choker. An instinctive self-preservation move? "Oh. No." She licked her lips, stalling for time. "No. It wasn't that."

"What then?" I pressed.

"No. I was just cold. I wanted to stand by the fire."

"You do know him, don't you?" I asked.

She looked confused. "Of course, he's the press liaison at the French consulate."

I leaned in a little closer and in my best conspiratorial voice said, "Kimberly, I know there're things you're not telling me. If you could level with me, it might really help. Don't you want Nancy's killer to be brought to justice?"

She pressed her shoulders back in indignation. "Of course I do! I just don't know what I could tell you to help."

"Do you know anything about Reparation Research? About the story Nancy was working on?"

Kimberly's eyes darted around the room. "No."

It was a lie. There was something about the way she looked around the room. So I did the same.

Who was she searching out?

"What were you doing at the consulate the day before Nancy was killed?"

"I wasn't there."

"You were. You're lying. I just don't know why."

Out of the corner of my eye, I could tell a figure was approaching. It gave Kimberly some courage.

"I wasn't there. Whoever told you that was wrong."

I didn't have the opportunity to tell her I was there and saw her. Calvin Rabara swept up to us. "Doll, are you hiding from me?" He wrapped an arm around Kimberly's shoulder and steered her toward the room. "Come here, there are some people I need you to meet."

He barely gave me a cursory glance. Kimberly shot me a pained look.

Maybe she did want to help me, but just didn't know how?

Was she afraid?

• • •

Paula hadn't budged from the buffet. She and Christophe were comfortably parked at a corner of the table. He was doting on her, fetching her seconds and thirds of any items she pointed out, while juggling his own plate and a champagne flute.

He smiled when he saw me approach.

"That got me nowhere," I said to Paula.

She nodded absently. "I can't believe this place. Isn't it gorgeous?"

I looked to the left side of the room where floor-to-ceiling arched windows provided a magnificent view of the San Francisco skyline. "Yes."

Christophe polished off his champagne. "Unparalleled!" he said, following my gaze out the windows.

I studied his features as he took in the city. He had a straight nose and a large, prominent Adam's apple. The last time we spoke he hadn't known about Armand, but by now the news most certainly would have reached him.

"Christophe, do you know anything about the investigation into Armand's death?"

He looked surprised. "Armand Remy? How did you know? I tried to keep his suicide out of the press."

Suicide?

He flashed a look in Kimberly's direction. "Was there a leak?"

"I'm the one who found him in his apartment."

Blood rushed to Christophe's face and it colored. "I didn't know." He dropped his gaze and looked at his shoes. "It's a shame. He was in a hit-and-run accident a few days before he killed himself. I think he didn't know how to cope. I heard he hit a woman and a small baby."

Paula's eyes widened and she gave me a quick shake of her head indicating I should keep my trap shut that I was the woman with the baby.

I swallowed past the lump in my throat. "When I was at his apartment, I noticed that the front lock had been broken. That's why I was able to go inside. Why do the police think it's suicide and not—"

"Oh, *non, non*. His apartment was broken into before. He came to work complaining about the neighborhood."

What about the bruising around his neck?

I had to speak to Galigani. He might be able to answer some questions by poking around with his contacts. Could he really be mad at me because of Mom?

Paula picked at her teeth with a meatball skewer. "What'd they take?"

Christophe glanced at her as if suddenly remembering she was there. "Em, I don't know. He didn't say."

Nancy's apartment had been broken into. Her computer had been stolen.

Whose computer did I have and who had sent it to me?

"Did they take his computer?" I asked, picking up a plate and perusing the buffet.

Christophe shrugged. "I don't think they took anything. He would have complained. The boy complained about everything! No. I think he said only that they broke into the apartment." He rumpled his unruly mop of curls and looked thoughtful. "How is it that you found him?"

I explained to him about getting Armand's address from Ramon. He sipped champagne as he listened.

"Do you know anything about the consul placing people at Reparation Research?" I asked.

Christophe's lips turned downward and he acted as though

I'd asked him the most boring question ever. "Reparation Research?"

"It's a biotech company in South San Francisco," I said.

"The consul is very talented at getting French nationals placed in American companies. He knows so many influential people. That's one of the reasons he's getting promoted."

Paula perked up. "He's getting promoted?"

"*Oui!* He'll be our ambassador next year."

Paula reached for the meatball platter and plucked another one off, but suddenly grabbed at her waist.

There was a look of alarm on her face. "Let's go to the ladies' room."

"Is it a contraction?"

She shook her head definitively, which made me think that perhaps her alarm was about Christophe.

"It's over there," I said, putting down my plate.

Paula grabbed my hand and rushed me to the restroom. As soon as we stepped into the elaborate foyer of the restroom, Paula bunched her dress in her hands and raised the hem above the knee. "Look!"

Paula's pantyhose had slipped down and the waistband was less than a hair away from falling down around her ankles.

We both started laughing so hard that we had to collapse onto a chaise that was in the foyer.

"If you'd ignored me any longer I don't know what I would have done!" Paula giggled.

"I wasn't ignoring you!" I wiped the tears of laughter that were trailing down my face and said, "I just didn't know you were having a fashion emergency."

Paula snorted. "Pregnant people should definitely *not* have to wear pantyhose!"

I rose to check my mascara in the mirror. The damage wasn't bad, but the thought of Paula's near miss made me burst out laughing again.

Suddenly the door to the ladies' room opened and two women entered. One was tall and painfully slim and frail, the other was probably wearing a size-two dress but seemed robust in comparison. They glanced at Paula and me but continued their conversation as though we posed no threat to their gossip.

The robust size two said, "I think she's going to break up with him though. She's obviously not interested in him now that she's got a bigger fish on."

The frail size minus two said, "Yeah. Big fish is going to be the ambassador and she's always wanted to get into the D.C. scene."

They each pushed on different stall doors and disappeared. I flashed Paula a look as the robust size two said, "Poor Calvin, he's going to be crushed. After he championed that commendation for her and now—"

An electrical shock zinged through my body.

"You'll be there to pick up the pieces. I predict he'll be your New Year's date," Frailly said.

A fit of giggles escaped the stalls.

The consul. The Christmas party. It had been Kimberly smooching with the consul on the balcony. She was the other woman.

·CHAPTER TWENTY·

To Do:

1. ✓ ~~Watch sling DVD.~~

2. Enroll Laurie in art class.

3. Upload Laurie's Santa pic on Facebook.

4. CHRISTMAS!!! Ahhhhh! (Need to buy wrapping paper, too!)

6. What kind of car should I get?

In the morning Jim and I discussed the case over coffee. The only help he gave me was to suggest it was time to check in with my client.

After breakfast I dialed Mr. Vann. I was in luck that he was free in the afternoon and anxious to meet with me also. When I hung up with him, I dialed Galigani. His voice mail clicked on but I was so disheartened I didn't leave a message.

My fingers automatically dialed Mom. I paused to think about what I should say to her. Something along the lines of "My boss is MIA. Are you happy about breaking his heart?" or how about, "I miss you?"

I wasn't surprised when her voice mail clicked on, but the only thing I came up with was. "It's me. Call me."

I hung my head and doodled on my to-do list, which seemed like it was growing longer each day. If I didn't find a better way to manage my time then I'd really need to hire an assistant. I'd have to make an honest man out of Kenny and give him a job.

When would I be able to finish my Christmas shopping? Although Laurie would have no recollection of this, it was still her first Christmas and I wanted to get her something special.

Maybe I could squeeze a trip to the mall in after meeting with Chuck Vann? I left Laurie with Jim and headed out. I was still amazed at how quickly I could pull myself together and leave the house when flying solo. I stopped by the café to pick up a latte and found Kenny planted in his regular spot.

His eyes were closed as he listened to music through his iPod and he seemed in a completely different world, the only tie to this one his ever-tapping foot. Butterfly was behind the counter busy chatting on her cell phone. I thumped Kenny on the back, enjoying the look of shock on his face.

"Why aren't you at home trying to figure out who that hard drive belongs to?"

Kenny pulled the earphones out. "Didn't your mom tell

you that if you hit someone on the back, hard like that, your face can get stuck in whatever position it's in?"

I laughed. "That is such a myth. Where did you hear that?"

"My mom."

"What position was your face in? Eyes oogling Butter-fly?"

He smiled. "It's Magnolia now."

I took a deep breath. "Let me guess . . . another tat-too?"

"This one is right above—"

"I really don't want to know."

Kenny laughed. "No, it's not like it's—"

I covered my ears and began to sing, "La la la la—"

He put his hand behind his back and motioned to above his hip.

I stopped singing. "So if you guys are dating now, you think you can get your boss a free latte?"

Kenny made a face. "We're not dating. I saw the tattoo when she bent down to fill the refrigerator case." He indicated the low case that lined the side wall and housed the readymade salads and sandwiches. "I can't ask her out because I don't have any money. You see, my boss doesn't *really* pay me."

"Here we go. It's because you don't *really* work for me."

Kenny laughed. "Whatd'ya mean? I did the computer thing. I know whose hard drive it is." He held out his hand.

I slapped it. "Spit it out."

He kept his hand outstretched. "A real five. I'm running out of caffeine here."

I slapped his hand. "Extortion! No info, no payo."

He smiled. "I have the user profile."

"Well, what is it?" I asked.

He wiggled his eyebrows and held his hand out. "No payo, no info."

I dug into my wallet. "What kind of date can you take her on with five bucks? You're pathetic."

He laughed. "The five bucks is just for starters. If you want any real info you have to add a zero, lady."

I turned on my heel and ordered my latte. Kenny chimed in that he wanted a hot turkey sandwich and an Italian soda. Butterfly hung up her cell phone and happily compiled.

"That was Carla, the supervisor here. I was helping her strategize on how to make manager at the other location. I'm hoping she does because then they'll need a supervisor here." She proudly pointed to herself.

I didn't want to mention the fact that she was the only person working. If she made supervisor, who was she going to supervise? Oh well, maybe she'd get a raise. The café had a hard time holding on to staff, so a raise wouldn't be a bad idea.

She piled extra turkey on Kenny's sandwich and smiled at me. "He's hungry all the time."

I laughed. "I know."

She gave him a dreamy googly look.

Aw puppy love. So cute.

Now, I wish she'd start on my latte. But instead she spent the next five minutes on Kenny's sandwich and garnishing the plate. She even pulled a batch of gingerbread cookies out of the oven and added one. She ignored me and carried it out to him. His face flushed when she approached.

They giggled together for a minute and then she returned behind the counter and started in on my latte.

I reflected on what Kenny had said about the hard drive. All joking aside, I suspected that the user profile may have been the only thing he was able to recover. Would it be enough?

I turned to Kenny. "I have those e-mails from Nancy to Chuck. Can you track down her user profile that way?"

Kenny took a bite of sandwich and shook his head, then through a mouthful of food said, "Not necessary. User NPickett."

So it was Nancy's computer? Who had sent it to me and why?

Butterfly handed me my latte.

I scooped it from her and turned to leave. On my way out I whispered to Kenny, "She likes you. You'd probably have an easy time dating her if you went out and got a real job instead of sitting here all day."

His shoulder went up. "Yeah. Real job. How's that working out for you?"

"Shut up," I said, thumping him on the back again. "Was there anything useful on the hard drive?"

He shook his head. "It was scrubbed pretty good."

I hopped into Jim's car and took off toward Chuck Vann's house. I sipped my latte as I drove, hoping it might make some of my brain cells connect.

What did I know? Nancy had been killed, probably strangled and left for dead in Golden Gate Park. She'd been at the French consulate on the day before she was killed investigating a story. I had yet to figure out exactly what she was working on. Chuck thought the story had gotten her killed. What could be that charged? She'd gotten the call from Kevin Gibson at Reparation Research. According to her notes, Kevin thought the consul was placing high-level scientists at Reparation Research for what? To leak formulas to *L'éternelle Jeunesse*?

Certainly that was a charged story. Would the consul go so far as to kill Nancy to keep her quiet? What kind of formulas could they be stealing?

Reparation Research specialized in the cosmetic industry. Fighting aging with human growth hormones and synthesized vitamins. They also had a line of 100 percent organic makeup that came in biodegradable packaging.

So, it's not like they were curing diseases, but they were the number one stock pick for the season.

And what about Kimberly? She was having an affair with the consul. According to the ladies in the restroom last night, Kimberly was eager to get onto the Washington D.C. scene. Could the consul's promotion to ambassador be in danger if the affair was made public? Would Kimberly kill her friend Nancy to make sure her affair stayed hidden?

How, if at all, was Armand's death tied to anything?

What about Christophe? Why had he been at the party last night? Was it simply part of his job? What about the day at the San Francisco Centre: Why had he fled from me?

Then, of course, there was Nancy's boyfriend, Ramon. He'd been the last one to see her alive. Could her death be simply a lover's spat? Maybe he'd desperately wanted to land a catering gig at KNCR and she was somehow preventing it?

I sipped on my latte trying to avoid the rapidly building pain in my head.

There was no parking on Mr. Vann's street so I pulled

around the corner and found a metered spot. I dug into my purse but could only find one quarter and two dimes. I dropped them into the meter. No matter, I wouldn't be there very long anyway.

I rounded the corner and walked the short distance to Mr. Vann's house. I climbed up the steps and rang the bell.

No answer.

Hadn't he been expecting me?

I glanced at my watch. Was I actually early? How had that happened?

I rang the bell again and noted three newspapers on the stoop. Soggy and wrinkled. How long had they been here?

I tried to breathe past my racing heart.

Now don't get ahead of yourself, Kate!

I'd just spoken to him this morning, hadn't I? He was fine. Maybe just at the back of the house or in the shower . . . .

I pushed the bell again and then bent over to exam the papers. Footsteps sounded behind me.

Chuck Vann was smiling as he climbed up the steps.

I clasped my hand over my heart. "You scared me!"

He was in running shorts and a sweatshirt. Even though it was December he was drenched in sweat. "Sorry. I didn't expect you until later."

"Do you want me to come back in a bit?" I asked.

He pulled a key out of a shoe pocket strapped to his laces. "No. If you don't mind the way I look. It's fine with me."

He stuck the key into the door, but as he twisted it he said, "Oh. That's weird. I forgot to lock the door?"

He pushed it open. The entire living room had been ransacked.

We stood on the doorstep and looked at each other.

"I haven't been gone that long," Chuck said in an urgent whisper. "Go to the corner and wait for me."

I grabbed his arm. "No. You come with me."

He looked annoyed and shrugged me off.

I pulled my cell phone from my bag and dialed 911.

Chuck nodded and descended the staircase with me. "You're right," he said, his face forming a determined look.

We spoke with the 911 operator, who instructed us to wait a safe distance from the house. So we hung out at the corner about ten houses down from Chuck's but with an unimpaired sight line to his front steps. No one could leave the house without being seen by us.

Chills fluttered down my spine. I'd been hovering around his stoop for about five minutes. Nancy's killer could have come barreling out of the house and taken me with him or her . . .

I brought Chuck up to speed on Nancy's apartment being broken into, Kimberly's affair, the call from Kevin at Reparation Research, and Armand's death. He listened intently, stroking his dark mustache.

Finally he said, "Whoever broke into my place, it must be the same person, right? They stole Nancy's computer, broke into Armand's place, and now mine."

I shrugged. "It's a logical conclusion."

Chuck squinted. "What are they looking for?"

Finally, a police cruiser pulled up, blocking Jim's car in the driveway. We walked down the street toward him and explained the situation. He told us to hold tight until he checked out the house.

The officer gave us the all-clear signal, so we walked up the stairs together. I stayed in the living room with the officer while Chuck took inventory of his house. When he returned he said, "As far as I can tell the only thing missing is my laptop."

"How long were you gone?" the officer asked.

"My run is forty minutes flat and then my warm-up and cooldown." He glanced at his watch. "Not more than an hour."

The officer and I exchanged glances. It could mean that someone had been staking out the house or someone knew Chuck's schedule.

An uncomfortable thought nagged at me.

An hour was such a short amount of time to get into the house and out. What if . . .

Chuck had known I was coming over . . . Could he have staged the break-in. But why?

CHAPTER TWENTY-ONE

I wasn't able to dwell on the thought. The officer was asking me a question.

"I'm sorry, what?"

"When did you get here, ma'am?"

"Only a few seconds before Mr. Vann."

The officer nodded and jotted something down on a notepad.

When the officer left, Chuck and I sat across from each other in the living room, much like we had the first day I'd come over.

He held his head in his hands. "I can't believe this. What do you think they're looking for?"

I thought about Nancy's hard drive. I knew I should tell him that someone had mailed it to me, and yet for some reason I kept it to myself.

And what about the files Galigani had copied from his

computer? Certainly, if it were me, I would want a copy of the data. After all, maybe I was the only one with a backup copy of his stuff.

"Do you keep a backup of your data?" I asked him.

He shook his head. "At work they take care of all that stuff. Here, at home, all I had was personal things, e-mails, tax records, and . . . photos." He cast his eyes downward and then with a sudden rage he sprang out of his chair and punched at the air. "They took the photos of Nancy! They took my photos! What do they want to do . . . erase her entire existence?"

I couldn't help him here. Galigani hadn't copied any photos. I pressed my lips together and watched him, feeling useless.

"Mr. Vann, have you had any more communication with the homicide detectives?"

Chuck's lips twisted in thought. "No. Why? Should I have? They certainly haven't called to give me any updates, but at least they haven't dragged me in for questioning again."

Did that mean McNearny no longer considered him a suspect?

Now in addition to feeling helpless I felt guilty for suspecting he'd staged the robbery. He paced the room, a torn expression on his face, a man dealing with insult upon injury. He stopped pacing and steepled his fingers over his mouth.

The rage left his body as suddenly as it had appeared, yet he remained thoughtful and distant. "What are they looking for? They think I have something? What? Did I have something and not even know it?"

I really hadn't found anything noteworthy in any of the files Galigani had copied. "I don't know. Did you ever communicate with Nancy about Reparation Research?"

Chuck made a pained expression and shrugged. "I don't know. She talked to me about a lot of things. But it doesn't really ring a bell. If I had my computer I'd search for it."

I left Chuck Vann's house and rounded the corner to my car. My heart dropped as I spotted Jim's windshield: There were two tickets on it.

One for an expired meter and the other for not curbing the tires. Anger flooded me. Had the cop who came to report on the robbery decided to ticket me? The tickets totaled $105.

I knew San Francisco was broke, but two tickets, really?

Images of the mayor and Calvin Rabara parading around at last night's fundraiser made my blood boil. Next time I saw Kimberly I'd make it a point to tell her to let her supervisor boyfriend know enough was enough. How could I be expected to run out and feed a meter in the middle of grief counseling!

And the tire curbing? Please, this was barely a hill. More like a small incline. If you didn't huff and puff while walking up it, it couldn't be considered a hill. And I hadn't huffed and puffed and I was completely out of shape! I looked up and down the block. Okay, it was a slight incline, but really, curb your tires? I walked down the hill and back. Nope, not out of breath at all.

How did they judge these things? Did the officer carry about a leveling gauge with him?

I climbed into Jim's car and threw the diaper bag doubling as my purse onto the front passenger seat. Before I could start the car I heard my cell phone ringing.

Please don't be Jim.

I wanted to avoid telling him about the tickets until I could find a bright side to it. Was there a bright side to getting tickets?

I looked at the caller ID display, but didn't recognize the number.

"Hello?"

"Kate, this is Kyra. I'm . . . uh . . . we met the other day . . . I'm Armand Remy's downstairs neighbor."

Something akin to an electrical current shot through me. She had to be calling me with a lead. "Yes! Kyra, of course, I remember you. What can I do for you?"

She let out a nervous giggle. "Oh, good. Good. Yeah. Armand's parents are in town. They're here with me actually. His mom wanted to speak with you."

I turned the engine over. "I can be there in a few minutes."

I couldn't find parking outside of Kyra's place that wasn't metered. And I'd already used all my quarters at the last worthless meter. I double-parked in front of a nearby convenience store and ran in. Now it would be just my luck to get a ticket for double-parking. Without taking my eyes off of Jim's car, I grabbed a water bottle and a bag of chips and threw five dollars down. The attendant barely took his eyes off the daytime drama he was watching. He charged me $4.85 for the water and chips, which left me with no meter money.

I sighed. "I need change for the meter," I said, pulling out another dollar.

He scowled at me, either because he'd already closed the cash register or because the transaction was taking more time than he wanted it to. He reopened the register and dished out the four quarters as if they were gold.

"Thank you," I said.

He'd already resumed watching the show.

On my way out of the store, I grabbed an auto trader magazine from the FREE newsstand rack. Stepping out onto the street, I clutched my four quarters, chips, and water and walked smack into Jean-Luc. My quarters spilled all over the sidewalk.

Great!

I knew he worked just down the street and that I was going to his girlfriend's house, but the sight of him still shocked me.

"Mrs. Connolly. What are you doing here?" he snarled.

"Shopping," I spat back, "for a new car." I flashed him the magazine. "You know, since my last one was smashed by Armand Remy. Remember—"

His eyes narrowed. "No stores in your neighborhood?"

I bent and picked up the quarters off the sidewalk.

Did he know Kyra had called me?

I straightened. "I got a lead that I'm *investigating*."

His jaw clenched and his head moved almost involuntarily in a nod. "*Oui*."

We stared each other down for a moment, but I quickly moved to the car. I drove up the street and looked for as close a spot as I could get. I was happy to see that this meter time limit was two hours, but when I dropped the four quarters into it, I only got thirty minutes.

Thirty minutes, really?

Each quarter was only worth seven minutes? Jeez, this was ridiculous.

I walked toward Kyra's building and stopped to turn around. The convenience store was around the corner so I knew Jean-Luc was behind me, and yet I felt like I was being watched. Creepy.

I looked at the corner where the French consulate loomed. *Yes.* The store around the corner was probably the closest place that wasn't a restaurant or café to grab something quick, so there was really nothing odd about Jean-Luc being there. And yet . . . a chill went through my body. Why did it feel like I was being followed?

I ducked into a stairwell a few buildings before Kyra's place and sat. I opened the bag of chips and munched. Within a few moments a man stopped directly in front of me. It was Christophe.

"Kate! I thought that was you."

I was right, I had been followed, and yet, if he was approaching me then it mustn't have been too secretive, right?

He was holding a large briefcase. It could easily hold a laptop, but if he was the thief who had ransacked Chuck's house would he so boldly flaunt it before my nose?

I stood. "Were you following me?"

He frowned and looked genuinely surprised. "Following you?"

I stared blankly at him.

He shuffled the briefcase nervously from hand to hand. "I was just heading back to work."

"The other day I saw you at the San Francisco Centre. You ran from me."

He looked confused.

"And then I ran into you at the party last night," I continued.

He smiled and shrugged. "We must be running in the same circles."

I dug my hand into the bag of chips and tried not to mash them in my hand. "Where are you coming from?"

He smiled. "Lunch."

I squinted at him. "Where'd you eat?"

He laughed. "Down the street."

I looked at him without saying anything and crunched on another chip.

His expression changed, his lips turning out in a small pout. "I had the eggplant and roasted red pepper panini at the café on the corner. It's not my favorite. They fry the eggplant in olive oil first, but that makes it too greasy."

Something about him was unconvincing, as though he was only giving me this information because he thought I was looking for it.

"Really? Maybe I should try it. I like eggplant."

His pouty expression turned into indecision. "If you like greasy food."

I waved a chip at him. "I love it."

He tapped his foot. "I have to get back to the office."

Before he could step away, I said, "I understand Armand's parents are in town."

Concern or something close to it flashed across his eyes. "Yes. How did you . . ."

"I'm about to meet with them."

His large Adam's apple bobbed up and down. "Why are you meeting with them?"

I shrugged. "They asked."

He was nervous, but about what? Armand's murder or suicide hitting the papers and giving the consul some kind of bad reputation? Or was he nervous that I was going to uncover something more sinister about Armand's death?

Suddenly Jean-Luc appeared. He clapped Christophe amicably on the shoulder but froze when he saw me. He fired off something in rapid French.

I ate my chips while they conversed and studied their

shoes. I did my best to look uninterested yet with every bite wished I was conversant in French.

Christophe was wearing brown sandals. The toes were closed, but had small slits every inch or so and the heels were open.

Very Euro.

Jean-Luc, in contrast, wore black oxford-style shoes. Laced up, wrapped tight, wrapped up as tight as he was. He tried to give off the *c'est la vie* attitude, especially with the buttons opened on his shirt and the hair peeking out, but it was a façade.

Suddenly, the sound of my chips crunching was deafening. I noticed it was because they were silent. The French chatter had ceased and they were both staring at me.

I crumpled the empty chip bag in my hand, enjoying the crinkling noise, then opened the water bottle and took a long drink.

Jean-Luc straightened, pulling himself up taller. "Mrs. Connolly, are you harassing our French citizens?"

"Harassing?"

"Armand Remy's parents are in town to collect his remains. They do not need to waste their time talking to you!"

They stared at me with their arms folded across their chests. I got the impression that I was supposed to go. Where? I wasn't sure, but they definitely were aligned against me. I nodded and stood.

I need to move my car anyway.

I waved at them as I retreated down the hill to my car.

I ended up driving around for a few minutes, then returned to make sure Jean-Luc and Christophe were securely out of sight. I pulled into the parking lot across the street from the consulate. The entire duck-and-delay procedure had cost me about thirty minutes—not bad, but I was dying to get home to Laurie. It was past feeding time and not only did my body feel overloaded, but my heart ached to see her little face and feel her fingers wrap around mine.

As I walked the short distance to Kyra's flat, I texted Jim.

> Got a call from Armand's neighborhood. Long story, but will be late. Please feed Laurie the dreaded formula.

I hiked up the steep stairs and rang the bell. Kyra opened the door and invited me in. Her expression was grave. Before stepping inside I asked her if she could step out onto the landing. She frowned but complied.

"What's up?" she asked.

"Are you still seeing Jean-Luc?" I asked.

She glanced at her feet. She was barefoot again, only this time her toenails were done in a clear gloss. The big toes had yellow sunflowers stuck on.

"I think so, but he didn't call this afternoon. It's the first lunch date he's missed." She shrugged. "I don't know."

"Tell me, were you home alone on Sunday . . . when Armand . . ."

Her brow creased. "No. Jean-Luc was here."

I nodded.

"He spent the night," she continued. "We didn't see Armand though . . . we kept to ourselves."

"Did you tell Jean-Luc that Armand's parents want to speak with me?" I asked.

She shook her head vehemently. "He wouldn't like that."

"Why not?" I pressed.

"He was very upset the other day when you were here. He thinks involving you in problems they have at the consulate is like airing their dirty laundry."

Her hand rested on the doorknob as she spoke and she looked eager to get back inside. I nodded and she pushed open the door.

Mr. and Mrs. Remy were perched on Kyra's couch. They both stood when we entered. Mrs. Remy looked anxious, while Mr. Remy looked despondent. After Kyra introduced us and we all greeted each other, Mr. Remy sank back into the couch. Mrs. Remy remained standing, nervously fiddling with her dress.

She was painfully thin and had sunken cheeks. Her hands twisted endlessly and she searched the room. She looked like a women who desperately wanted a cigarette.

"Do you want to go to the back porch?" Kyra asked.

Mrs. Remy dove for her handbag while Mr. Remy waved us on. She pulled out a pink leopard cigarette case from her purse and followed us outside. As soon as she lit her cigarette the energy in her body changed. She focused on me with clear brown eyes.

"You're a private investigator. You have to help us. Armand didn't kill himself like the police say."

"The police have closed the case," Kyra clarified.

While Mrs. Remy looked into the sun, Kyra mouthed "*Suicide*" to me.

Mrs. Remy turned to us. "I know my son. He wasn't depressed or *fou*—" She pointed to her head with her index finger and twisted it, sign language for crazy. "—like the police say. We spoke all the time. He was happy."

Her accent was thin and she pronounced "happy" as "appie," which for some odd reason endeared her to me.

Her eyes were dark with pain, but she was a fighter. She was determined to get justice for her son and I hoped that might equate to justice for Nancy.

"Kyra told me his apartment was broken into. How can they say he killed himself when someone broke into his apartment?"

"I thought the apartment was broken into a few days before . . ." I said.

Mrs. Remy waved the hand with the cigarette around, dismissing my comment. "Someone broke in. They were looking for him the first time and didn't find him. But it only made it easier for them to come back." Her other hand clenched her cigarette case, making a fierce fist. "Why didn't he get the door fixed!" she cried.

Kyra and I exchanged pained glances.

"It's a theory," I said. "Especially since nothing was taken from his apartment—"

"Nothing taken?" Mrs. Remy asked, outraged.

"It is my understanding that he told Christophe Benoit at the consulate that nothing was stolen from his apartment."

Mrs. Remy's brow furrowed as she took a hit from the cigarette. "But then where is his computer? He was on it all the time. And it's not in his apartment."

I looked to Kyra; she gave me a small shrug.

Another stolen computer?

I thought back to his apartment. There had been a table with stacks of papers and a space on it. I'd assumed that a stack of paper had been moved, but I understood now that the space on that table probably had been previously occupied by his computer.

"Have you noticed anything else that is missing?" I asked.

Mrs. Remy shook her head. "*Non*."

"Do you have any idea who might want to hurt him? What was going on in his life? Was he mixed up with something— "

She stubbed out her cigarette. "We spoke all the time, e-mailed almost every night. He never said anything about any problems." She gave Kyra a sad look and said in a whisper, "Only about a girl he was in love with."

By the way Kyra reacted, I didn't have to guess that the girl was standing right in front of me. Unrequited love.

Had Kyra known Armand had been in love with her?

I couldn't tell.

She leaned against the fire escape and brought her foot to the bottom rung. She rubbed the little sunflower on it and made a noise not dissimilar to a *tsk*.

Was unrequited love enough of a reason to kill yourself? Knowing the girl you loved was sleeping with your boss? Just plain having Jean-Luc for a boss might be enough to send someone over the edge and then knowing he'd ended up with your girl instead . . .

Well it was *something*.

What did it have to do with Nancy though? There had to be some information connecting them, information that had probably been sent via e-mail, thus the computer thief, but what was it?

"Do you know that the consul will be your new ambassador?" I asked.

Mrs. Remy looked disinterested. "Oh. Yes."

I looked from Kyra back to Mrs. Remy. "I think he's having an affair."

Kyra looked surprised, but Mrs. Remy seemed not to care. She pulled out another cigarette and lit it. "What does this have to do with Armand?" she asked.

"I don't know," I admitted.

Kyra tugged nervously at her sweater. "What happens at the consulate when the consul moves on? Do they get a new boss or . . ."

I waited for her to continue.

She stared at me. "I mean, ambassador, that means he moves to Washington, D.C.? Right?"

I nodded.

"Well, does the staff go with him? Or do they stay here?" she asked.

Ah. She was concerned Jean-Luc was going to leave. Obviously he hadn't said anything to her about it.

I shrugged. "I guess it depends."

Mrs. Remy made an impatient gesture. "What does that matter?"

Kyra's eyes darted back to her sunflowered toe and she looked contrite. "It doesn't matter."

It was a good question though. Who would be impacted by the consul's promotion? Was someone's job on the line? Could anyone be trying to prevent the promotion?

Did anyone beside the consul have anything to lose? Or gain?

CHAPTER TWENTY-TWO

To Do:

1. Enroll Laurie in art class.

2. Upload Laurie's Santa pic on Facebook.

3. Figure out who killed Nancy so I can get on with holiday prep.

4. Write letter to DPT protesting tickets.

5. Decide on New Year's resolutions.

6. Need more formula.

I arrived home in a panic. I hadn't planned on being away from Laurie so long and now felt an urgency to be with her that I couldn't contain. I sprang up the garage stairs two by two and pushed the door open, calling out, "I'm home!"

Mom stood in the living room with a smile on her face. "She just flipped over! Look at this."

My body surged with emotion. "Where's Jim?" I demanded.

Mom put her hands on her hips. "Well, I know you're still mad at me, but not even a kiss for your old mom?"

I walked over to her and kissed her cheeks. "I'm not mad at you," I lied.

Mom laughed. "Yes, you are. You're still upset about the other day."

"No, I'm not. I think it's spectacular that you were able to share that milestone moment with Laurie for her first Christmas photo. And the fact that I was put in the middle of you and your two boyfriends is certainly not your fault. You're not even to blame that Galigani is refusing to speak with me. And I couldn't be more happy that you have personally witnessed Laurie flipping over, another of your granddaughter's milestones. I couldn't be happier."

Mom ignored my sarcasm. "Look, look, she'll do it again. It's a game we've been playing all afternoon!"

Mom flipped Laurie onto her tummy and placed a little stuffed whale I'd never seen before in front of her. Mom indicated the whale. "An early stocking stuffer."

She winked at me and pressed the center of the whale. It vibrated and played a tune. Laurie screamed in delight. Mom picked it up; Laurie pushed up on her arms and craned to see the whale. Mom brought the whale all the way up on Laurie's right side. Laurie flipped onto her back. She had a shocked expression on her face like she couldn't imagine how she'd gotten onto her back.

When she saw the whale again she screeched. Mom

tickled Laurie's face with the whale and Laurie clutched at it. Mom smiled proudly at me.

I collapsed onto the couch unable to feel like anything but a failure. The first time Laurie had flipped over had been a fluke. It happened last month when I had been out of the room and she hadn't done it since. Now, Mom was able to get her to do it on demand.

Mom frowned at me. "Want some tea?"

I shook my head. "No. I'm sorry I've been avoiding your calls."

Mom squinted.

"I just . . . sometimes, when you beat me to the punch at things with Laurie, like the Christmas photos . . . I feel like a failure."

Mom came to sit next to me. She rubbed my back. "Darling! No. I'm only trying to help you. I know you're busy. I was busy when you were small, too. Helping you with Laurie is my way of making it up to you."

I hugged her. "You don't have anything to make up to me. You're an awesome mom."

"So are you," she said.

"Well, I don't know about that, but thank you for saying it. I need to feed Laurie," I said.

"Oh." A guilty look crossed Mom's face. "I just gave her a bottle."

I covered my face. I knew, of course, that I'd texted Jim and told him to feed her, but when I saw Mom here I somehow held out the hope that maybe Laurie hadn't been fed yet.

"I didn't know when you were coming home," Mom said.

This meant I'd have to bond with the dreaded breast pump and not my darling.

I got up and picked Laurie up off the floor. I inhaled but instead of Laurie's sweet, pink freshness I smelled Mom's moisturizer. I laughed despite myself.

"Okay, peanuckle. I'll see you in a few minutes. Please try not to be walking by then."

Mom smiled as I handed Laurie off to her.

"Have you talked to Galigani?" I asked.

Mom looked surprised. "Yes, this morning. Why?"

"He's been avoiding my calls. I thought he was mad at me."

"About what?" Mom asked innocently.

Oh brother, if I had to explain it to her . . .

"About you dating Hank. About me knowing it and not saying anything to him."

Mom waved me off. "He doesn't care about that."

"Why do you say that? Of course he does."

"No. Don't be ridiculous. At our age, we're not that possessive. He's probably happy that he doesn't have to entertain me full-time."

"Have you talked to him about it?"

"As if I need his permission for something? We're not married!"

Okay, if she didn't care and he didn't care, why should I care?

After I pumped, Mom went home, promising to drop my stack of Christmas cards at the post office.

All of Laurie's turning over had exhausted her and she only seemed to want to snooze. I found this a good enough excuse to crawl into bed with her and nap myself.

I finally got out of bed around 4 P.M. to make dinner.

Just as I was taking inventory of the fridge, I heard Jim slip his key into the lock.

"Hello?" he called out.

"In the kitchen," I replied.

There was some rustling in the living room and then his footsteps down the hall. He came into the kitchen and gave me a big kiss. "What's for dinner?"

"Eggs? Cereal?" I asked.

He laughed. "I guess I should have gone grocery shopping. Who's eating all our food?"

"You," I said.

Jim pulled a beer out of the refrigerator and offered it to me. I declined. He opened it and took a swig.

"What was all that rustling around in the living room and where have you been?" I asked suspiciously.

Jim smiled but didn't say anything.

I went into the living room and spotted two small boxes underneath the Christmas tree. They were wrapped in bright red Christmas wrap and had gold bows. I picked up one of the small boxes. It was for me from Jim. The other box was for Laurie.

He appeared in the living room. "Don't shake it," he said.

My shoulders slumped. "I don't have anything for you yet! And I don't have anything for Laurie either."

"You don't have to get me anything," he said, picking up the box for Laurie. He pulled a pen out of his breast pocket and wrote something on the box. "There. Now you don't have to get anything for her either."

He showed me the label where he'd added *And Mommy*.

"It's not the same! I want to . . . do the shopping . . . to do the . . ."

He wrapped his arms around me. "Don't cry, honey."

"I'm not crying," I said, swallowing back the lump in my throat.

He pressed his lips against mine. "Good. I don't buy crybabies dinner."

Laurie let out a wail from the other room.

I smiled. "I guess she's not invited."

I called Kenny and convinced him to baby-sit while Jim and I popped down the street to the Irish pub near our house. When Kenny came over, I showed him how to do a proper diaper change, and promised that I would actually pay him for baby-sitting.

At the pub Jim ordered shepherd's pie and drank Guinness while I brought him up to date on the investigation. I ordered fish and chips and sipped on my favorite chardonnay.

"Nancy's hard drive was mailed to our house?" Jim asked. "Who has our address?"

I flipped through the case file I'd brought with me. I'd given business cards to practically everyone I'd met and I'd made the mistake of putting my home address on the cards.

Jim looked at my cards. "Yeah. Let's take that off. We're lucky someone sent you a hard drive and not a bomb or anthrax or something." He rolled his eyes at me. "I can't believe I didn't catch that the first time you printed the cards."

I grimaced. "I didn't have it on the first batch I made. But then I was carrying around two sets of cards, one that I was giving out to Mommy-type people, like the lady who gives the infant art class, and the other one that—"

Jim nearly spit out his beer. "What? What did you say? Infant *art* classes?"

Under the table, I rubbed his leg with my foot. "How's your shepherd's pie?"

"What the hell kind of kook gives infant art classes? And then what kind of crazy person is actually interested in those?"

"Well, it's not art like that. It's art like an introduction . . ."

"She can't even sit up yet," Jim said.

"She rolled over today," I said brightly.

"She can't hold a paintbrush. She's not ready for art classes."

I sipped my chardonnay. "Okay, okay, my point was—"

"Right. You're going to take our address off these cards."

I flipped through the case file and found the envelope the hard drive had come in. "Yes. I will. First thing tomorrow. I promise. I'll put it on my to-do list."

Jim's eyes went wide. "No. Not on the list! I want you to actually do this."

"What do you mean, not on the list?"

"That list is just an excuse to pretend you're going to do something."

"What!"

Jim frowned more to himself than me. He picked up his pint glass and guzzled some Guinness. "Never mind. Forget I said anything."

"I do everything on my list."

Jim nodded. "Of course you do, honey."

"Except, you know, the stuff I cross off."

Jim seemed suddenly interested in his dinner. He began to shovel food into his mouth. "Mmm hmm."

"But I only cross stuff off that I'm not going to do," I

said defensively. "You know, stuff that I've changed my mind about."

Jim smiled. "Like the art classes."

"I haven't changed my mind about the art classes."

He ignored me and looked over his plate at the envelope in my hand. "Do you think a woman wrote our address or a man?"

I examined the writing. "There's a little flourish on the S in street."

Jim nodded. "Feminine, right?"

I shrugged. "Not necessarily. Some men might write like that."

I looked at some of the men at the bar. Most were dressed in jeans or Ben Davis work pants and had boots on. Christophe's sandals flashed across my mind. Jim wouldn't be caught dead in those shoes.

"What about a European man? Someone who wears sandals. He might write with a little flourish, right?"

Jim polished off his Guinness and nodded. "Yeah. Euro guy. Okay, French guy, right?"

I nodded, flipping through the rest of the file. I had paperwork from Chuck Vann. His notes were in block lettering. Very engineerlike, precise, anal.

"What does Kenny write like?" Jim asked.

I stared at him. "Don't be stupid. Kenny didn't send me the hard drive."

Jim laughed. "Not him, exactly. I mean, someone like him. An artistic young guy. Or a young French guy, like Armand."

I shook my head. "Armand couldn't have sent it to me. He never had my address and he was dead when this was mailed." I continued to flip through my file and then I saw it.

My breath caught as I tried to wrap my brain around what I was seeing. "Foreign guy. Not French, but not American either."

Jim looked at me. "Who?"

"Cooking's an art, right?"

Jim squinted at me. "A Mexican chef." I held out the cell phone bill that Ramon had jotted names on for me.

"Bingo. Want to take a drive across the park with me?"

CHAPTER TWENTY-THREE

Jim and I checked in with Kenny. He'd played the trombone for Laurie and had lulled her into a deep sleep. He said her favorite song had been "Twinkle, Twinkle Little Star."

How appropriate. She was a little star! My little star.

Jim and I drove across Golden Gate Park and to Ramon's house. We parked across the street from it and studied his place for a minute. The lights were on, but there didn't appear to be any movement. We climbed up the stairs together and rang the bell.

After a few minutes, when we hadn't gotten an answer, Jim pounded on the door and I rang the bell again, holding my finger on it so it gave a continuous ring. Suddenly the door flew open and a naked Ramon stood before us.

"What's going on?" he demanded. "Oh! Kate." He looked from me to Jim, confused but seemingly not embarrassed. He pulled the door open farther. "Come in out of the cold," he said, retreating down the hallway. "I'll get some pants; have a seat."

Jim held my elbow and ushered me to the living room. I tried to suppress my laughter. Jim scolded me. "It's not funny!"

I shrugged. "I can't help it. I think it is." The harder I tried to suppress my giggles the more furious they became until I was only shaking with no sound coming out.

"You're supposed to be a professional," Jim said.

I probably wouldn't have been laughing if I'd been alone. I'd probably have been horrified, but something about seeing the man naked while I was standing on his doorstep with Jim brought on the fit of giggles.

The way we had pounded on the door and rang the bell, he must have thought the house was on fire.

There was a rustling sound down the hall, then the sound of voices. He was with a woman. Jim and I exchanged glances.

Nancy had only been dead for two weeks and already he had a new squeeze. After a moment, he appeared, still bare-chested, but with a pair of loose-fitting jeans on.

"This is my husband, Jim," I said to Ramon.

Jim gave Ramon a cool nod. Ramon nodded back.

"I know you sent me Nancy's hard drive," I said.

Ramon shook his head as though to deny it and for some reason glanced at Jim. Jim gave him a stoic look, which seemed to prompt honesty because Ramon said, "How did you know I sent it?"

I shrugged. "How did you get ahold of it? Did you steal it from her apartment?"

Ramon looked aghast. "No! Of course not. Steal it?"

"Her apartment was broken into and her computer was stolen," I explained.

A perplexed look came over him. "No . . ."

Jim and I glanced at each other.

"When? I didn't know . . . she didn't say . . . I don't know anything about a break-in . . . She never told me that," Ramon said.

"You had the new key to her apartment," I said.

Ramon shook his head. "She didn't tell me it was a new key. She left it here . . . She said I should have it just in case."

"In case of what?" I asked.

Ramon looked saddened. "She didn't say."

Jim and I exchanged looks.

"Where'd you get the hard drive from?" Jim asked.

"I took it from her computer!"

Jim grit his teeth. "We know you took it from her computer, but where was her computer when you took it?"

Ramon's jaw clenched. "It was at that apartment on Bush Street—the one I gave you the address to," Ramon said to me.

Armand's apartment?

"Is that why you gave me the address? Because her computer was there?" I asked.

Ramon looked down the hall as if afraid his new honey would overhear us.

Jim stepped toward him. "You're wasting our time here. And clearly you have other things you'd rather be doing. Spit it out."

"I found that address in Nancy's jeans. When she didn't come over that night and she didn't call either. . . it wasn't like her. I thought she'd hooked up with someone else." He shrugged. "I got jealous. It's my Latin blood. I went there and no one answered the door, even when I carried on like you two tonight, banging and ringing and banging.

So, I forced my way in. No one was there, but her computer was there. I knew she was cheating on me. Figured I'd screw her the way she was screwing me and I took out her hard drive." He squeezed at the bridge of his nose.

Jim flashed me a look.

"I didn't know she was dead. So help me, I didn't know that. Whose apartment was it? Do you know?" Ramon asked.

How had Armand ended up with Nancy's computer?

I squinted at Ramon. "Yes. I do know."

Ramon waited for me to speak, watching me with his dark eyes. I looked at Jim: He shrugged and nodded ever so slightly, giving me a nonverbal queue to go ahead and tell Ramon.

"I found the inhabitant dead. His name was Armand Remy. He was an intern at the French consulate. The police think he killed himself."

Ramon, clearly shocked by what I'd just said, staggered back.

A woman appeared in the doorway. We all turned to look at her. It was Karen Nolan, the station manager at KNCR.

Karen Nolan was Ramon's new squeeze?

"Kate? Do you have an update about who killed Nancy?" she asked.

Ramon quickly went to Karen's side and grabbed her elbow. It seemed an almost protective response. Was he protecting her or himself?

I looked directly into Karen's eyes. "I have some updates," I said.

Jim moved closer to me. Definitely demonstrating it was two against two.

Karen looked at us, confused by the semi-standoff. "Who is it? What's going on?"

I explained about finding Armand dead and also Chuck's house being broken into today. "Someone is still trying to get information. I need to know what it is."

Karen frowned and looked at Ramon. "Do you know?" she asked him.

He shrugged, almost too readily.

"Ramon, when you were at Armand's place, did you take anything else?" I asked.

Karen looked at me sharply. "What do you mean when he was at Armand's place?" Her head jerked in Ramon's direction but his eyes were on me.

"No! Of course not! I didn't taken anything, besides, you know, Nancy's hard drive. I'm not a thief . . . I was just—"

Karen grabbed at Ramon's arm, but before she could ask anything he said, "I'll explain later."

I wonder how he was going to explain to his current lover that he'd tried to sabotage his past lover. But I guess, given the circumstances, if all he did was hack into her computer, it was better than the alternative.

"Karen, I'll need to reach Kimberly tomorrow, can you tell me what time she gets to the station?"

Karen shook her head. "She doesn't come in on Fridays. I can give you her cell number."

Jim and I headed to the door. "Thanks. I have it."

Jim and I walked in silence to his car. Karen had been distressed when we left, but Ramon was happy to get rid of us.

Jim opened the passenger-side door for me.

"I know why he didn't stop."

Jim looked puzzled. "Who?"

"Armand. He didn't stop when he hit Laurie and me because he was on his way back from stealing Nancy's computer. He must have had it in the SUV when he hit us."

"Wait. I thought Ramon just admitted that he took Nancy's hard drive."

"He did. But he took it from Armand's house. I know from Nancy's apartment super, who has no reason to lie, that Nancy's computer was stolen from her place. How did it get to Armand's?"

I got into the car and watched Jim move around to the driver's side. He opened the door and sat behind the steering wheel.

"Did Nancy live anywhere near where you were hit?"

"Yes. On Chestnut; we were hit on Lombard Street."

"We saw her at the consulate the same day," Jim said.

"Yeah, we also saw Kimberly, who to date has denied even being there," I said.

"She owes you some answers."

"She's at the top of my to-do list."

Jim laughed and started the car.

The following morning, after feeding Laurie and snuggling in bed as long as possible, I rose to make breakfast. Jim was on a conference call, so I scrambled some eggs and made toast then brought them to him in the office. His eyes widened in excitement as he saw the food.

I motioned to him that I needed to go. He nodded and I proceeded to get myself ready. I left him a note with Laurie's feeding schedule, like I always did every time I left the house.

I dialed Kimberly from the car but when she didn't answer I drove straight to her house anyway. I wasn't entirely sure what I'd say to her, but I figured she was the key to solving everything. I rang the bell and waited.

It was still early morning, only about 9:30 A.M. I wonder if she was with the consul or maybe at Calvin's. Where did he live anyway? Should I try to track him down?

I thought of my parking tickets. I could certainly give him a piece of my mind about that.

I rang Kimberly's bell again.

If she was with the consul, where would they be? At some five-star hotel? The Ritz or the Mark Hopkins.

Maybe she wasn't with either one of them. Maybe she'd gone for a cup of coffee or a run.

At the thought of a run, goose bumps rose on my arms.

Nancy had gone for a run, or had been planning on it . . . what could have happened that morning? She'd left Ramon's and then what?

I dialed Galigani; he picked up on the first ring.

"Kid, where've you been?"

"What do you mean? I've been trying to reach you for days."

"You have?"

"I left you a bunch of voice mails."

"Oh. Sorry . . . this stupid thing. My box filled up and I think I accidentally deleted stuff while I was out of town."

Sounded like a sorry excuse. Maybe he was trying to backpedal for being mad at me.

"Out of town for what?" I asked, testing him.

"My daughter invited me up north for Christmas, but she couldn't do Christmas so we did this week, only it was short notice."

His daughter?

"I didn't even know you had a daughter."

He laughed. "Yeah, well, there's probably a lot about me you don't know and probably a lot about me you don't want to know. I talked to McNearny, though, sounds like they got the perp."

My blood drained to my toes, leaving me feeling chilled. This was ridiculous, I should be happy that McNearny had figured it out . . . and yet.

I wanted to be the one to solve it first.

"Who?" I asked.

"Armand Remy. His DNA was on Nancy. They got some fibers off her, too. Looks like she was strangled with one of his bedsheets."

Just like that? They could make a decision about some-thing so important from fibers?

I couldn't stop myself, the words just tumbled out. "Is that all they got? His apartment was broken into. Whoever it was could have taken a sheet!"

"The gangs in Chinatown and the Mission are really heating up, and we got the holidays going on and every-thing—"

"What? So! So, McNearny's looking for a tidy close? Is that it? Blame Nancy's death on the intern and then say he killed himself over the guilt?" I asked. "What about the bruising around Armand's neck? Did he strangle himself?"

I listened to Galigani exhale. "Look, the ME says the kid bled out. If something was around his neck they can't prove that he did or didn't do that. Maybe he tried to hang himself first and it didn't work. None of the neighbors saw anyone coming or going from his place on Sunday. At any rate, no one wants to deal with the consulate on this thing. You know, make a big international hoopla. The Board of Sups got wind and didn't like it at all. There's a lot of pressure to—"

"Who on the board? Calvin?"

"I don't know exactly."

"I'm sitting on his girlfriend's steps right now. She's two-timing him with the consul."

Galigani whistled. I watched the sailboats in the marina bob up and down.

"Did you say you're sitting on Kimberly's front steps?"

"Yeah."

"What the hell kind of way to do a stakeout is that? And how do you know she's not inside listening to every word you're telling me?"

"I wasn't staking her out exactly . . . I was . . ."

"Get the hell out of there! She's your missing key. She's already lied to you, you think she's gonna open up to you now that the police have someone they like for this?"

I gathered up my bag and stood. "I dunno," I muttered.

I walked down the steps and back to the car. "What do I do now?" I asked him.

"Get out of sight and wait for me. I'll join you."

"Okay."

Before I could hang up he said the words I was dreading, "Oh, one more thing, kid. How's your mom? She with the other guy today?"

·CHAPTER TWENTY-FOUR·

I waited in Jim's car for Galigani, flipping through the auto trader magazine I'd picked up yesterday and thinking about my next car. While I waited, a woman rounded the corner. She was wearing blackout sunglasses, a large hat, and a gold-trimmed scarf. The silk scarf was wrapped around her neck and she had her face ducked into it. Nevertheless I knew it was Kimberly. She was moving rapidly toward her house and reached inside her bag, presumably to click an automatic garage-door opener because at that same moment, her garage door started to rise slowly.

Thank God she hadn't been home listening to my conversation with Galigani!

Every inch of me wanted to jump out of the car and follow her into the house, but I was on strict instructions from Galigani to stay put. I watched as she disappeared inside and the garage door closed again.

I texted Galigani.

She's here. Where R U?

My cell phone buzzed. I picked it up.

"I can't text and drive!" Galigani said.

"Sorry. She's here. How far away are you?"

"About fifteen minutes."

I watched in horror as the garage door opened again.

Had she spotted me?

I prepared myself for her to come out of the house, armed and screaming. Instead I saw red taillights flash.

"Uh oh," I said.

"What?" Galigani asked.

I watched as the red lights went out and then white reverse lights came on. She was backing out of the garage.

"She's in the car. She's leaving."

"Follow her but, for God's sake, don't be obvious!"

I slouched down in the driver's seat until she drove past me, then I started up the car and did a quick U-turn.

"We're heading down Marina Boulevard toward Van Ness," I said to Galigani.

"Okay. Stay on the line with me. Do you have a headset?"

"Of course," I lied.

"Good, I don't want you getting pulled over and ticketed for being on the phone."

I shuddered. "Speaking of tickets—"

Galigani groaned.

Kimberly made a right onto Van Ness and I followed her. We could be going anywhere, of course, but we did happen to be heading toward Bush Street, which was where the French consulate was.

When we got to Grant Street, which was a block from the consulate, Kimberly pulled into a parking garage.

I filled Galigani in.

"Don't approach her. Just watch. Can you ditch your car?"

"No! Grant is Chinatown. There's less parking here than up the street!" I whined.

"Just pull up to a meter. If you're in the car they're not going to ticket you."

"Ha!"

I did as instructed and parked in a metered yellow zone. Between the stress of looking for Kimberly and watching for a meter maid I thought my head would explode.

While I waited, I asked Galigani, "So, can you do anything about a couple of tickets I got? I mean, do you know anybody?"

Galigani guffawed into my ear. "What are the tickets for? Speeding?"

I didn't want to tell him about not curbing my tires and thankfully I didn't have to because Kimberly walked out of the parking garage.

"I see her. She's heading up the street."

But she didn't continue to the consulate. Instead, she stood at a corner café. There was outdoor seating, but the day was chilly and most of the crowd was inside. She stepped into the café, but because of the large glass windows I could still see her.

"You think she's meeting the consul?" I asked Galigani.

"I don't know. Take pictures."

"Seriously? For what?"

"For what?" Galigani barked. "Do I have to spell everything out for you? You think the consul's wife might be interested in those? You think Kimberly might not want the wife to see them? You think—"

"Okay, okay. Then I have to hang up now. My camera's on my cell—"

"You don't have a digital with a good zoom in your kit?"

What kit? Was I supposed to have a PI kit or something?

Christ! Another thing to add my forsaken list!

"Yeah. I have a knuckle sandwich for you in my kit," I said hanging up.

I took a few shots of Kimberly sitting in the café, but I was so far away and the camera phone so poor you could barely make her out.

Could I risk getting any closer? With the amount of people in the street, I doubted she'd see me. It was getting another ticket that worried me.

Oh well, no pain, no gain.

With my hand on the door I looked in the rearview mirror toward the consulate. Christophe was bouncing down the block. I watched as he headed straight for the café. Christophe.

He'd been at the supervisor party, at the San Francisco Centre, and now . . .

He pulled open the café door and joined Kimberly, kissing both her cheeks. Their conversation seemed to be agitated. Kimberly's movements were jerky. She was angry. Suddenly she pulled off her sunglasses to reveal a massive black eye.

Christophe buried his head in his hands and Kimberly quickly put the glasses back on.

What was this? Had the consul beaten up Kimberly?
Maybe Calvin?

No, that made no sense. If Calvin had hurt Kimberly she wouldn't be running to the French consulate's chief press guy.

Could she be threatening to report the consul?

How I wished I could hear their conversation. I day-dreamed about having the entire café rigged with listening devices, Hollywood style.

I should probably purchase some recording devices and keep them handy in a PI kit. Okay, I should probably get a PI kit first.

I looked around at the crowd. Could I ask someone to go in and eavesdrop? I thought of Kenny; too bad he wasn't with me. Kimberly had never seen him before and he would easily fit in with the café scene.

Before I could come up with a solution so I could over-hear them, they both rose from their chairs. They sepa-rated at the exit and went in opposite directions. No farewell kisses. Christophe headed up the street—presumably to the consulate—and Kimberly turned back to the parking garage.

I dialed Galigani. "I think we're leaving."

He groaned. "Man, I'm just getting to Montgomery!"

"I'll call you back," I said.

Then on impulse I got out of the car and crossed the street to where Kimberly was. She was walking rapidly and seemed distracted.

If I were to follow her, it would inevitably lead to a confrontation, so why avoid it? I'd only waste time and it was already the fifteenth—I had Christmas shopping to do and I already missed Laurie like crazy.

Kimberly was looking down trying to fish something

out of her purse. I took advantage of this and rammed straight into her with my shoulder, aiming for sunglasses. Her sunglasses flew off her face and she lost her balance. I grabbed her to keep her from toppling over.

"Oh my God! I'm so sorry!" I said. "I tripped."

Her eyes widened in recognition. "Kate! What are you doing here?"

"Kimberly?" I asked in mock surprise.

She fumbled for her sunglasses, bending down to pick them up.

I bent with her. "I'm heading over to the consulate," I lied. "One of their staff ran into me the week before last. Totaled my car. What happened to you?"

She replaced her glasses and straightened. "Nothing—"

"Did Calvin do this to you?" I asked.

"Calvin? No. No. Of course not. I fell."

I leaned in close to her. "Did Eloi do this to you?"

She pulled away from me. "What do you know about Eloi?"

"More than you want me to, I'm sure."

Her hand moved to her throat, a small protective gesture, one she didn't even realize she was making. "I don't know what you mean."

"Are you moving to Washington with him?" I wiggled my eyebrows at her and in my best Pepé Le Pew accent said, *"L'ambassadeur."*

I had no idea how to say "kept woman" in French, otherwise I'd have thrown it in for good measure.

She scowled at me. "What are you saying?"

"I know about your affair with him. I know you were at the consulate with Nancy the day before she disappeared. I just saw you meeting with Christophe Benoit, the chief press and communication guy."

She took a step back. "How did you . . ."

A crowd of people pushed past us, the lunchtime rush beginning.

"Did you kill Nancy?" I asked.

"What?" She looked at the people around us. "No. No! Of course not. Are you crazy? She was my friend."

"Why aren't you helping me find out who killed your friend?"

"The police know who killed her. It was the intern from the consulate. Christophe just told me, the case has been closed."

She yelled this last comment at me and it drew looks from passersby, but in typical San Francisco style no one interfered.

I whispered to her, "I think that's a lie. I think the intern's a fall guy. Why would he kill Nancy?"

Her shoulders shot up. "He was probably in love with her and she wouldn't—"

"Where was Eloi last Thursday? The morning Nancy was strangled in Golden Gate Park? Was he with you? Or does he just want you to say that? Is that why you have the shiner?"

Kimberly looked aghast. "Eloi didn't kill Nancy!"

"And you know this how?" I pressed. "Because you were with—"

"It was the intern. I wasn't with the consul. We're not having an affair—"

I smiled. "I saw you and him together on the balcony the night of his Christmas party."

A wave of indignation rose around Kimberly. She secured her scarf and hat, then through gritted teeth said, "You don't know anything. I'm not going to let you ruin this for me."

She pushed past me and raced to the parking garage entrance. My phone buzzed in my pocket.

"Where are you?" Galigani asked.

"I'm walking to Union Square."

"What? Did you lose her?"

"No. I need to park legally first, then I'm going Christmas shopping," I said. "Wanna come?"

CHAPTER TWENTY-FIVE

Galigani joined me at the shoe counter in Macy's. I was purchasing Laurie a pair of tiny black patent leather shoes, size one, for our Christmas dinner.

"What happened?" he asked.

"I blew it," I said, pulling out my credit card and handing it to the clerk. "She denied everything."

Galigani gave me a halfhearted pat on the back.

After a moment of silence he said, "What can I get your mom?"

We collapsed into a fit of laughter. He shopped with me for the balance of the afternoon. We talked about everything under the sun except the case and my mom and his daughter, who he refused to talk about as soon as I'd brought her up.

I found a beautiful leather valet tray for Jim. For Laurie, I bought a "Baby's First Christmas" toy collection.

Inside a soft, zippered Christmas ornament bag was a silver frame ornament that I had engraved, a little peppermint stick rattle, a tree-shaped plush toy, and a gingerbread man teether.

I bought baskets to package the fudge I planned to make Paula and David, Galigani, and to ship back to my brother and his wife. For Danny I selected a portable train station. I had a hard time picking out anything for Mom and finally decided on a photo collage tote that I could put photos of Laurie in.

Galigani hemmed and hawed over what to buy Mom, but ended up purchasing a bracelet made up of rose-colored crystals.

As we left Macy's I saw signs for the San Francisco Ballet performance of *The Nutcracker*. I sighed. I'd love to see the ballet with Jim and Laurie. How old did Laurie have to be to take her to a show?

Suddenly Galigani said, "So, you suspect the consul?"

I nodded.

"We need proof," he said. "You are not allowed to fly off the handle and confront him." He looked me square in the eyes. "Do you understand?"

"Of course," I lied.

Well, technically it wasn't a lie. I understood him, I just wasn't going to promise that I wouldn't try to meet with the consul.

I arrived home exhausted and depressed. After feeding Laurie, I lay down for a nap with her hoping to sleep off some of my sluggishness.

How could SFPD just close the case like that? Surely they couldn't really believe Armand had killed Nancy. And then again, what did I know? Maybe he had and I should be glad the case was over.

But I wasn't glad. I had a terrible feeling in the pit of my stomach that not even a nap was curing.

Jim puttered around doing laundry. I awoke to a pile of clean clothes in a basket by the bed. I dumped them out on the bed to fold and was completely disheartened to find that my favorite sweater and pajamas had shrunk.

"Did you dry these on hot?" I yelled down the hall.

From the office Jim said, "What?"

"Hot. Hot! You shrunk my favorite stuff."

Jim peeked out of the office. "I didn't dry them on hot."

I glared at him, then his head disappeared back into the office.

"We've gone through this before. You can't dry my stuff on hot," I said to the space where his face had just been.

At that moment, Laurie began to wail from the bassinet; I pulled her out and found that her diaper had leaked. I grabbed a pair of clean pajamas out of the basket and headed to the office/nursery to change her.

I tried to squeeze her into the pajamas, but they were too small.

"You shrunk Laurie's pjs, too," I said.

"No, I didn't," Jim protested from behind the computer. "She's growing."

I pulled a pair of pajamas from the top drawer of the changing table. They didn't fit her either. I went through about four pairs all with the same results.

My breath caught. None of her zero-to-three-months clothes fit. I grabbed a jumper that read 3–6 MONTHS and tried it on. It fit perfectly.

I hugged her to me. "My baby's growing!" I said.

Jim laughed. "That's what I just said."

What did it mean about my clothes? I hadn't tried them on, but they looked smaller. Was I getting larger, too?

I handed Laurie to Jim. "Hold on to her a minute, I'm going to get the sling."

Laurie's eyes remained on me. As I left the room, she craned to see me then cried out. I peeked back into the room and she stopped crying.

"Did you hear that? She cried when I left the room."

Jim looked at me as if I was insane. "She always does that."

"No. No, she doesn't. She's never done that."

"She always stops crying when you pick her up."

"This is different."

I tested her again by leaving the room. Her eyes were trained on me and as soon as I disappeared she cried out. I reappeared and she stopped crying.

"She knows I'm her mommy!"

"Of course, she does," Jim said.

"I mean, by sight. She recognizes me!"

Jim shook his head back and forth, unable to grasp my excitement.

I pulled her out of his arms. "You try it."

Jim returned to working on the computer. "No."

"Killjoy," I said to him. To Laurie I said, "Daddy doesn't want to play. Bad mood Daddy, grumpy Daddy."

"Our insurance called while you were out," Jim said.

"Uh oh."

"No, it's good. They're going to invoke our uninsured motorist clause. So you can officially start shopping for a car. Merry Christmas."

• • •

In the evening I poked around online for a while. When I decided to upload Laurie's Santa photo onto my Facebook page, I saw that I had a message from Kevin Gibson.

> Forgive me for my tardy reply. I did contact Ms. Pickett, but it was a false alarm. I am saddened by the news of her death. The Bahamas are great.

What a strange message. He'd contacted her but it was a false alarm? What kind of false alarm? He'd been wrong about the leak at the office? Is that what he was trying to say?

I clicked through his updates on his profile page. He'd posted once a day since being in the Bahamas, mostly updates about the weather or the kind of drink he'd just ordered. Maybe he was drunk when he sent me the note.

There were no posts prior to his vacation so I couldn't get an idea about his being maybe a bit looser in the Bahamas than usual. There were no photos either.

Who goes on vacation and then opens a Facebook account? Why wasn't he posting pictures of himself on the beach or in a bar? His account photo was a picture of an iced rum drink with a little umbrella sticking out, but it was a stock image.

I thought about the Facebook pages I'd visited: Paula's; my brother, Andrew's; even mine. We all had activated the privacy settings. Yet, Kevin Gibson's page was public . . .

As I clicked the info button on his page, my phone rang. It was Mom. I filled her in on the SFPD's findings.

"Hmmm," Mom said. "You're not satisfied."

"No, but—"

"Let's go talk to the consul tomorrow," she said.

"Ummm, no. I can't. What would I say? Besides, Galigani told me—"

"Oh don't worry about him dear. You have to listen to yourself."

"Well, I wouldn't even know where to find the consul. Every time I've been to the consulate he doesn't seem to be around."

"Let's stake out his house."

I laughed. "What? I don't know where he lives."

"I'll find out. You take everyone on a stakeout. I want to go."

"But, Mom, I—"

"We'll start early in the morning. I'll be over at seven o'clock. I'll bake some chicken tonight for us to take as lunch. It'll be fun."

"Oh, no, Mom. I . . ." I heard a click. "Hello?"

She'd hung up.

The following morning, Mom appeared on my doorstep at exactly 7 A.M. She had a picnic basket and cooler with her. In the basket, she'd packed homemade breaded and baked chicken, fresh rolls, macaroni salad, a thermos of minestrone soup, and chocolate chip cookies, along with plates, napkins, and flatware. In the cooler was iced tea, sodas, and bottled water.

Why hadn't Mom ever gone with me before on a stake-out?

What a mistake! From now on she'd be my right-hand gal.

"We have to take Laurie with us," I said. "I don't want to be away from her all day again."

"That's no problem," Mom said happily. "I'd love to have her with us."

We packed up Jim's car and headed out. To my surprise,

Mom had actually found out where Eloi Leppard lived. She'd found his address by calling the consulate and pretending she worked for FedEx. Apparently, the receptionist at the consulate was all too happy to give her the shipping address to where the fine art he'd ordered was to be sent.

He lived, not surprisingly, in Presidio Heights—a neighborhood that was home to several congressman and senators. The consul's residence was a limestone mansion surrounded by large hedges. From where we were parked, we couldn't see much, except the garage door was visible and we figured we'd see him leaving.

I spied on Laurie through the Elmo mirror pinned to my backseat. Her pacifier was dangling out of her mouth and she was snoring. Was her tiny nose stuffed up?

Mom pulled a knitting project out of her tote. It was a fuchsia and green–striped Dr. Seuss–style scarf.

"What are you working on?" I asked.

She pulled on some yarn. "It's a scarf for your brother for Christmas."

"It's fuchsia."

"No. It's red and green."

"Mom, that's not red, that's fuchsia."

Mom squinted at it. "Really? It looks red to me."

I laughed. "I'm sure he'll love it."

I cringed, thinking about what Mom might have made for me, Laurie, or Jim.

"Of course, he'll love it. It's cold in Pennsylvania. This'll keep Andrew warm." She eyed me. "If he doesn't like it then Tracy will. What are you going to send them for Christmas?" she asked.

"Well, I was going to make some fudge and send them a basket, but I don't think I'm going to have time, so I'll probably just order something from Baskets.com—"

Mom frowned. "That's totally impersonal!"

"Well . . ."

"Why don't we send a basket of goodies together? We can include the scarf and maybe a gift card, so they can get whatever they want."

"I'm not sending him that scarf."

Mom pursed her lips. "He's going to love it."

After a moment, Mom asked. "Do you want a piece of chicken?"

"It's eight-thirty in the morning."

Mom shrugged.

We killed some time by playing I Spy. Mom finished the scarf and pulled out the chicken. I nursed Laurie and ended up giving her a diaper change on the backseat.

Finally after a few hours, we saw a Lincoln Town Car meander down the street. We watched as it pulled up to the consul's house. Within minutes the consul was coming down the front steps and getting into the backseat of the car.

"We're in business," I said to Mom.

She clapped. "Oh goodie!"

CHAPTER TWENTY-SIX

We followed the Town Car to the Ritz-Carlton. The Ritz happened to be around the corner from the French consulate. Which I had assumed was where we were heading.

"What do we do now?" I asked Mom.

"Let me out. I'll follow him. He's never seen me before. I'll call you."

Before I could even pull over properly, she opened the car door and popped out.

I decided to park in Saint Mary's Square parking garage, because even though it was pricey, I couldn't bear the thought of another meter or worse, another ticket.

My phone rang.

"Park the car," Mom whispered into the line.

"I did."

"Come in then. He's meeting someone for lunch. Second floor. I got the table next to him."

I pulled Laurie and her car seat bucket out of the back-seat and snapped the bucket into the stroller. I pushed her up the huge hill to the Ritz. The view of the Bay, Alcatraz, and downtown San Francisco was absolutely worth the calf strain of the hike.

The hill was almost a seventy-degree angle. Now this was the type of hill you'd need to curb tires on. Anything less, forget it!

I smiled at the doorman outside the Ritz. He pulled open the door for me and I immediately felt pampered. Jim and I had spent our wedding night at the Ritz and entering the ornate lobby now brought back warm memories. I crossed the oriental rug to the elevator bank and pressed the button.

Because the hotel was on a hill, when I pressed the button for the second floor the elevator went down instead of up. I smiled when the doors opened and I spotted Mom in the restaurant. She had her menu up to block her face, but the top of her head was visible.

Seated at the neighboring table was the consul and a man in a business suit. They were deep in conversation, but the conversation was in French so a fat lot of good it was going to do us to overhear them.

Mom ordered the lobster knuckle risotto with local as-paragus and baby carrots. I ordered the Dungeness crab with hearts of palm, avocado, and orange-infused olive oil. I kept glancing at the consul's table hoping they wouldn't finish before us, because if I had to leave even one bite of the delicious dish behind, I'd be mad.

I did, however, refrain from licking my plate. Barely.

The consul was enjoying a pasta dish and the business-man picked at a salad. Finally the consul stood, buttoned his Brooks Brothers suit jacket, then shook hands with the businessman. He moved toward the exit of the restaurant. I popped up to follow him, leaving Mom and Laurie at the table to deal with the bill.

He was a few feet in front of me, heading for the elevator bank.

Should I talk to him here? Or ride the elevator with him to the lobby?

No time like the present.

"Excuse me, Consul, may I have a word?"

He looked at me, trying to recall where he might have seen me before. "Ah, the girl from the balcony! *Mademoiselle*, I am so sorry you had that terrible experience at the party. I told my staff to take care of it. Sometimes, with the outdoor part of the building and the gardens, it's hard to control rodents."

He gave me a patronizing pat on the shoulder and pressed the elevator button.

"No, Consul, I have to speak with you about another matter. Armand Remy."

His brow creased. "Armand?" He held his hands open, palms up in a "what can you do" gesture. "It's unfortunate that the poor boy killed himself. And this business about the American reporter . . ." He tsked. "But how does this matter concern you?"

"His parents are in town. I met with them. They don't believe that Armand killed himself and I can't imagine they're buying the idea that he killed Nancy Pickett."

Anger flashed across his face, but ever the diplomat, he put it in check and said politely, "If they are dissatisfied with the way the police have handled the investigation, they must come to see me or my staff. However, if they simply disagree with the verdict, then that is a different matter."

The elevator beeped its arrival and the doors opened invitingly.

The consul moved forward to step into it.

"Consul," I called, in an effort to detain him. "Are you placing French scientists at Reparation Research?"

The consul froze and looked as if I'd hit him in the solar plexus. "What concern is this of yours?"

The elevator buzzed and its doors closed.

I handed him my card. "I've been hired to investigate the murder of Nancy Pickett."

He held his hand up, palm out to halt me. "But we know who killed—"

"Nancy was covering the story of your *Légion d'honneur* award."

He looked confused and dropped his hand. "What does the award have to do with anything?"

"Your promotion to ambassador—congratulations by the way—do you think receiving the award clinched the decision?"

He squinted at me, his jaw set. We stared at each other for a moment; he was evaluating me. Trying to size up how formidable of an opponent I might be.

I must have not registered on the formidable meter, because his expression relaxed and he glanced at his watch. "*Mademoiselle*, I'm afraid I have no time for this discussion." He pressed the button for the elevator.

"Off to meet the mistress?"

His head jerked toward me. "What?"

I smiled. "On the balcony, Kimberly Newman. I saw you together."

He shrugged and waved a dismissive hand at me. "So, what of it? Women desire men of power and influence all the time."

Right. No big deal. His wife was probably used to his indiscretions. As long as her status as wife to the ambassador was safe, maybe she didn't care.

He gave a cynical laugh. "You didn't think you were going to blackmail me with that, did you?"

"I'm not trying to blackmail you. I don't care if you have an affair or not. That's between you and your wife. The beatings bother me a bit, but certainly that's not murder."

He repelled from me. "What beatings?"

I smiled at him. "Oh come on, Ambassador, as long as we're talking to each other, why not get it all out in the open? Kimberly's walking around with a pretty nasty black eye. Was that her warning to keep quiet?"

His eyes flicked to the right and left. "I have no idea what you're talking about." He pressed the call button repeatedly. "You are wasting my time."

"I'll be brief then. This is how I see it. Nancy figured out that you've been placing scientists over at Reparation Research—"

"There is nothing wrong with that!" he snapped. "That is my duty as consul. I am to facilitate meetings with *learned men*."

He sneered at me, clearly indicated I was as far away from being a learned man as humanly possible.

"Does that *facilitating* include having the scientist take back corporate secrets to France?"

He sneered at me. "If a cure for cancer is found faster because scientists are sharing information then the world benefits, *mademoiselle*. You should be happy and thank me."

I laughed. "It's not sharing, it's stealing. Corporate espionage or at best several intellectual property laws are being violated." I leaned in close to him and almost whispered, "And Reparation Research isn't working on a cure for cancer. They're a cosmetics company. They're patenting formulas to make lipstick last longer without drying your lips."

The elevator opened and beeped at us.

He looked toward it, glad for an escape.

"Nancy knew you were to receive the Legion of Honor because of your *aid* to science, is that right? Certain influential French cosmetic companies stand to make a lot of money, don't they, Ambassador? The cosmetics industry is a fifty-billion-dollar industry. But hey, everyone wins, we get great skin, they make a fortune, and you get an award. The award leads to an ambassadorship. Who could possibly be mad?"

He stepped into the elevator.

My arm shot out to stop the elevator from closing "You had Nancy Pickett killed because you wanted the story to die."

"No! I didn't even know the reporter. You're wrong!"

"Not wrong about much." I waved a finger at him. "I may not be a learned man, and I don't have the cure for cancer, but you can bet I'm going to get justice for Nancy Pickett, Ambassador."

I released the elevator door and watched it close on his shocked expression.

I returned to the restaurant fuming. The businessman was still picking at his salad and chatting with Mom.

Mom immediately saw my expression and jumped out of her chair. She nodded to the gentleman. "So nice meeting you."

He looked at me curiously, but waved to Mom.

I grabbed Laurie's stroller. "Let's go."

We waited for the elevator, Mom pestering me for details.

"He says he didn't know Nancy."

Mom shrugged. "Well, what did you expect him to say? Yeah, I had her killed, but hey, I have diplomatic immunity so go pound salt?"

I thought of Christophe running off at the San Francisco Centre and being at the supervisor party when he'd told me he didn't know Kimberly. He'd already lied to me. What else was he hiding?

"No," I said to Mom. "I didn't expect a full mea culpa, but I think he may be telling the truth. I don't think he knew she was working on the story. But the press guy would, right?"

Mom and I decided it would be best to leave the car safely parked and walk the short distance to the consulate. Mom strolled around with Laurie in the lobby while I asked for Christophe.

The receptionist informed me he was off-site. I imagined he'd have to deal with a lot of inquiries right now as the news was breaking about Armand killing Nancy.

On impulse, I requested to speak with Jean-Luc. The receptionist frowned but nodded and walked me down a hallway to his office.

She rapped on the door, peeked in, and announced me. They had a quick exchange in French. I heard Jean-Luc groan. After a moment, the receptionist waved me inside and closed the door behind me.

It was a small office, similar to Christophe's. A desk

with a computer, from which Celtic music played, a round table in the corner, and tall filing cabinet against a wall, the only difference was that Jean-Luc was packing up this office as though he was moving. Several cartons were stacked near the door.

"I know that Armand stole Nancy's computer." I launched in without preamble. After all, what else was I going to say? Good to see you and your chest hair?

"That's why he didn't stop when he hit my car," I continued. "He didn't want to get caught with stolen goods."

Jean-Luc smiled. "Do American men find nosy women attractive?"

"Do French women appreciate sarcasm?"

"Mrs. Connolly. The police investigation showed that Armand killed Miss Pickett. None of us here at the consulate are proud of that fact. We are deeply saddened by it."

"Are you my Facebook friend?" I asked.

Jean-Luc frowned although something else flashed across his eyes. "Face, what?"

"Oh, of course, you're not. Jean-Luc Gaudet is not on Facebook, but Kevin Gibson is."

Jean-Luc set his jaw. "What are you babbling about? Who is Kevin Gibson?"

I smiled. "You know who Kevin Gibson is, he's the leak. He's the one who started this entire mess. He's the scientist at Reparation Research who contacted Nancy about the consul placing corporate spies over there. He likes Celtic music." I shrugged. "At least that's what his Facebook profile says."

"If Mr. Gibson is accusing the consul of something as grave—"

"It is grave, isn't it? We certainly wouldn't have wanted that to leak out before the *Légion deux honneur*!"

"*De* not *deux*!"

"Right. *Deux* is two, right? As in two sides, duplicitous."

Jean-Luc gritted his teeth. "Accusations are easy. You have no proof of this and if Mr. Gibson does he can come forward."

"Oh, Mr. Gibson can't come forward, he's dead."

The blood drained from Jean-Luc's face. "What?"

"Well, either that or he's in the Bahamas. But I won't know for sure until after New Year's when he's scheduled to return." I gave an exaggerated shrug. "At least that's what his Facebook status page says."

"Is all this about the insurance situation? I'm deeply sorry Armand hit your car, you need to work with—"

Suddenly a missing piece of the puzzle clicked into place for me. "You were at Kyra's the night Armand *committed suicide*, weren't you?"

Jean-Luc's lips twisted. "What does that have to do with anything?"

"While Kyra was sleeping, you climbed up the fire escape and got into Armand's apartment. That's why none of the neighbors saw anyone coming or going into Armand's the night he was killed."

"You don't know what you're talking about."

"Really? Having access to Armand's apartment through the back of the house must have been important though. How else were you going to take one of his bedsheets?"

"Please leave."

I reached out for the doorknob, my hand shaking uncontrollably. "I have Nancy's hard drive."

Jean-Luc's eyes twitched. "What?"

"And a backup copy of Mr. Vann's data. It's a long story, but I do have the proof."

He laughed. "If you had proof of anything, the police would be here."

He was right. There was nothing on the hard drive or in Mr. Vann's data, but if he was behind all this nasty business, then it was something he probably feared.

"Would they? You have diplomatic immunity. They'd just deport you or something, right?"

Jean-Luc snarled.

"What do you get out of it? Why put yourself in jeopardy for the consul? So what if his dirty secrets about corporate espionage leak out? He doesn't get his award? His promotion . . ." I looked around at the state of the office. Jean-Luc was moving . . .

"Oh. Are you going to Washington with the ambassador? Kyra will be disappointed . . .

"I'm not going to Washington." He smiled wide, the cat who ate the canary. "I'm the new consul for San Francisco."

My breath caught. "Get your boss promoted and you get promoted, too. Nice. What about poor Armand? Why did you kill him? Because he knew too much?"

Jean-Luc pressed his lips together tightly, staring at me but saying nothing.

"What about Kevin Gibson?" I asked. "What am I going to find if I go over to his place?"

"Why don't you go and find out?" he challenged.

"I think I will," I said, turning on my heel.

As I left his office, I heard him mumble almost inaudibly, "*Merde*."

CHAPTER TWENTY-SEVEN

To Do:

1. ~~Enroll Laurie in art class~~ Jim says ridiculous. Maybe should find another class for her in New Year.

2. ✓ ~~Upload Laurie's Santa pic on Facebook.~~

3. ✓ ~~Figure out who killed Nancy so I can get on with holiday prep~~ Prove it!

4. Write letter to DPT protesting tickets.

5. Decide on New Year's resolutions.

6. ~~Need more formula.~~ N.Y. Res. #1—no more formula. Breast is best!

I'd called Galigani as soon as I'd gotten home, but he more or less dissuaded me from going to McNearny with anything about Jean-Luc. The evening news was taking the Armand story and running it full force. There had been a press conference with Christophe and the consul. They were aggrieved by the news. A reporter had captured Armand's parents' heads ducked in a photograph.

I took a call from Chuck Vann. He thanked me for helping him and told me a check was in the mail. That was it. Case closed. I was free to go about my business, cash my check, and prep for Christmas dinner.

Instead, I tossed and turned all night wondering about Kevin Gibson.

The following morning, Jim ran to the grocery store to buy all the supplies for our Christmas Eve dinner. Mom was bringing Galigani to dinner as Hank was going back East to join one of his daughters.

I wrapped the presents and put them under the tree.

Still thoughts of Kevin Gibson haunted me.

When Jim returned, he agreed to watch Laurie while I closed this last loop.

I pulled up to the small blue house on Cherry Street in San Carlos and parked in the driveway. The home was detached with a graveled walkway that led behind the house. It was made of cider blocks and looked about as sturdy as one could hope for in earthquake country.

I got out of my car and stepped up to the front porch to ring the bell. I picked at my nails while I waited. No one answered, which made perfect sense if its occupant was truly vacationing in the Bahamas. I ignored the pit in my stomach and rang the bell again.

The front window shades were pulled and no holiday decorations were visible. In contrast, the neighbors on either side of the house had the full-tilt Christmas décor, complete with reindeer and a blow-up Santa on the front lawn.

I took the gravel walkway to the back of the house. A wooden fence surrounded the garden. There was a large grass area bordered by flower beds. At the back sat an empty doghouse and an enclosed potting shed.

From the neighbors backyard I heard a dog bark.

I stared at the doghouse.

Did Kevin have a dog?

If so, who was taking care of it while he was on vacation? A neighbor? A dog sitter?

I fingered the lock on the potting shed. It was shiny and bright, a new lock in contrast to the rusted door.

I banged and pulled on the door to no avail, which was fine. What had I expected to find anyway?

Kevin Gibson was probably getting sunburned on a beautiful beach right now. Nothing to worry about except the potency of the sun and the Bahama mamas.

When was the last time I had a fruity cocktail with an umbrella sticking out from it?

Suddenly, I heard a crunching sound on the gravel walkway. A mid-sized chocolate Labrador tore down the path, its owner trailing it.

The dog sprang on its hind feet, ready to claim me as its own. The owner yanked on his leash, saving my blouse and jeans from the wonderful muddy mess the Lab would have bestowed upon me.

The Labrador began to sniff at me. I held out my hand to let him smell it, then patted his head. He moved on to sniff at the potting shed door.

The owner was a man in his mid-forties, fit with a square face and a crew cut.

"Are you Kevin Gibson?" I asked.

He shook his head. "No. I'm Jason, Kevin's neighbor. Are you looking for him?"

I nodded.

The dog let out a bark followed by a whimper and started to scratch at the dirt surrounding the potting shed.

"He's on vacation. Is there anything I can help you with?"

I dug out a card from my pocket and handed it to him. "Do you know when he'll be back?"

Jason studied my card. "After New Year's." He pulled the dog's leash. "Come on, Buddy, don't tear up the place."

The dog growled and barked.

Jason yanked on the leash again and started to walk me out. The Lab followed us, still barking and resisting.

Why did the dog like the potting shed so much?

Why was there a new lock on the shed?

"Do you know what's in the shed?" I asked Jason.

Jason looked confused. "What?"

Visions of a dead Kevin Gibson, crumpled in the potting shed, crowded my mind.

"Your dog liked the shed."

Jason laughed and waved his free hand. "Ugh, Buddy sniffs and digs up everything. Probably just a raccoon scent or something."

I indicated the doghouse. "Does Kevin own a dog?"

"No. Kevin's way to busy for a dog. He's never around. I think the doghouse was here when he bought the place."

We stopped in the front yard. I thanked him and got into my car.

Only one way to know for sure what was in the potting shed.

Fortunately, there was a Home Depot only a few miles away. I drove straight there and purchased a bolt cutter and a new lock.

I decided against calling Jim for fear that he would talk me out of it and since the drive to San Carlos was about forty minutes from San Francisco I didn't want to have the thought nagging at me enough to cause a return trip.

Instead, I thought about what I'd tell Jason if he and Buddy came back.

In the Home Depot parking lot, I emptied my diaper bag and placed the bolt cutter inside. I returned to Cherry Street.

I wished for the cover of night, but since it was only noon and I had to get back to Laurie I didn't have that luxury.

The best strategy would be to do it quickly.

I parked a block away, so Jason or any other neighbor wouldn't be alerted to my presence.

I walked as if I belonged there, with purpose and direction. I crunched down the gravel path to the potting shed, removed the cutter, and proceeded to attempt to snip the lock.

Only it was extremely difficult. The cutter scratched at the lock, but I wasn't able to cut it. Why hadn't I bought the bigger cutter? Because it was expensive as hell! As it was I'd paid over a hundred for this one. The bigger ones were priced around three hundred and thirty.

I opened the bolt cutter again and readjusted my position to get some leverage on the tool. I squeezed the shears together and felt the lock snap in two.

Yes!

The hinges squeezed as I pushed open the door. Inside, it was cold and smelled of musty earth. I could make out a shelf of small ceramic pots and some bulky burlap sacks. No dead body stench assaulted me as I'd feared.

I entered and poked the burlap sack with my bolt cutter. The sack gave. I peeked inside.

Just dirt.

No Kevin Gibson, dead and decaying in the potting shed. Only me unable to leave any stone unturned.

And yet . . .

What if Kevin was dead in some room of the house? Should I try to break into the house?

I heard crunching on the gravel path.

Shoot! Caught red-handed.

I took a breath and pasted my best smile on my face to greet Jason and stepped out of the potting shed.

My heart stopped.

Jean-Luc was crossing the garden toward me, his face dark with anger.

I gripped the bolt cutter. "What do you want?"

Not waiting for an answer, I hurled the tool at his head. It smashed him in the temple and blood spurted out. I took advantage of his shock, running straight into him and knocking him to the ground.

I stumbled over him; only three yards separated me and the gravel path leading to freedom.

I took one desperate step forward but a hand gripped my ankle. I fought the unbalance, kicking at him with my free foot and screaming at the top of my lungs.

With one brutal yank, he pulled me to the ground. He

was on his feet and dragging me across the lawn. I gripped at the grass, only succeeding in taking it with me.

"Let me go!" I screamed, flailing about.

I tried to wring out of his grip, flipping over on to my back. It didn't faze him.

"Shut up," he said. The wound on his temple was gushing now and the intensity of his eyes had dimmed a bit. He was in pain.

He made a retching sound, his body convulsing with a dry heave.

I kicked at him with my free leg, but despite his pain his grip was locked around my ankle.

He swung open the potting shed, dragging me inside.

Damn that dog and his stupid nose. If he hadn't made a fuss, I would have gone straight home instead of to buy a bolt cutter.

Home!

Laurie! Jim!

I kicked at Jean-Luc with my free leg. He released me and twisted toward the shelf. Before I could get to my feet he grabbed a mid-size pot and heaved it at me.

My arms reflectively covered my eyes and face and I screamed. "Did you kill Kevin, too?"

The pot hit my forearms, then crashed to the ground. He threw another pot at me, this one hitting me on the forehead. Black spots appeared before my eyes.

I ducked my head and pulled my shoulder up, trying to turn my back on him and protect myself.

He flung another pot at me, hitting me directly on my shoulder blade.

The room was spinning now; I grabbed at the floor.

As if from a distance, I heard him groan and mumble something like, "*Merde.*"

Then a retching sound. This time the stench made it
clear he'd vomited.

Merde, indeed.

I struggled to get to my feet, but couldn't get off my
hands and knees. I crawled toward the door. Only I couldn't
make out where it was. There had been light just a moment ago coming from the . . .

Where was the door?

The room was spinning out of control and I was fright-
fully dizzy. Suddenly I felt as if someone had just pushed
me off the merry-go-round. One final spin and darkness.

I awoke in the dark. My tongue felt thick and dry. The
room smelled horrid, vomit mixed with something sweet
and metallic. My head throbbed and I couldn't quite lift it.
Where was I?

I felt around the ground, which was cool . . .

Dirt.

The potting shed.

Oh God! I'd passed out in the potting shed. Where was
Jean-Luc?

In a panic, I struggled to my hands and knees, deciding
not to try for my feet. I was unsteady and didn't want to
risk another fall. I felt around the ground. My hand bumped
into a pot, then brushed something wet and sticky.

It was too dark to identify it. I wiped my hand in the
dirt. It was either vomit or . . .

Yes, the sickening metallic smell was blood.

I found the wall and traced along the interior with my
hand until I found the telltale grooves and hinges of the
door. I pushed on the door; it opened a crack and then
held. A new lock had been placed on the shed.

A sob escaped me. I cried out at the top of my lungs.

Could anyone hear me? Jason? Buddy?

What if no one came? I had to get out of here. My breasts were burning and sore, knotty lumps forming with the backed up milk.

Laurie!

My baby! My darling! I had to get to Laurie and Jim.

Would Jim know where I was?

I vaguely remembered not calling him from the Home Depot! Oh God, why hadn't I called him? Had I told him where I was going? I couldn't remember, the pain in my head was making everything foggy.

I had to find a way out.

I banged on the door again.

Please, please, let me find a way out.

No light came from the small crack in the door. It was night out. What time was it? How long had I been out? Did I have my phone with me? I fumbled around the shed trying to locate my diaper bag/purse.

Then I recalled I'd emptied the bag in my car and only put the bolt cutter in it. I'd left the bag at the foot of the shed before I'd entered it the first time.

What had Jean-Luc been doing here?

Had he followed me or was he coming to move the body . . .

Where was Kevin Gibson? Was he really in the Bahamas?

My head was throbbing and the shed seemed even darker than before. I realized my eyes were closed. I forced them open.

I must stay awake!

I banged on the door and screamed at the top of my lungs. "Jason! Buddy!" repeatedly.

Finally I slumped to the floor, exhausted and in pain. I thought of Laurie and sobs wracked my body.

My hands squeezed the dirt. Could I dig my way out? I scrapped and pushed the dirt around. Digging as quickly as I could. The effort was making me dizzy, but I chanted, "Laurie, Jim," over and over again to keep myself going.

My tongue felt thick with thirst and bending forward to dig was making the dizziness worse.

I couldn't stop though, I had to keep digging. Fearing that if I stopped I'd pass out again, I persisted until finally the ground seemed to tilt up to meet me and darkness ensconced me.

Sounds.

I heard sounds. Was it gravel crunching?

My eyes fluttered open and I screamed out and resumed my banging on the door.

Footsteps approached. A man's voice called out. "Hello?"

"Help me! Oh God. I'm locked in here. Please help me."

"One moment, ma'am," the voice said. "Hey. I need bolt cutters over here."

I closed my eyes, rested my head against the door, and prayed.

I couldn't make out who was outside or how many people but when the door opened I was relieved to feel the cold night breeze on my face.

Strong hands grabbed at my arms. "Are you injured?"

"Yes. My head . . ."

"Hold still. I need a gurney."

There were more voices. It was dark and things were fuzzy to me, but I could make out a star on a uniform.

"Are you . . . ?"

"I'm Bill O'Sullivan. San Carlos PD. We're going to take you to emergency. Okay? Is there someone I can call?"

I was being lifted on a gurney. I was able to squeak out Jim's name before blankness overtook me again.

I opened my eyes and took in the bright surroundings. A hospital room, someone holding my hand.

Jim!

He was sitting on a chair next to my bed, clasping my hand in both of his. His head was lowered in prayer.

I squeezed his hand, but emotion overtook me and I cried out before I could speak.

Jim's head popped up and clutched my hand. "Kate!"

"Where's Laurie!" I sobbed.

"Laurie's fine. She's great. She's with your mom."

"I want to see her. What am I doing here?"

"You don't remember?"

"I think I do. I remember the shed and Jean-Luc, the cops. I guess I don't remember coming to the hospital. When can I go home?"

"The doctor has to release you. I hope soon. How do you feel?"

"My head hurts."

Jim laughed and rubbed my cheek. "I would think so. They did an MRI, you have a slight concussion, but the overall opinion was that we're lucky you have such a hard head."

"What day is it?" I asked.

"Christmas Eve," he said.

"Did they catch Jean-Luc?" I asked.

Jim's expression grew grave. "Yeah. Honey, they got him."

"Is he here at the hospital, too? He was bleeding pretty bad—"

He squeezed my hand again. "Kate, he's dead."

CHAPTER TWENTY-EIGHT

I stared at Jim, the news sinking in slowly. "Wh . . .what do you mean? Do you mean that I . . ."

"He died of a head injury. One of the neighbors saw him slumped over the steering wheel of his car and she called the police. That's how they found you. He'd left a trail of blood to the potting shed. He was rushed to ICU, but he didn't make it."

Jim and I looked at each other for a few moments.

"I killed him," I whispered.

Jim nodded solemnly. "It was him or you, Kate. He left you to die."

I closed my eyes and took in a sharp breath. There was a strange pressure over my heart, a fear, an indescribable heaviness. In a matter of a few life-altering moments, I had become another person. I'd become a killer.

"Don't get stuck in that place, Kate," Jim said.

I opened my eyes. "What place?"

"You're thinking that somehow you're a bad person."

"I just killed a man."

"We can regret that he's dead, the loss of life, but you can't regret defending yourself. You can't apologize for saving your own life," Jim said.

He stared into my eyes and I knew he was right as I held on to his hand. "I love you," he said.

"No matter what?" I asked, starting to cry.

"No matter what," he replied.

"I got two tickets the other day. One for an expired meter and the other for not curbing my tires," I said through my tears.

Jim burst out laughing.

The door to my room opened and Galigani peeked in. "Kid! You're awake!"

He held the door open for Mom, who was cradling Laurie.

Tears poured from my eyes. I tried to jump out of bed to grab Laurie, but Jim stopped me.

Mom placed Laurie in my arms and hugged us both. I squeezed Laurie to me and wept. Laurie's blue eyes peered up at me, her hands pulling at my hair. She smiled and cooed.

I held her to my heart, feeling all her goodness and trying to absorb her innocence.

Suddenly I remembered Kevin Gibson. "Galigani, did they search Kevin's house? Is he in the Bahamas?"

Galigani and Jim exchanged looks.

My heart sank

"Gibson was strangled to death. They found his body in a bedroom closet," Galigani said.

"Was Jean-Luc working alone?" Jim asked. "Or was the consul behind it?"

"Looks like the consul was ignorant of everything. When he found out from Kate that Kimberly had been banged around he started cooperating with homicide. Apparently, Jean-Luc had paid a visit to Kimberly to pry information out of her. She didn't know much but that didn't stop him from giving her a black eye. She ran to the press guy, Christophe, to try and piece things together and, mostly, I think keep her name clean," Galigani said.

"Will the consul still be ambassador?" I asked.

"They're transferring him to Sudan," Galigani said.

"To a comparable post?" Jim asked.

"I'm not sure," Galigani said. "It's clear they want him out of the U.S. He obviously wasn't watching things too closely and they won't want to reward that. We don't know who will get the ambassador post yet, but word has it that Christophe will be the new consul here," Galigani said.

"What about Kimberly? Will she go to Sudan?" I asked.

Galigani shook his head. "No. She's all over the papers. Calvin Rabara announced their engagement and his intention to run for mayor next year."

"What?" I asked.

Galigani laughed and patted my shoulder. "Oh, kid, you've only seen a tiny bit of the city's political underbelly; it could always be worse."

Silence took over the room, each one of us reflecting on the unnecessary loss of life.

Galigani cleared his throat. "McNearny's not happy about the extra paperwork, but he did call me to make sure I wish you a merry Christmas."

Several hours passed and while waiting for my doctor to release me from the hospital, Galigani and I conferred with Gary Barramendi. Barramendi agreed to provide San Carlos PD. with a carefully crafted statement that he, Galigani, and I had worked on.

Finally the doctor gave me a clean bill of health, along with some strong pain relievers and we were on our way.

Jim tried to reassure me on our way home that Christmas dinner could still be salvaged. Our tradition was a honey-baked ham on Christmas Eve, and fortunately all that was required for that was a bit of warming.

"Anyhow, Galigani and Mom will be happy just to be with you," Jim said.

As we approached our house we saw someone standing on our front steps.

"Who's that?" I asked.

The man turned and waved at us as we pulled into our driveway. He was holding something in his hands.

"That's Ramon," Jim said.

We got out of the car and greeted him.

"Kate! Your head! Are you all right?"

I absently touched the bandages. "Yeah."

Jim carried Laurie up the steps and opened the door. We all marched inside and settled into the living room. Ramon set the tray he was carrying on my coffee table, and then fussed over me while Jim put Laurie down in her crib.

"I saw the story on the news. You're amazing," he said, propping up my feet and sticking a pillow behind my head. "I brought this for you and your family." He pulled the tinfoil off the tray. "Traditional Mexican Christmas dinner. Tamales!"

The aroma filled the room.

Jim returned to the living room; his jaw dropped. "You shouldn't have. Let me get some plates," he said.

The bell rang.

"Do you want me to get that?" Ramon asked.

I nodded.

Ramon let Galigani and Mom inside. Mom was holding a shopping bag full of wrapped presents that she popped under the tree. She eyed the tray of tamales and clapped her hands. "What a treat!"

The doorbell rang again. Mom and I looked at each other. We were all present and accounted for, so I couldn't guess who it could be.

"I'll get it," Mom said.

Paula, David, and Danny marched in.

David was carrying two brown sacks from the grocery store. "Merry Christmas! I brought beer," he said.

Before I could introduce Paula to Ramon, she was already digging into the tamales. Danny came to sit on my lap and play with my head bandage. He kept repeating, "Auntie Kate have an owie?"

"This is a surprise," I said to Paula.

"We heard about your near miss," Paula said. "Celebrating with you trumped eating David's mother's dried-out dinner. We didn't know about the tamales, that's just a bonus." She smiled at Ramon.

The doorbell sounded again. I smiled to myself. It had to be Kenny. That boy could smell a party a mile away. Mom opened the door. Kenny and, to my surprise, Butterfly marched in.

Kenny was holding a gold envelope. His eyes danced when he saw the tray of tamales.

Jim, who had made several trips to the kitchen for plates, now placed one in Kenny's hand. "Here, bud."

Kenny handed the envelope to Jim. "The ballet called. I play tomorrow. Closing show of *The Nutcracker*. These are comps for you and Kate. Merry Christmas!"

Suddenly my throat closed up and tears sprang to my eyes.

Jim's hand shot toward me and he squeezed it. "Honey, what's the matter? Is it your head?"

The room was silent; all eyes were on me.

Tears rolled down my cheeks. "You all are the best family and friends anyone could ever ask for."

To Do:

1. Eat (all the leftovers).

2. Love (the wonderful people in my life).

3. Sleep (until New Year's).

The new Scrapbooking Mystery from
New York Times bestselling author

LAURA CHILDS

FIBER & BRIMSTONE

• A SCRAPBOOKING MYSTERY •

While Carmela Bertrand prepares a monster puppet for the
Halloween Monsters and Mayhem parade, a fight breaks
out between her friend Jekyl Hardy and Brett Fowler—
and just minutes later they find Fowler's dead body.

Carmela has known Jekyl for years and can't believe he'd
ever resort to murder, despite the fact that Fowler owed
him money. But when another victim is discovered—who
also had an unfriendly relationship with Jekyl—Carmela
is convinced someone is framing her friend and now must
find a way to unmask the real killer.

penguin.com

DON'T MISS THE FIRST NOVEL IN
THE BOOKS BY THE BAY MYSTERIES FROM

ELLERY ADAMS

A Killer Plot

In the small coastal town of Oyster Bay, North Carolina, you'll find plenty of characters, ne'er-do-wells, and even a few celebs trying to duck the paparazzi. But when murder joins this curious community, writer Olivia Limoges and the Bayside Book Writers are determined to get the story before they meet their own surprise ending.

WELL-CRAFTED MYSTERIES
FROM BERKLEY PRIME CRIME

- **Earlene Fowler** Don't miss these Agatha Award–winning quilting mysteries featuring Benni Harper.

- **Monica Ferris** These *USA Today* bestselling Needlecraft Mysteries include free knitting patterns.

- **Laura Childs** Her Scrapbooking Mysteries offer tips to satisfy the most die-hard crafters.

- **Maggie Sefton** These popular Knitting Mysteries come with knitting patterns and recipes.

- **Lucy Lawrence** These brilliant Decoupage Mysteries involve cutouts, glue, and varnish.

- **Elizabeth Lynn Casey** The Southern Sewing Circle Mysteries are filled with friends, southern charm—and murder.

M5G0610

PO #: 0003188976

M2G0610#